Finding Noelle

— A NOVEL —

Finding Noelle

— A NOVEL —

JANICE WILLIAMS

PRIMIX
PUBLISHING
THE WRITE CHOICE

Primix Publishing
11620 Wilshire Blvd
Suite 900, West Wilshire Center, Los Angeles, CA, 90025
www.primixpublishing.com
Phone: 1-800-538-5788

Published by Primix Publishing   02/04/2022

ISBN: 978-1-955177-68-9(sc)
ISBN: 978-1-955177-69-6(e)

Library of Congress Control Number: 2021924630

Contents

*Sometimes, it's not the memories we've lost that have such
an impact on our lives, but rather the creation of new ones.*
Janice Williams

Prologue

Reaching over to change the station on her radio would be Noelle Carrington's last memory of her former life. Tragically hit head-on in a blinding snowstorm, her life instantly changes forever. Perhaps wiping out your life history at the young age of twenty-four might come with some advantages. Noelle's life had not been easy. She was born into a world with no living parents. Sgt. Ben Carrington, her father, had been drafted during the Viet Nam War and was tragically killed in Cambodia in 1970. Noelle's mother, Cindy Carrington, passed due to complications from cancer during her birth. Cindy was only two months into her pregnancy when given the unfortunate news. Dealing with the tragedy and trauma of losing her husband at such a young age, Cindy struggled to keep her pregnancy viable. It seemed the odds were heavily stacked against her. Diagnosed with breast cancer in her first trimester, Cindy fought desperately to carry her unborn child to term. However, the added strain of losing her husband only further complicated a high-risk pregnancy. At eight months, Cindy lost her courageous battle with cancer during childbirth. Delivering a beautiful baby girl only moments before she passed on Christmas Eve, Noelle was placed into the loving hands of her maternal grandmother, Edith Edwards.

Edith was a frail older woman, totally unprepared to take on the burdens of raising a newborn. Cindy had been the only child of Edith's and her late husband, Frank. With Frank having died years earlier and her declining health, Edith suddenly faced the responsibilities of caring for an infant. Despite her age and health problems, Edith loved Noelle and, without hesitation, stepped up to provide a loving home. However, being retired and a widow meant money was scarce. Life for Noelle was a daily struggle where money was concerned. As a result, she grew up learning to do without many material things. Then, fate would step in at the young age of twenty-four, erasing all her memories. Unexpectedly, a tragic auto accident would change her life forever.

Noelle's life teetered precipitously on the edge of death as she closed her eyes at the point of impact. Would she go willingly, or would she be pulled back from the precipice? A voice softly beckoned as the brilliance of white light embraced her. Noelle felt an unexplainable peace that compelled her to stay in the heavenly realms. However, this was not to be the case.

"Noelle, it's not your time. You cannot stay. You must go back," the angelic vision instructed.

Chapter One

Noelle would never remember the horrific sounds of squealing tires trying to grasp the wet, slippery asphalt on the narrow two-lane road, the excruciating crushing metal, or shattering glass. She would have no recollection of the truck driver who fell asleep at the wheel of his big rig and unknowingly swerved into her lane. Likewise, Noelle would never recall the memory of being hit head-on during the blinding snowstorm—the toxic smell of smoke, fuel, burning rubber, or plastic.

After a crucial exam at the University of Missouri in Arlington, driving home late at night, an inclement weather system caught Noelle unaware. It appeared November 1994 had brought with it much cooler temperatures and an excessive accumulation of snow. However, knowing these mountainous roads like the back of her hand, Noelle never gave a second thought to the drive. The roads had been freshly plowed, and she knew every hairpin turn, every steep incline, and every downward slope. But unfortunately, these familiarities would do nothing to stop fate. In an instant, things would tragically change the course of her life.

Hurriedly, the paramedics pushed the gurney through the double doors of the emergency room at Methodist Hospital. Noelle was desperately clinging to life as she was rushed into an exam cubicle.

"Someone page Doctor Bennington. She's unconscious, and her

blood pressure is plummeting. We're losing her," the EMT shouted. "She's lucky to be alive."

Running in, Doctor Alex Bennington took a glance at his patient. She was young and beautiful. Her long blonde curls flowed effortlessly over the pillow like silk. She showed no visible signs of injuries other than normal bruising and minor lacerations on her forehead. However, after years of working in military hospitals in Iraq, he knew many critical injuries never presented themselves by appearance. After his initial assessment, extensive tests, and ordering a CT scan, it indicated his suspicions were correct. She required emergency surgery.

"We've got to get her upstairs. Immediately," Doctor Bennington ordered. "She's bleeding internally. I'll scrub and meet you in the operating room."

"Where's Noelle? Where's my precious baby?" Edith Edwards screamed hysterically, running in through the double doors of the emergency room.

"I'm sorry. You'll have to wait in the waiting room," the young nurse quickly instructed, stopping her in the hallway.

"I have to see my granddaughter. Clint Harper called to tell me she was in a horrible car accident. He was only a few cars behind her and witnessed the terrible crash."

"I understand. However, you'll have to wait outside. There's a waiting room at the end of the hall."

Not adhering to the nurse's orders, Edith panicked. Immediately, she began pulling back the tall curtains, which divided each exam room. Frantically, Edith searched each small cubicle for a glimpse of Noelle. Suddenly, finding Noelle's seemingly lifeless body, she stopped, frozen in her steps.

"Noelle. Oh my God. Baby, you have to hang on. Can you hear me?" Edith exclaimed, rushing over to touch her granddaughter's hand.

"I'm sorry. You must wait in the waiting room. We're doing everything possible," Monica, an emergency room nurse, reiterated. Then, sympathetically taking Edith by the arm, she gently ushered her out of the exam room and into the corridor.

Edith watched from the hall as the nurse wheeled Noelle's motionless body out of the emergency room and toward the elevator. Again, Edith felt overwhelmed with grief.

"We're taking her up to surgery. So, please, just take a seat in the waiting room. Someone will be out to speak with you in a few minutes," Monica compassionately instructed.

Walking over to the waiting room, Edith found a chair and sat down. The past few minutes had been unbelievable. How could things have tragically spiraled out of control so fast this evening? Noelle had simply left to take a test at the university, which she'd frequently done during the past year.

"Mrs. Edwards, I'm Kristina Caldwell, a social worker. During emergencies, I'm often called to help the families involved. As you know, your granddaughter was in an auto accident. Unfortunately, she has internal injuries and has been taken to the operating room. But I'm sure she will be fine, she's in excellent hands. So please don't worry," Kristina said sympathetically, reaching for Edith's hand. "Doctor Bennington is the best trauma surgeon at Methodist. There is another waiting room on the next floor. Please follow me, and I'll take you upstairs," Kristina kindly suggested.

Reaching the waiting room, Kristina smiled.

"You can wait here. As soon as your granddaughter comes out of surgery, either Doctor Bennington or one of his colleagues will come out and speak with you. Is there anything I can get for you?"

"No. I just want to see my baby girl," Edith pleaded desperately, wiping her eyes.

"I'm sure you will be allowed to see her as soon as she's out of surgery. There are vending machines inside, and the hospital cafeteria is located on the first floor. Try not to worry. I'm sure she'll come through surgery just fine."

Edith felt alone, helpless, and scared. Hopefully, Clint Harper, who called to inform her about the accident, would notify the ladies at church. It was uncanny how he'd been only two cars behind Noelle when it happened. Having been a deacon at First Baptist Church for many years, Clint knew everyone in Arlington.

Edith noticed some magazines on a table near the vending machines and checked out her selection of reading materials. Now in her late sixties, Edith's face reflected the strains of a hard life. Her short stature revealed a noticeably hunched frame due to years of crippling arthritis. Wiry gray hair, a narrow face inundated with wrinkles, and brown eyes enhanced with horn-rimmed glasses easily portrayed the worries of a woman whose life had not been easy. Wearing a drab cotton house dress didn't add to her appearance. After reading magazines for over an hour, she sat nervously, wringing her hands, waiting for any news regarding her precious granddaughter. Finally, after what seemed like an eternity, she stood up, noticing the young doctor who entered the room.

"Mrs. Edwards, I'm Doctor Bennington. Your granddaughter made it through surgery. She's a lucky young woman. However, she's still in grave condition. She has a ruptured spleen, and the trauma of the accident has resulted in swelling near the brain. I've medically induced a coma and given her diuretics. She's temporarily being sustained on life support at this time. We're doing everything possible. The next few hours will be critical. I'm sorry to give you such devastating news this evening. Do you have any questions?"

"Oh, Doctor Bennington, I can't lose her. I can't. Do you understand? Noelle is the only family I have," Edith cried. "Can I see her? I need to see her?"

"Mrs. Edwards, I assure you we're doing everything possible. Yes. Certainly, you may see her. One of our nurses will be in a few minutes and take you up to Intensive Care." Compassionately putting his arms around Edith, he smiled. "If you need anything or have questions, one of our staff in the Intensive Care Unit will be happy to help. Again, I'm sorry. Someone will be right in." Turning to leave, he'd never become comfortable giving such unexpected news to loved ones. "One last thought, is there anyone you would like our staff to call or contact concerning your granddaughter's condition?"

"Oh, no, it's just Noelle and me. There's no one of importance in her life. She received a scholarship to study journalism at the University of Missouri in Arlington, and she's extremely busy with school." Edith nervously rambled, giving more essential details, hoping it would breathe life into Noelle.

Doctor Alex Bennington found this bit of news fascinating as he walked out the door. He knew the rigors of studying and competing for scholarship money. Born in Athens, Greece, Alex, and his parents immigrated to the United States when he was ten. After eight years of medical school, he had graduated at the top of his class. He was by far the best trauma surgeon available at Methodist, and at the young age of thirty-one, his reputation for being the best in his field kept him busy and on-call. His charm and handsome appearance made him popular with the nurses. Dressed in green scrubs, his jet black hair, striking blue eyes, and tall, lean muscular physique complimented his dark olive complexion. Alex's Greek ancestry was discernible in his stunning chiseled profile. Being a trauma surgeon with the Air Force Reserves demanded he stay physically fit. He kept in shape and was an avid bicyclist. The mere fact he had remained single kept the young nurses vying for his attention.

"Mrs. Edwards, I'm Gloria. I work in ICU. Doctor Bennington asked me to take you to the third floor to see your granddaughter. Please, follow me."

Nothing could have ever prepared Edith for what she was about to see as she walked into Noelle's room. The love of her life was lying motionless on the stark white sheets of the hospital bed. Tubes and hoses were the only things at this point, keeping her alive. Unbelievably, her beautiful sculpted face was unscathed except for a few abrasions and minor cuts on her forehead. It seemed almost miraculous that outwardly Noelle showed no significant visible signs of having been involved in an accident. Her long blonde curls encased the white pillow. She appeared angelic and peacefully sleeping, minus all the medical equipment and the ventilator's constant hum.

Rushing over, Edith grabbed her grandaughter's hand. "Baby, can you hear me? I wish it had been me in that accident instead of you. I'm so sorry. Noelle, you have to be strong. Sweetheart, you have to fight to stay alive. You can do this. I need you." Leaning over Noelle's hospital bed, Edith sobbed relentlessly. "Please, don't leave me," she pleaded, holding onto the bed rail. Overcome with emotions, she felt faint.

Noticing Edith's frail condition, Gloria knew the stress was overwhelming.

"Mrs. Edwards," Gloria smiled sympathetically. "Why don't you go home and come back in the morning. She's receiving the best care possible. There's nothing you can do at this time. We'll call you if there is any change in her condition."

"I think I would like to stay with her for a while if that's alright?"

"Certainly. I'll get you a chair. Is there anything else that I can get you? Would you like a cup of coffee?"

"No thanks," Edith sighed, trying to make herself comfortable in the hard high back chair.

Within minutes, Edith was informed that Clint Harper was downstairs in the waiting room. He was accompanied by two women from Edith's Sunday School Class, Mary Godwin, and Ethel Peters. They were longtime friends of Edith's and loved Noelle deeply. Their familiar faces gave Edith some much-needed comfort as she went downstairs to meet them.

"Edith, how are you holding up?" Clint questioned, putting his arm around her.

"Well, as good as can be, I guess," Edith answered, wiping her moist eyes.

"How is Noelle?" Mary asked thoughtfully.

"Well, she made it through surgery. But she has a ruptured spleen and swelling on her brain from the trauma. So they've put her in a coma. She's in critical condition, and I'm so worried about her."

"Edith, please try not to worry. We'll add Noelle to the prayer chain at the church. Clint told us about the accident. Thank goodness he was only a few cars behind Noelle when the accident occurred. Did the truck driver make it?" Ethel inquired.

"No. The man driving the truck which hit Noelle didn't survive," Edith looked up with tears welling in her eyes.

"That's right. The other driver died instantly," Clint interjected, handing Edith a tissue.

"Oh, dear, we're so sorry. Noelle is such a beautiful young woman. You've done such an amazing job raising her. Everyone at church loves

Noelle. She's done an amazing job teaching Bible studies for the young people," Mary added.

"Ladies, we should be going and let Edith go back upstairs to the ICU. So if there isn't anything further we can do, I better drive you both home," Clint suggested.

"Yes. We better be going," Ethel agreed.

"I'll call you tomorrow. If you need us, please don't hesitate to call," Mary smiled, giving Edith a warm hug.

"Thanks for coming to the hospital. It means a lot to me that you came to check on Noelle. I'll be in touch with you tomorrow."

Returning to Noelle's room, Edith felt twinges of pain in her shoulder as she tried to get comfortable in the hard, straight-backed chair. Tonight would be grueling trying to sleep under these conditions. Just at that moment, Doctor Bennington walked into the room.

"Mrs. Edwards, why don't you go home for the night? You need to get your rest. I promise your granddaughter is receiving the best care," he thoughtfully suggested as he walked over to Noelle's bedside. After thoroughly checking the ventilator and evaluating Noelle's condition, he walked over to Edith. Lovingly, he put his arm around her, trying to give her some comfort. "We're keeping her in a medically induced coma. I believe I spoke with you earlier regarding this, so there's no need for you to stay. Why don't you go home for the night? I'm sure you'll be more comfortable. Hopefully, tomorrow, if the swelling subsides, we can discontinue her medications and begin to bring her out of the coma and remove the breathing tube."

"Oh, thanks, Doctor Bennington, but it doesn't feel right to leave her. Although, I'll have to admit this chair isn't very comfortable. If you're positive that someone will call me if her condition changes, I guess I might go home and try to get some rest. But I'm sure that I won't be able to sleep a wink even at home," Edith mentioned.

Walking over to Noelle's bedside, Edith lovingly took her hand.

"Sweetheart, I love you. I'm going home for tonight, but I'll be back first thing in the morning. Rest peacefully." Edith knew there was no way Noelle had heard a word spoken. However, she felt compelled to talk to her as if she could easily understand.

"Thank you, Doctor Bennington. Please call me at home if there's any change. I gave my phone number to Kristen Caldwell."

Before leaving the room, Edith paused. Turning around, she took another glance at her gorgeous granddaughter encumbered with all the medical equipment. She found it truly unbelievable that a horrific tragedy could unexpectedly happen in such a short time. Before the accident, Noelle had always been very athletic and vibrant. Her long blonde hair, gorgeous blue eyes, and sculpted facial features, along with her tall, lean frame, made her easily noticeable.

Alone with his young patient, Doctor Bennington felt drawn to the beautiful young woman lying in front of him. He felt compelled to know more about her. It was unfortunate that someone so young had to endure such misfortune. However, the mere fact she was single and had no significant other in her life made her alluring. He was captivated by her angelic appearance.

Looking down at his watch, it was almost midnight, time for his shift to end. Rubbing his five-o'clock shadow, he was tired. He would grab a cup of coffee and change before heading back to his apartment. Leaving his patient's room, he prayed she would make a full recovery.

Chapter Two

Waking up early, it seemed Edith would not be the only person to encounter a sleepless night. Slowly opening his eyes, sleep had eluded him. Alex had always considered himself to be a kind, compassionate physician. A doctor, his patients, could trust and confide in. However, he could not recall when he had cared so profoundly or felt an unexplainable connection to any of his patients.

Looking over at the clock, it was 5:00 a.m. Alex never got up this early when he worked late the previous night. Usually, he got home from the hospital around midnight and slept until 7:00 a.m. Wondering why he was awake at this time of the morning, he knew before he could even give it a second thought. His new patient, Noelle Carrington, was mysteriously finding her way into his heart without a single word having ever been spoken between them.

Reaching across his bed, he grabbed the phone sitting on the nightstand. He had to know Noelle's condition. Dialing the Intensive Care Unit, he was surprised to hear Jodie Connor's voice, the head nurse in charge of the ICU.

"Intensive Care, this is Jodie."

"Jodie, this is Doctor Bennington. I'm calling to check on the status of a new patient, Noelle Carrington. She was admitted last night."

"Good morning, Doctor Bennington. Hold just a second while I get her chart. It appears the diuretics have been effective, and the brain edema has greatly decreased. Would you like to continue her course of treatment?"

"Yes. Continue with the current instructions. I'll be in later this morning to check on her and make a decision concerning the medications."

"Certainly, Doctor Bennington."

"Thanks, Jodie."

Jodie was the managing supervisor in the Intensive Care Unit. She had been employed as a registered nurse at Methodist Hospital for over twenty years. She was dedicated and loyal. Her premature gray hair indicated her long hours and hard work.

Getting out of bed, Alex walked into the kitchen to make coffee. Perhaps a jolt of caffeine and a hot shower would revive him. Without hesitation, he decided to go to the hospital. He had to see Noelle.

Standing underneath the warm water, it felt invigorating. Finally awake and ready to start the day, Alex dried off, wearing a sweatshirt with sweatpants. Walking back into the kitchen, he prepared a small bowl of oatmeal, poured himself a glass of orange juice, and sat down. He was a creature of habit and his morning ritual always included oatmeal and juice.

Finding his backpack, he filled an insulated travel mug with coffee for the short bike ride to the hospital. His apartment was only two blocks from the hospital. It was small by any standards. However, the location made it ideal for a busy doctor who typically spent more hours at the hospital than at home. The one-bedroom, one-bath apartment basically met his needs. In addition, the covered balcony provided him a place to store his bike, his preferred method of transportation. Finally, grabbing his helmet and pushing his bike out through the front door and downstairs, he began his usual morning ride over to Methodist Hospital. Reaching the hospital, he quickly changed into his green scrubs. He was ready for the day ahead.

"Good morning Jodie. I'd like to see the chart for Noelle Carrington," Alex smiled, walking up to the nurse's station in the ICU.

"Certainly, Doctor Bennington. How was your ride into work?" Jodie, also a biking enthusiast, shared his passion. She never missed an opportunity on the weekends to ride with her group, the Cycling Divas.

"Energizing. Nothing like a brisk ride to get the day started," Alex smiled, taking the chart. "You're right. It seems the swelling has significantly been reduced. Please stop the medications gradually and keep a close watch for any changes. Page me if she begins to wake up."

Noelle's room was right across from the nurse's station. Taking a glance, he was surprised to find Edith already sitting next to Noelle's bed.

"Good morning, Mrs. Edwards. How was your evening?" Alex inquired, walking into Noelle's room.

"Oh, Doctor Bennington, not very well. I wasn't able to sleep a wink last night. I was so worried about Noelle."

"I'm sorry. I was hoping I might have given you some reassurance last night. The good news, it appears the swelling has significantly subsided. Hopefully, this afternoon, if she continues to improve, she'll begin to wake up, and you'll be able to speak with her. She's a lucky young woman," he remarked, checking Noelle's pupils and vital signs. "From what I know about the accident, her prognosis could have been far worse."

"Thank you, Doctor Bennington. I couldn't ask for anything better. I can never thank you enough."

"You certainly don't have to thank me. I love my job. So tell me more about this young woman. I arrived early this morning, and I have a little time before making my rounds. Has she always lived with you?" he questioned. He knew learning more about his patients and their families was always beneficial. It was evident that Mrs. Edwards, at her advanced age, was finding it difficult to cope with Noelle's amnesia.

"Yes. Noelle's father was killed in Viet Nam before she was born. Cindy, her mother, my only child, was pregnant with Noelle when we heard he died. She was devastated and later diagnosed with metastatic breast cancer. Her pregnancy was high-risk. Cindy's health had never been good, even from a child. We lost her on Christmas Eve after she gave birth to Noelle. Naturally, being the only family Noelle had and her grandmother, I didn't hesitate to take responsibility for her. Life hasn't been easy for either of us. My being a widow and retired has certainly had its downfalls. However, she's a gorgeous reflection of her mother, and I adore her."

"I'm sure your daughter was beautiful. You have to be commended. You've raised a lovely girl. The fact you mentioned that Noelle received a scholarship to study journalism speaks volumes about her strength of character. I'm sure it will give her the willpower to make a full recovery."

"Yes. I pray that you're right. Noelle had a mid-term test on the evening of the accident. She's a straight 'A' student, and she's always been a determined young woman and works hard."

"That's a pretty impressive goal. However, I'm sure with your granddaughter's gorgeous appearance, she would be an asset to any news crew. Well, I should be going. I've got rounds to make this morning. If you need anything, just check with one of the nurses at the ICU desk. I've left instructions to bring her out of the coma slowly. If you notice any movements in her hands or elsewhere, just let one of the nurses know. It was nice talking with you."

"Thank you, Doctor Bennington, you've been a great help."

Putting his stethoscope around his neck, he walked toward the door. Maybe coming in early today had its perks. He was now more knowledgeable than ever about sleeping beauty. But, regardless of the fact they'd never spoken, Noelle strangely consumed his thoughts.

Before he started his daily rounds, he went downstairs to the cafeteria.

"Good morning, Doctor Bennington," Angie smiled, busily ringing up his coffee and a bran muffin. "You're doing rounds early this morning."

Angie was young and energetic. She loved her job and could always be counted on for a warm smile when you entered the cafeteria. Cute with flaming red hair and freckles, she wore her long hair pulled back into a ponytail. Angie had worked at Methodist since graduating from the local high school. She knew Doctor Bennington was a hot commodity. All the single women who worked at the hospital never missed an opportunity to subtly let the handsome young doctor know they were interested and available.

"Good morning, Angie. I had to check on a patient. How are you?"

"Oh, I'm fine. Have a wonderful day," Angie smiled demurely.

"Thanks."

Taking his coffee and muffin, he decided to eat upstairs in the physician's lounge. He'd hardly taken a bite of his muffin when he heard a familiar voice.

"Doctor Bennington, I'm surprised to see you here so early," Doctor Trevor Reed inquired, walking into the lounge.

Alex and Trevor Reed had been best friends since medical school. They humorously referred to each other by their professional names. Trevor was two years older than Alex, Hispanic, tall, dark, and handsome with wavy black hair and brown eyes. But, unlike Alex, he'd married his high school sweetheart, Becky, shortly after medical school.

"What brings you in so early? I know you love this place, but a double shift. Really?" Trevor chided.

"I needed to check on a patient I admitted last night. She was the victim of a car accident. I had to induce a coma after surgery, and I wanted to come in and personally check on her this morning."

"Oh, you're referring to the young woman in ICU. From what I heard, that accident was horrendous. I'd say she was fortunate you happen to be available. Alex, if you don't have any plans this weekend, why don't you come over for dinner on Saturday," Trevor insisted, quickly changing the topic of their conversation. "I'll throw some steaks on the grill, and Becky can make one of her famous potato salads. You could use a break from this place. Why don't we say around 6:00 p.m.?"

"I'll have to check my schedule. I think I'm on call at the hospital this weekend."

"Well, check your schedule and let me know," Trevor replied, closing his locker.

"Okay. Talk to you later," Alex answered, taking a sip of coffee. Then, anxious to get the day started, he hurriedly finished his muffin. Alex loved his job as a surgeon. However, not having a significant other in his life, he overcompensated by spending too much time in the hospital.

Suddenly, hearing his name being paged to the emergency room, he immediately put down his coffee and rushed downstairs. He arrived in the emergency room just in time to notice a gurney hurriedly pushed inside a cubicle.

"Doctor Bennington, this young man fell from a second-floor scaffold. Thankfully, he landed on a thick row of shrubs, which cushioned his fall. However, he's complaining of significant lower back pain."

After a quick assessment, x-rays were ordered. It appeared Doctor Bennington's morning was off to a hectic start hearing the approach of an incoming ambulance. Finishing his cup of coffee would have to wait even longer. Finally, taking a moment, he glanced up at the clock in the emergency room. He had spent over two hours frantically taking care of patients in order of their severity. Some mornings, it seemed the arrival of incoming patients never slowed.

"Doctor Bennington, you're wanted in ICU," Kaitlin, an emergency room nurse, yelled urgently, quickly catching sight of him.

"I've got this," Doctor Reed exclaimed, rushing past him. "You're needed in ICU," he continued.

Leaving Trevor to attend to the incoming patient, Alex hurriedly made his way to the elevator. His only thoughts were of Noelle.

Reaching the nurse's station in ICU, he could hear screams coming from Noelle's room.

"What's going on?" he demanded, running in.

"Doctor Bennington, Noelle's grandmother, noticed she was beginning to move her hands and arm. So she came running out to the nurse's station and informed Gloria. When Gloria checked, it seemed the patient was conscious and trying to remove the ventilator tube. So Gloria carefully removed the tubing and turned off the assisted life support," Jodie explicitly explained.

"Why is she screaming?"

"She's in shock. She remembers nothing regarding the accident or why she's in the hospital. She doesn't even remember her name or her grandmother," Jodie added.

"I'm Doctor Bennington. Please, there's no reason to scream. You were in a car accident last night and brought to Methodist Hospital. You are in a safe place, and you're going to be fine. You had a small cut on your forehead and internal injuries, which required surgery when you arrived," he explained. "I temporarily put you in a coma, but you've made a miraculous recovery, and I don't often get to use those terms. Trust me. You're going to be fine. There's no reason to scream or panic."

"Doctor Bennington, I can't remember anything. This woman claims to be my grandmother, but I've never seen her before," Noelle hysterically insisted. "I don't want her in my room." Then, grasping his hand like a child who's afraid of the dark, she harshly demanded Edith be asked to leave.

"Noelle," Edith quickly interjected. "Please, I love you. I'm Edith, your grandmother. You have to remember. I've raised you since you were born." Completely confused by Noelle's words, Edith stepped away from the hospital bed and sat down. Rubbing her forehead, she was utterly overwhelmed and distraught.

"Mrs. Edwards, why don't we step outside for a moment."

Compassionately taking Edith by the arm, Doctor Bennington gently escorted her outside to the hallway.

"Please, don't take her words to heart. I'm afraid your granddaughter has amnesia. It's not uncommon for someone involved in a major accident to suffer from a temporary loss of memory. We just need to give her some time. Since your presence appears to be somewhat disturbing, why don't you go home and get some rest? Perhaps by tomorrow, she'll be more cooperative. We're taking great care of her."

"Okay. Maybe you're right. I certainly don't want to agitate Noelle by staying. Will you call me if anything changes?" Edith reluctantly agreed. She knew he was right. The last thing she wanted was to see Noelle continue to be upset and angry.

"You have my word. Your granddaughter is in good hands. Please go home and try to get some rest."

"Thanks. I'll come back tomorrow morning."

Observing Alex as he walked back into her room, Noelle called out to him in a state of panic.

"Doctor Bennington, please don't leave me. I don't want to be alone."

Feeling the anxiety in her voice, Alex felt compelled to stay with her for a while. As a surgeon in the Air Force Reserves, he knew the fear and apprehension she felt. It was all too common in war zones where soldiers were suddenly and critically injured. War casualties were often in shock and unable to cope with the unexpected loss of limbs or significant injuries. So he sympathized with her sudden trauma of learning about the accident.

"Jodie, you can go. I'll try to reassure her that she's in a safe place and needs to remain in the hospital."

"Okay, thanks, Doctor Bennington. I'll be at the ICU desk if you need me," Jodie smiled.

"Thanks for asking Edith to leave," Noelle mentioned as she continued to grasp his hand in a vice-like grip. "Honestly, I swear I've never seen her before," she quietly whispered. "You have to trust me."

"She's your grandmother, and she loves you dearly," he smiled. "However, I've asked her to leave and get some rest. She's extremely worried about you. I don't think she has slept at all since the accident," Alex explained, releasing her tight grip to take her blood pressure. "Your blood pressure looks good. You need to calm down and let us take care of you."

"That's just it. I don't want you to take care of me. I want to go home."

"So where's home?" he quizzed, knowing that she wouldn't possibly know the answer.

Suddenly quiet, she looked up at him like a lost child, finally answering after a long pause. "Um, I'm not sure."

"Just as I thought," he remarked, noticing her perplexed gaze.

"You've repeatedly called me Noelle. I suppose that's my name?"

"Yes, and I'm Doctor Bennington, but you can call me Alex."

"Alex, you're a doctor at Methodist Hospital? According to the nurse, I believe that's the name of this place," Noelle hesitantly questioned.

Then, smiling demurely, she stared at him intently. She found him to be exceptionally handsome.

"Yes. At least you've got that right," Alex smiled.

"Doctor Bennington, you're needed immediately in the emergency room," Jodie stated, running into the room. "It's urgent."

"Sorry. I have to go."

"Please, don't leave me. Please," Noelle begged, quickly grabbing his hand.

"I'll prescribe something to help you relax. Then, try to get some rest."

"No. You can't leave. I need you to stay," Noelle insisted.

"Listen, Sweetheart, you're in great hands." Wow, had he really used the word sweetheart. It had merely rolled off his tongue like a Freudian slip. "Your room overlooks the nurse's station. Here's the call button if you should need one of the nurses. I've got to go, but I'll stop by later if you're awake. Now, be a good girl," he smiled, placing the control in her hands.

Rushing out of the room, he paused for a brief second as he walked past the huge glass window which separated her room from the nurse's station. Taking another glance, he was mesmerized by her beauty. Never before had he felt such an attraction to any of his patients. It seemed she needed him for strength and relied on him for guidance. Hopefully, later tonight, he might be able to help her reconnect with her past. But, unfortunately, his thoughts turned to more urgent matters at hearing his name once again paged to the emergency room.

"How's sleeping beauty?" Trevor teased, walking briskly to catch up with him.

"Awake."

Hearing the sirens from numerous ambulances, they both ran to meet the incoming casualties.

"What's going on?" Alex inquired quickly, making his way down the corridor towards the entrance to the emergency room.

"A tour bus overturned on Interstate 50. Tragically, it appears there are numerous victims. We're getting at least twelve with the more critically injured being taken to St. Mary's," Monica answered briefly, hurriedly pushing a gurney towards the emergency room entrance.

Doctors Bennington and Reed worked vigorously to stabilize and comfort their incoming patients for the next four hours. Stabilizing victims according to the severity of their injuries was a concerted effort between doctors, nurses, and staff. Hurriedly they raced between cubicles, urgently ordering x-rays, suturing lacerations, and monitoring vital signs. At last, their efforts had been successful. Finally, the incoming casualties had been admitted and were resting comfortably.

Exhausted from the rigors of the past few hours, Alex needed a break.

"Doctor Reed looks like we're finally done. Let's take a quick break."

"Good idea," Trevor acknowledged following him down the corridor towards the exit doors. The massive onslaught of casualties had taken a toll on the young doctors.

Walking outside and away from the emergency room entrance, Alex paused for a moment to light a cigarette.

"Geez, Alex, I thought you gave up that nasty habit. Seriously, you just spent hours in the emergency room, then you come outside and light up a cigarette. Doctor Bennington, I assume you know the stats regarding those."

"Trevor, the last thing I need this evening is a lecture from you. It's an old habit and my way of dealing with stress. A throwback from the hard hours I work when I'm on duty with the reserves. I can't exactly stop to take a stiff drink as critically wounded soldiers are arriving with missing body parts, now can I?" Alex reprimanded.

"Okay, Buddy, calm down. I get it. So tell me more about sleeping beauty," Trevor insisted, changing the topic of conversation. Sitting down on a worn, weather-beaten bench, they were finally able to relax.

"You know, she does have a name," Alex insisted, somewhat agitated. "It's Noelle." Taking a long draw on his cigarette, the heat from the sun felt warm and soothing. "She's conscious, somewhat miraculously. But she has amnesia, and she didn't even remember her grandmother, who was standing next to her bed. She was extremely agitated and apprehensive when she woke up. In fact, she was screaming. I was paged to her room in the ICU." Slowly exhaling, Alex finished his cigarette. Throwing the butt on the ground, he briskly stomped it out.

"Well, that's easily understandable. Who wouldn't be? Waking up after an accident with no memory can be confusing. But, Alex, I've known you for a long time, and I think it's safe to say you appear somewhat attracted to her. Heck, you even came in early this morning. Do you think that's wise?"

"Trevor, I would never do anything to jeopardize my career. I've worked too hard to get where I am, and I love my job. Trust me. I know as a doctor it's not ethical and against hospital policy to get personally involved with a patient. However, I can't explain it. Things just happen. Don't worry. As I said, I'm not going to risk my career."

"Got it, Doctor Bennington. How you handle your patient relationships is your own business. So are you coming this weekend? I talked with Becky, and she's excited about the possibilities of you coming over for a cookout."

"Yes. It looks as if I'll be free on Saturday. What can I bring?" Alex answered, standing up to stretch his long legs.

"Nothing. We've got it covered. However, after talking with Becky, she's decided to change the menu. Instead, she's excited about cooking one of her favorite recipes, herb-crusted salmon, and of course, your favorite potato salad. Adding to that, I'll throw a couple of steaks on the grill and make a pitcher of my fabulous peach slushies," Trevor grinned, looking down at his watch. "It's five o'clock. My shift is over. I'll talk with you later, and don't forget about dinner."

"What? No cold beer? You're not getting all feminine on me, are you?" Alex grinned. "You make your peach slushies, and I'll bring the beer. Speaking of food, I think I'll head down to the cafeteria and see what's on the menu."

"Listen, Alex, I didn't mean to pry earlier about Noelle," Trevor apologized, walking back inside the emergency room. "You're an awesome Doc, and you definitely deserve someone special in your life. And, honestly, I don't know where I would be without Becky."

"No offense taken. I'll see you on Saturday."

Walking into the cafeteria, it appeared lasagna and salad would have to suffice.

"Good afternoon, Doctor Bennington back again," Angie teased, ringing up the cost of his meal.

"Yes. It's been a hectic day. I'm starved." Alex smiled briefly, reaching inside his scrubs for his prepaid meal card.

"Oh, the bus accident was horrible. Jodie told me all about it. We've been extra busy serving the family and friends of the victims. Enjoy your lasagna."

"Thanks," Alex smiled, taking his tray.

Walking toward the back of the cafeteria, he found a table with open seats. He needed a place to eat his meal in silence and decompress. He knew that Trevor was only looking out for his best interest. Still, the fact he mentioned the risk of his career felt somewhat offensive. However, there was no denying it. He was attracted to Noelle, and strangely, he sensed it was mutual on her part. Cutting into his lasagna with his fork, he ate quickly. He was hungry, not having eaten a lot earlier. Noelle consumed his thoughts while he ate. Hopefully, she didn't forget his promise to check on her. He wanted to help mend her relationship with her grandmother.

Putting away his tray, he noticed the time. It was almost 6:00 p.m., his shift at the hospital had ended. Walking towards the elevator, he smiled. Hopefully, he might be able to help Noelle with her memory loss. Feeling the sadness in Edith's voice earlier that morning, maybe with a bit of help from him, there might be a slight chance that Noelle would at least begin to remember her.

"Hey, Jodie, surprised you're still on duty. So how's our amnesia patient doing this evening? Any outbursts since I last saw her?"

"Good evening, Doctor Bennington. No. Things have been quiet. I gave her the sedative you prescribed, and she's been sleeping most of the afternoon," Jodie explained.

"Thanks."

"You're welcome. We're all working a few hours overtime this evening. The victims from the earlier bus accident took up our extra beds and created the need for extra staff tonight," Jodie explained.

"You're right. We admitted a dozen new patients earlier. I'm going in to check on Miss Carrington. Have a good evening."

"If you need anything, just let one of us know," Jodie added.

Wow, had she heard him correctly. He'd just addressed his new patient by her proper name. Jodie knew if there was the slightest hint of an attachment to his new patient that he would keep his relationship on a professional basis. Jody laughed, knowing that he could never fool the nurses in the ICU. Doctor Bennington, or Adonis as the nurses teasingly referred to him, after the Grecian God easily wore his feelings on his sleeves. They were all astonished he'd remained single.

Entering the dimly lit room, Alex walked over to Noelle's hospital bed. Instantly, she opened her eyes. Why had he not remembered the color of her eyes? They were strikingly azure blue. Reaching out, she took his hand.

"You came. I was beginning to think you were a figment of my imagination," Noelle smiled.

"I promised to check on you after my shift ended. So how are you feeling this evening?" Alex inquired. But, first, reaching for the blood pressure cuff, he checked her vital signs. "Well, I must say that looks good," he smiled, reading the results. "Let me check your pupils." Then, quickly, he flashed a small penlight directly into the center of each eye. "Great. Now let's check your memory. Do you remember the accident, your name, or recollect anything from your past?"

"No. But I remember that you're Doctor Alex Bennington and that you referred to me as Noelle. Sorry, I can't recall anything before this morning. However, I do remember an elderly lady being in the room. She claimed to be my grandmother, but honestly, I've never seen her before. So, you have to believe me."

"I know that's why I decided to stop by this evening."

Watching as Alex walked to the back of the room to get a chair, she panicked.

"Please don't leave me. Please," she begged tearfully, trying to pull herself up from the hospital bed. "You're the only person I know. The only person I trust."

"Noelle, I need you to lie down and relax. I was just walking over to get a chair." Quickly leaving the chair in its place, Alex walked over to the bed's edge and sat down. "Listen, I understand you're a little apprehensive, but you're completely safe. You're going to have to trust the fact we're all here to help you recover," he smiled, pulling the blanket upward to her chest and gently tucking it under her chin. "Now, stay calm. I'm simply walking over to get a chair."

Pulling it next to her bed, he sat down. "Truthfully, you don't remember anything about your accident?" he asked, placing his stethoscope around his neck. Staring into her gorgeous blue eyes, he was mesmerized by the beauty of the young woman lying in front of him.

"No. I told you. I don't remember anything. Maybe you're the one with amnesia."

"Wow. Do I detect a bit of sarcasm and humor?" Alex smiled.

"How long before my memory returns?"

"That's a hard question, and I'm not sure you're going to like my answer. It could take a few days or even longer. There's no definitive answer. There's no physical reason for your amnesia other than the trauma which resulted from the accident. I'm going to refer you to a specialist, Doctor Adams, she's the best in her field. She will stop by tomorrow. Hopefully, she can help."

"Thanks. Now, I want to know more about you. Did you always want to be a doctor?" she asked curiously as her lips slowly curved, reflecting the hint of a smile. She was captivated by the handsome young doctor sitting next to her bed.

"There's not much to know, and yes, I always wanted to be a doctor. Guess you could say I was fortunate. Some people take years before they find their true calling. However, my grandfather and uncle are both doctors."

"Not your dad? What happened?"

"Let's just say that my father wasn't exactly doctor material, and leave it at that."

"Alex, did you learn anything regarding my past from Edith? The woman whom you claim is my grandmother," Noelle inquired, changing the subject.

"Edith is, in fact, your grandmother. You have to know she loves you.

And yes, she gave me information regarding your past. But, honestly, I don't know how to tell you. I'm not sure that I should or even if you're ready to hear more facts regarding your past."

"Alex, you have to tell me. I don't care how horrific the details might be. You have to tell me. Do you understand?"

Staring pensively at Noelle, Alex thought it was uncanny that she could almost read his mind. How could she possibly have known her past included so much tragedy?

"Because you're insistent, I will answer your questions. However, I feel it would be better coming from your grandmother. I hate being the one to tell you," he hesitated. "Noelle, I'm sorry. Your mother died during childbirth the night you were born. Unbelievably, it was Christmas Eve," Alex explained. "I also lost my father when I was fifteen. He was killed in a motorcycle accident. So, we have some things in common. I mean that we both grew up without one or both of our parents. I guess you could say my father was the black sheep of our family."

"What else did she tell you?"

"Maybe you should wait and ask her. But, as I said, I'm not sure that I'm the one who should be informing you of your past."

"Well, since you've brought it up, I'd like to hear it from you. What else did Edith tell you?" Noelle demanded as she once again slowly attempted to sit up.

"Are you sure you're ready to learn more about your past? What I'm about to tell you might be hard to hear."

"Yes. You said I could trust you. So, please, get on with it. I'm not getting any younger," Noelle smiled firmly, grasping his hand. "Wow, speaking of age, how old am I?" she asked inquisitively. Even something as simple as age had easily escaped her mind.

"Well," Alex smiled. Noelle's child-like curiosity amused him. "According to your chart and the conversation I had with Edith, you are twenty-four. I'm sorry that I had to give you such devastating details regarding your mother," Alex explained sympathetically. Waiting for her reaction, he felt terrible having to divulge such facts.

Noticing tears streaming down her cheeks, Alex paused, reaching for a box of Kleenex sitting on the table next to the bed. Pulling one of the tissues from the box, he lovingly wiped her face.

"Maybe we should stop for the night?"

"No. I want to know more. What about my dad? Did she say anything about him? Anything at all?"

"Seriously, it can all wait. I see the hurt in your eyes."

"Seriously, it can't," she reiterated, rejecting his notions of leaving things unsaid. "I want to know everything. Everything that Edith told you."

"I don't see how learning more about your past will help. I feel as if I will only continue to hurt you and cause you more pain by giving you more details," Alex pleaded empathetically.

"Listen, Alex, not only do I trust you, but you are the only person I really know right now, at this very moment. I have to know," Noelle insisted with tears in her eyes.

"Okay, if you insist," he reluctantly questioned.

"I'm sorry. You also lost your father, Sgt. Ben Carrington in Viet Nam in 1970, just a few years before the war ended. Edith said your mother, Cindy, received the tragic news not long after discovering she was pregnant with you. It seemed afterward her health quickly spiraled downward. I'm so sorry. Your mother was diagnosed with stage four breast cancer," Alex frowned, quickly handing her another tissue. "I feel like the worst person on earth right now, having told you about your parents."

"Alex, thank you. I didn't mean to make you feel like a bad guy or even uncomfortable. That was never my intention. I simply needed to know," she added, wiping her moist eyes.

"Sweetheart, I'm sorry. Truly, I am."

"Is there more? Is there anyone significant in my life? I mean, at this time?" She had to know.

"No, not that Edith mentioned. She made it sound like you were studying remarkably hard to earn a degree in journalism. But, look at you, you're absolutely gorgeous. Trust me. I can't even imagine that being true," Alex winked.

"Well, maybe there is now," Noelle blushed. "Alex, there is no reasonable explanation, but when I first saw you, it felt as if I'd known you my entire life. How is that even possible when my whole life has been wiped from my memory? You asked me to trust you. I trust you explicitly. If my memory never returns, I can only thank God that you entered my life at the right moment and not a day sooner."

"Do you even know what you've just said? We've only known each other for less than a day. So how can you conceivably know that your feelings for me are real?"

"I can't explain it. Just like I can't rationally understand the loss of my memory. I feel as if I've known you forever, and yes, my feelings for you are real. However, ask me again in the morning just to be sure," Noelle teased. "Alex, it's a joke. You trust me, right?"

"Explicitly," he winked, getting up from his chair to close the curtain, which exposed the entire room to the ICU desk.

"Wait, come back. You can't leave. I didn't mean to scare you."

"Sweetheart, scare me? Honestly," he laughed, closing the curtain.

Walking toward her hospital bed, surely, this was madness. However, if it was total insanity, he never wanted to be more insane than at this very moment. Holding Noelle in his arms, he gently kissed her. Nothing mattered, only what transpired between the two of them this evening. Alex discovered that life had a way of mysteriously bringing them together under the direst set of circumstances.

"Be a good girl. I've got to go. I'll see you tomorrow," Alex winked with a smile as he opened the curtains.

Chapter Three

The following day Noelle woke early. Then, sitting up in bed, she buzzed for the nurse.

"Can I help you?" Jodie answered.

"Yes. Could you please tell me what time Doctor Bennington usually makes his rounds?"

"Usually, he picks up charts around 8:30 a.m. Is there something I can do for you?"

"Oh, no, thanks. I was just curious. Thank you."

Glancing at the clock above the ICU desk, it was only 7:00 a.m., Jodie smiled.

"Hey, Gloria, remember I told you Doctor Bennington closed the drapes last night in Noelle Carrington's room," Jodie whispered. "Well, she just buzzed to see what time he makes rounds."

"So, what's your point?"

"Well, I told you that I sensed a connection between those two."

"Jody, get a life. Who cares? He's been single a long time. I think he deserves a little happiness. You're going to be known as the hospital gossip if you don't keep your crazy thoughts to yourself," Gloria insisted. "You know doctors aren't allowed to have relationships with patients. I think you're reading too much into this."

Gloria Brown, a senior nurse in the ICU, worked with Jody. They had gone through nurse's training together and had remained close. In fact, Jodie had been the primary reason Gloria was hired at Methodist. Even though best friends, Gloria was quite Jodie's opposite. She was tall and slim, with gorgeous green eyes, and hated all outdoor sports. Wearing her brown hair pulled up in the back, she wore glasses and wasn't as outspoken as Jodie. However, they easily kept each other laughing when they worked together.

"Oh my gosh, speaking of the devil, look who just walked out of the elevator. It's Doctor Bennington. I told you," Jodie whispered with a smile.

"Good morning, Doctor Bennington. You're certainly doing rounds early again this morning," Gloria questioned.

"Yes. I have some errands to take care of later, so I decided to come in ahead of schedule. Can I please have Noelle Carrington's chart?"

"Yes. Just a moment."

Quickly retrieving the chart, Gloria handed it over to the handsome young doctor, who was now sporting a rather sexy dark growth of facial hair. "Have a good morning Doctor Bennington."

"Thanks."

Watching as he walked toward Noelle's room, Jodie and Gloria desperately tried to hide their laughter.

"I told you," Jodie reiterated once more with a grin.

Entering Noelle's room, now he was the one who felt apprehensive. What if her feelings had changed since last night?

"Good morning. How's my gorgeous girl?" he asked quietly. He was unable to contain his huge smile as he walked over to Noelle's bedside.

"Alex, you're early? I haven't even had a chance to comb my hair, and I have no make-up."

"Sweetheart, you don't need a thing. How are you feeling?"

"I feel fine, especially after last night. I was afraid it might have been a dream."

"Not a chance, not as far as I'm concerned," he winked.

"Alex, did it really take such a tragic event and my loss of memory for us to find each other?"

"Regrettably, I suppose it did. I'm truly sorry about that aspect, but

I thank God you were brought into Methodist and that I happened to be in the hospital."

"Me too. Come closer. Wow, Doctor Bennington, that's sexy," Noelle whispered, running her fingers through his five-o'clock shadow. "Your cologne smells amazing."

"You like it?" he smiled curiously, giving her a quick kiss on the forehead.

"There's so much more I want to know about you," she lovingly whispered into his ear. "I may not remember my past, but I want to know all about yours. I want to know everything there is to know about this handsome doctor that I've fallen in love with."

"Noelle, you used the word love. In my culture, that word isn't spoken without meaning behind it."

"Alex, do you believe in love at first sight? Honestly, I can't explain it or how it happened so suddenly. I just know that it's true," Noelle replied, her eyes quickly filling with tears.

"Sweetheart, I didn't mean to make you cry." Then, grabbing a tissue, he leaned over, wiping her eyes. "To answer your question, yes," Alex smiled.

"Sorry. I seem to be rather emotional," Noelle tearfully apologized.

"No apologies. I'm trying hard to keep things on a professional level until I get you out of here. It's not easy," Alex whispered. "I can't stay long. Doctor Julianna Adams will be coming in to see you about 9:00 a.m., and I have some errands to run. Everything looks good. Your vital signs are excellent. Hopefully, by the end of the week, you'll be able to go home. I've got to go. One last thing, if Edith calls, please think about seeing her today. She's devastated, and losing you further, I'm afraid, would be detrimental to her health. She's not a young woman."

"Okay. I'll do my best to make sure Edith isn't upset. It's hard. I feel no connection to her. It's going to take time for me to adjust to my new surroundings."

"Maybe Doctor Adams can help with that aspect of your amnesia. Just explain it to her as you've told me. I'm sure it will be fine. I have to go. I love you. Be a good girl. I have a prior commitment, and I might not be available this evening, but I will see you tomorrow morning."

Quickly kissing her forehead, Alex hoped to get past the nurses sitting at the ICU desk before they noticed him.

However, it was not to be the case. Instead, it appeared that Jodie and Gloria were both smugly smiling as he turned in Noelle's chart.

"Have a good day, Doctor Bennington," they grinned blatantly.

After seeing Noelle, he focused on his other patients, especially the tour bus casualties, which he'd admitted through the emergency room. Even coming in early, he would have little time to pull each medical chart, and see each patient before changing into his military uniform for the drive out to Arlington Air Force Base. His reserve weekend was coming up. An urgent message had been sent out regarding a mandatory meeting at his squadron later that morning. Keeping an extra military uniform in his hospital locker and a shaving kit always came in handy. It saved time on mornings like this when there was no time to return to his apartment.

Looking down at his watch, he raced to the physician's lounge. Opening his locker, he heard a familiar voice.

"Good morning, Doctor Bennington. Geez, it seems like you can't stay away from this place. How's sleeping beauty this morning? Oops, I meant Noelle. That is the reason you're here so early, right?" Trevor grinned.

"Trevor, she's fine, and no, it's not exactly the reason I'm here this early. I have a mandatory meeting at the squadron in less than an hour. How's your morning?"

"Busy, but not as busy as your's it seems. So Major Bennington, how are things at the base?" Trevor inquired.

"I'm not sure. Hopefully, I'll still be around for dinner on Saturday. If not, I'll let you know."

"What? Are you being deployed?"

"Guess that's what I'm going to find out. Just keep it under wraps. I'm not sure. Please don't say anything to anyone at the hospital. I'll let you know. I've got to run. Talk to you later."

Saluting the guard at the gate, Alex drove onto Arlington Air Force Base. Arlington wasn't a huge base. However, it did house numerous cargo aircraft and tankers. Quickly finding a place to park, it seemed he'd made it on time.

"Hey, Major Bennington. How's it going?" Major Dan Matthews, another reservist, yelled, quickly running to catch up with him. What's going on?" he inquired.

"I'm not sure. Guess we'll find out."

"Yes. Short notice," Dan acknowledged catching up to Alex as they entered the squadron offices.

It wasn't long before everyone arrived and was seated.

"At ease, gentlemen," Colonel Williams announced, walking up to the podium.

"It appears we're deploying early next week. I wanted to inform you personally. This will give each of you a few days to take care of any personal issues at work or at home with family. We're on our way to Aviano Air Base in Italy. Aviano will support our troops and coalition forces in an ongoing black-ops campaign. I don't have to remind you this is a covert operation, and Aviano is simply our jumping-off point. Some of you will be transferred immediately upon our arrival at Aviano. You'll be moved inside the theater. We're going to provide hospital support. This deployment could easily extend into next year, so don't go home and make any long-term plans. That's all I have for today. You're free to go. Oh, make sure you're packed and ready to deploy when called. Thanks. Gentlemen, you're dismissed."

Colonel Williams, a distinguished officer at Arlington Air Base, was well respected by the men under his command. He was easily expected to attain the rank of General before retiring. Having deep blue eyes and salt and pepper hair, it hadn't exactly hurt his career that he was extremely handsome. His tall, lean athletic physique was evidence he kept in shape. It was paramount his troops followed his exercise routine.

Walking out of the meeting, Alex rubbed his forehead. He knew the timing couldn't be worse. How would he ever break the news to Noelle? She'd been through so much, the accident and the loss of her memory. Now to be hit with this so soon after they'd just met was too much. He had quickly become her source of strength, but more than that, they had fallen in love. There was no denying it. How would he ever be able to tell her? The possibilities of him being away for a year were more than troublesome. He was perplexed by his dilemma. What if Doctor Adams couldn't provide her the help she needed? There would be no one to help her if he were gone. This was the worst possible timing to be deployed. Why had he let himself get persuaded into signing up with the Air Force Reserves in the first place? He didn't need the money. It wasn't even significant. It was his ego and the fact it made him feel patriotic and macho. Now, his decision might cost him the love of his life.

"You look worried. Is everything alright?" Dan asked, patting him on the back.

"Yes. It's just a small personal problem at work."

Heck, it certainly wasn't a small personal problem at work. It was a huge personal problem, Alex thought to himself.

"Sorry. You want to join me at the Officer's Club for a drink before we leave the base?"

"Thanks, but yesterday I admitted some of the accident victims from the tour bus that overturned Interstate 50. I need to check on a few of those patients this evening. Maybe a rain check?"

"Sure. Give me a call. See you in a few days," Major Matthews grinned, walking outside. "Take care, Buddy."

"Yes. You too."

Walking over to his car, he did need a stiff drink. However, now wasn't the right time for that either. With the news he'd just been given, he was caught between a rock and a hard place, as the old saying goes. There was no way on earth he wanted to hurt or, worse yet, lose Noelle. They hadn't even had the chance to see each other outside of the hospital. He couldn't wait to be alone with her, and now that might never happen if she knew what he was facing, what they both were facing. The odds of finding each other under their present circumstances had been astronomical. Yet, it had happened. It was real, and he wouldn't change a thing, not even the unfortunate circumstance of her tragic accident and loss of memory. But, heck, she didn't need memories of her past. She had him now, and the future was all theirs, or at least he had certainly hoped before hearing Colonel Williams' words this afternoon. Deciding a stiff drink was in order, he called Trevor at the hospital.

"Hey, Doctor Reed, this is Doctor Bennington."

"Hey, Alex, what's up? Buddy, you never call me anymore. I feel neglected."

"Trevor, knock it off. I need you to cover my patients this evening. At least the ones I admitted from the bus accident."

"Okay. What's wrong? Are you being deployed? Got a dilemma with sleeping beauty?"

"Listen, Trevor, I don't need any smart remarks from you. Trust me, now isn't the time to push my buttons. I'll explain later. Whatever you do, don't mention anything about a deployment. I'm not coming into the hospital this evening. So, I won't be doing rounds. You will cover for me. Right?" Alex questioned.

"Yes. Don't worry. I've got this. However, you'll owe me?"

"Not a problem. Talk with you tomorrow."

"I love you, Buddy. It will all work out," Trevor assured him.

"Thanks. Talk to you later."

No words of encouragement could ever help the way he felt. However, Trevor had given him some time to gather his thoughts. Remembering an unopened bottle of Jack Daniels at his apartment, it would have to suffice. Now that he had driven off base and was wearing his uniform, there was no other available option.

Walking into his apartment, he instantly unbuttoned the shirt to his uniform, removed it, and threw it over the sofa. Wearing only his T-shirt and pants, his hands shook as he lit a cigarette. Taking a moment to relax, he sat down on the sofa. What was he doing? He needed a drink. Walking into the kitchen, he quickly found a bottle of Jack Daniels. Pouring himself a drink, he tossed it back in one gulp. Afterward, he grabbed the bottle and a glass and walked back into the living room. He poured himself a larger drink and downed it in one long continuous swallow as he sat down on the sofa. Stopping to enjoy his cigarette, he lounged back. What was he doing? He had to slow down. Maybe one more, he thought. Downing a third shot, he finally laid his head back on the sofa. He felt somewhat better. However, thoughts of Noelle still swirled relentlessly in his mind. Just his luck, he'd finally found the girl of his dreams, and in less than twenty-four hours after their meeting, there was a high probability she would never want to see him again.

Staring at a small oval frame sitting on the coffee table, it contained his parent's photo. He knew the passion and love which connected them. He wanted what they had together. Fate had brought Noelle into his life, and he was resolved to do everything possible to keep it that way. Deciding not to give her the news of his impending deployment, he wanted to enjoy the next few days. He wanted to spend every possible second with her waiting until she was out of the hospital to break the news. Hopefully, over the next few days, she would be so smitten with him that she would never want to be without him other than maybe a few short deployments. With Trevor having covered for him, Alex called it an early evening and retired with his glass of whiskey.

Making rounds the following day, he was anxious to see Noelle after first checking on patients admitted from the bus accident. Finally, walking into her room, he smiled.

"So, how's my amnesia patient this morning? Did you see Doctor Adams?" Alex inquired, closing the curtain which surrounded her bed.

"Oh, Julie. She was wonderful."

"Wow. You referred to her as Julie. So you must like her?"

"Yes. It appears Doctor Adams is very knowledgeable about amnesia. But, of course, she reiterated what you said in regards to how long it might take before my memory returns, and she also agreed with you on other things as well."

"Oh, really, concerning what?"

"The fact my memory could never return. Alex, what would I do if that happened? I'm not sure that I could deal with that."

"Sweetheart, let's give it some time. However, if the worst happens and your memory doesn't return, we'll deal with it. No worries."

"Alex, I'm nervous about going home with Edith on Friday. I'm sure she's a good person, but I don't really know her. I might not remember anything about my home or my belongings. What would I do if I felt uncomfortable living there? I have no other place to go," Noelle questioned, becoming emotional as tears gently rolled down her cheeks.

"If you feel that you would be uncomfortable staying with Edith, that's not a problem. The solution is a no-brainer. You can stay with me, no questions asked. In fact, you have no idea how happy I would be to know that you are coming home with me. However, it won't be possible for you to be seen leaving the hospital with me. So instead, I'll have Becky, Trevor's wife, pick you up and bring you to my apartment.

He wanted and needed every second he could have with her. Maybe this was his lucky break. Even though he would never deny Edith the right to have her granddaughter back at home, he needed Noelle desperately. He wanted her more than she could ever know at this moment.

"Really. Alex, are you sure? I would never want to be a burden."

"Sweetheart, you trust me, right?" He waited with bated breath for her answer.

"Alex, yes. I trust you," Noelle smiled.

"Then I don't see a problem with us living together. Unless you don't want to share living arrangements and are saving yourself for marriage," he wickedly teased with a wink.

"Alex, that's absurd. I would love to move in with you. If you're positive, I won't be an inconvenience?"

"Positive. However, discretion is key until you're released and out of the hospital. Sweetheart, thank God you were involved in the accident and lost your mind," he laughed.

"You're funny. I didn't lose my mind, just my memory. However, you might begin to lose your mind if I move in with you."

"Oh, I love to live dangerously. I'll take my chances," Alex grinned. Then, looking down at his watch, he noted the time. I have to go. I've got rounds to make, and you need to get some rest."

"Do you have to leave?"

"Yes. I'll check on you tonight before I leave the hospital.

"You promise."

"Oh, you're going to be trouble. Aren't you? I love it. We'll make great roommates."

"But, you never told me anything about your past, and I want to know everything. Everything," Noelle insisted.

"Somehow, I believe we'll have plenty of time to discuss my past. But there's not much to know, come to think of it."

"Well, I'll be the judge of that."

"Sweetheart, I have to go. I'll see you later tonight. Get some rest," Alex smiled, leaning over to give her a quick kiss.

"Thanks, Alex," she whispered.

Then pulling back the drapes, he was out the door.

Tomorrow would bring another day. One more day to spend with the girl who was now consuming his every thought.

Chapter Four

I t was Friday. Noelle had been downgraded from the ICU and was finally being released from the hospital. So ultimately, the question of where she would go had been settled, at least in Alex's mind.

"Good morning, Sweetheart. Are you excited to be leaving?" Alex inquired with a huge smile.

"Most definitely. However, I want to speak to you regarding that. It seems you've been so busy the past few days that we've hardly had time to talk."

"Okay. What's on that cute little mind of yours?"

"Alex does the possibility of me moving in with you still exist?"

"Yes. Of course, you're moving in with me. I thought we had already agreed on that."

"Alex, are you sure?"

"Well, let's see if this helps," he winked, kissing her discreetly. "Noelle, nothing, and I do mean nothing could make me happier," he added.

"Thanks, because I've already told Edith."

"How did she take the news?"

"I think she was a little disappointed, but she said she understood. I'm not sure. However, this is about me and how I feel."

"Sweetheart, let me think, you're twenty-four. Isn't that correct?"

"Yes."

"Well, then I think you're old enough and completely capable of making your own decisions. Surely, Edith had to know that you might decide to move out at some point in your life. Is she stopping by to see you before you leave the hospital?"

"No. But she said we were welcome to stop by her house and pick up my things."

"Why don't we get you settled into the apartment, and then I can run over and pick up whatever you need. How does that sound?"

"Geez, Doctor Bennington, it seems you have everything worked out."

"Would you like to hear some good news? I have a surprise."

"Of course. What is it?" Noelle smiled, intrigued at hearing the word surprise. Don't keep me waiting in suspense."

"I have this weekend off from my job at the hospital. So now, we'll have the entire day to get you settled. Plus, if you feel up to it, we've been invited to dinner tomorrow evening. I'd like you to meet my friends, Doctor Trevor Reed, and his wife, Becky. I think you'll like them. Becky has offered to pick you up today when you're released."

What he'd deliberately omitted was the reason he had so many free days. The hospital had already been informed of his impending deployment. Everyone had been made aware of his leaving, everyone except Noelle. He needed more time to figure out how he would tell her. However, telling her could wait. He had more important things to take care of at the moment. Getting her settled into his apartment took priority.

"Wow, Alex, you're kidding. So you're free for the entire weekend?" she eagerly questioned.

"Yes. It looks like you'll have me all to yourself. Does this mean that you're excited?"

"Excited. Are you kidding? I'm thrilled. Let's get out of here," Noelle demanded, getting out of bed.

"Sorry. You'll have to stay until I go down and sign your release. One of the attendants will bring you a wheelchair. You're not allowed to walk out unassisted. Just hang loose for a few minutes. I'll be right back."

Almost a half-hour later, there was another knock at the door.

"Good morning Miss Carrington. I'm Jeffrey. I'll be taking you downstairs and out to your car," Jeffrey explained, pushing a wheelchair into her room. The orderly was tall and lanky. His blonde hair and tan, slim physique made him appear like an avid surfer. She was amused, knowing there was no possible place to surf in Missouri.

"Oh, thanks. I'm just waiting on Doctor Bennington," Noelle mentioned.

"Not any longer," Alex smiled, walking into the room.

"Good morning, Doctor Bennington," Jeffrey grinned.

"Good morning, Jeffrey. I'll push Noelle down to the entrance. I'm actually on my way out.

"Yes, sir."

Becky drove up within a few minutes to drive Noelle over to Alex's apartment.

"Goodmorning, I'm Becky, Trevor's wife. It's nice to meet you. Alex is going to meet us at the apartment. I must say your accident sounded horrible. But Trevor and I are happy that you made such a remarkable recovery."

"Thanks. It's nice to meet you too. I don't know if Trevor told you, but I still don't remember the accident or my previous life. I'm praying that will all change soon."

"I'm sure it will happen. If there's anything I can do to help, please don't hesitate to call. We've been friends with Alex since medical school," Becky smiled.

Reaching the apartment, they arrived behind Alex.

"Wow, Alex has a Porsche?" Noelle laughed.

"Yes. Trevor says it's his baby."

Driving up to a gated community, Alex pushed his code into the security box. Immediately, the large wrought-iron gates swung open.

"Sweetheart, I live upstairs. Stay put. I'm going to come around and carry you. I don't want you climbing stairs, at least not now."

"Well, I'll leave you in the capable hands of Doctor Bennington,"

Becky laughed. "It was nice to meet you. We're looking forward to having you both join us for dinner. See you soon. Oh, Alex, I almost forgot, I picked up the pizza."

"Thanks, Becky."

"Alex, I feel strong enough to walk up the stairs."

"Really? Babe, who's the doctor? I believe that would be me," he winked.

Scooping Noelle into his arms, he carried her up the stairs and inside his apartment.

"I'll be right back," Alex mentioned, gently sitting her on the sofa. "I had Becky grab some pizzas earlier."

"Okay. I'll just be sitting here waiting." Noelle smiled.

Looking around the apartment, it appeared typical for a single guy, especially someone who didn't spend much time at home. The furniture and décor were very modest. The living room contained only the necessities, a rather unpretentious beige sofa, matching loveseat, and a glass coffee table with matching end tables. The décor was almost nonexistent. Two small paintings depicting Santorini, Greece, hung on the wall above the sofa. The apartment definitely lacked a personal touch from someone of the female persuasion. She could easily make it feel a lot more elegant and cozy, given a bit of time. However, that discussion could easily wait for another time. She was thrilled to be out of the hospital and with someone who loved her as much as Alex.

"What do you think?" Alex asked, walking in with the pizzas and wine.

"Alex, it's really nice. So who was your decorator?"

"Okay. I know. You don't have to rub it in. Maybe you can give me some ideas to freshen the place up. It's a pretty basic one-bedroom apartment. However, I'm hardly ever here. I practically live at the hospital. The complex does have awesome amenities if you'd like to use them later once you're completely recovered. Speaking of recovering, I think you probably should get some rest. You'll take my bedroom. I'm going to sleep on the sofa."

"Alex, I didn't come here to take your bed away from you. So why don't I sleep on the sofa and you stay in your room? Honestly, I would feel bad knowing that you are sleeping in your living room. And no disrespect, but I'm afraid your sofa doesn't look very comfortable."

"Sweetheart, don't worry about me. Honestly, you're talking to a carefree bachelor. I don't think there's anything in here that's really comfortable. Truthfully, as I said, I'm never home. I simply crash here at night when I get off work."

Thankfully, surveying his apartment, he'd remembered to put away his military uniforms. And anything which might make Noelle suspect that he was a member of a reserve unit. He would deal with that later next week. Right now, he just wanted to spend quality time with the beautiful young woman sitting on his rather modest sofa.

"Come. I'll show you the bedroom," Alex smiled, taking her hand. "It's not much. Don't get your hopes up."

Again, it was much the same as the living room. A queen-size bed covered in a simple blue duvet sat against the back wall. An armoire sat opposite the bed, holding a small television and workspace. The bedroom was simplistic, containing an adjoining bathroom. Sliding glass doors opened onto a small patio.

"Oh, I see you used the same interior decorator who designed your living room."

"Geez. Don't be so cruel. *Mi Casa Es Su Casa,*" he winked.

"I think you should lay down, Miss Carrington, and get some rest. It's only your first day out of the hospital," he suggested turning back the duvet. "Doctor's orders, I'm afraid. Where are your prescriptions? I did prescribe you some pain medications, didn't I?" he questioned with a quizzical expression. "I'll bring you a slice of pizza and something to drink."

"Oh, Alex, I'm not taking anything for pain. I don't need it or anything to help me relax. As long as you're here, I'm fine. Oh my gosh," Noelle panicked. "Alex, we didn't go to Edith's house. I have no clothes, not even anything to sleep in. What am I going to do?"

"Sweetheart, it isn't the end of the world. I'm sure I have something you can wear. You can borrow a pair of my pajamas and wear my robe.

We'll go over to Edith's house tomorrow and get some of your things. How does that sound?"

"Well, I suppose I have no other choice."

"I like your way of thinking," Alex agreed as he rummaged through his closet. "What about this, Miss Carrington? I do believe it's the latest fashion," he teased, handing her a pair of camouflage pajama pants.

"Alex, I'm not going hunting, and I need a shirt," she laughed.

"I guess you're right. Let me keep looking. Would you prefer a tee-shirt or pajama top?" Alex asked, handing her a pair of navy sweatpants and a sleeveless tank. "Will this do?"

"Let me try them on."

Walking into the bathroom, she tried on the sweatpants and tank. It appeared Alex's clothes were way too large. They completely hung off her petite frame. Walking out, they laughed hysterically.

"Okay. Let me rethink this. How about one of my shirts?"

Once again, he went back into his closet and pulled out a very soft and comfortable white shirt with buttons.

"Try this. I know it's a dress shirt, but it buttons down the front, and it's really soft. I think you'll find it comfy."

"Okay. Let me try it on, but I'm not making any promises."

Walking out from the bathroom wearing his white dress shirt, she wore her hair pulled back into a ponytail. Noelle had never looked sexier. She took his breath away. He was speechless, and he was never at a loss for words.

"What do you think?"

"Wow, Sweetheart, you're absolutely stunning," he whistled.

"Really, Alex? You make me feel pretty even wearing your white dress shirt."

"Noelle, you're gorgeous. I can't take my eyes off you. Would you like pizza?"

"Of course. Can we eat in the living room?"

"Anywhere you want," he smiled. Taking her hand, he pulled her back toward the living room. "Sit down on the sofa. I'll get the pizza. Oh, have you taken any medications today?"

"No. Why?"

"Well, I'll pour you a small glass of wine. Be right back."

Quickly returning, Alex carried two glasses of wine and one of the pizza boxes along with napkins.

"Oh, I'm sorry. Do you need a plate?"

"Alex, sit down. It's fine. We don't need plates. You have napkins."

"Okay. I never have anyone over, so you'll have to forgive my manners."

"You worry too much. Everything is awesome," Noelle remarked, shoveling a large slice of pizza into her mouth. "This is delicious," she smiled with a smidgeon of tomato sauce clinging to her bottom lip.

He took his napkin and wiped her mouth, afterward giving her a quick kiss.

"Wow, it appears you do love pizza. Geovany's is my favorite." Reaching for another slice, Alex handed it to her. "Eat up, doctor's orders," he winked, taking a sip of wine.

"The wine is amazing. I love it," Noelle mentioned finishing her last sip.

"Sorry. No more wine. You might need pain meds later tonight. Be right back." Alex went into the kitchen and retrieved the bottle.

Pouring himself another glass, he stared into the depths of her gorgeous blue eyes.

"Sweetheart, I'd like to make a toast...*Here's to our journey together. Wherever it takes us.*"

Unexpectedly, she pulled him toward her, giving him a quick, passionate kiss.

"Wow. My kind of girl. Can we try that again?" Alex teased, setting his wine glass down on the coffee table.

Affectionately pulling her close to his chest, he kissed her with such intensity it took her breath away. She felt like putty in his hands. Suffice it to say, for the next few minutes, the pizza was quickly forgotten.

"Would you like another slice?"

"No, thanks. I'm suddenly feeling exhausted," Noelle yawned.

Picking up his beautiful girl, he carried her into the bedroom. Turning back the duvet, he gently slipped her under the covers pulling the blanket around her shoulder. Kissing her on the forehead, it appeared she was already asleep. He quietly closed the drapes and shut the door.

Walking back into the living room, he poured himself another glass of wine and lit a cigarette. Knowing that she was with him, even if she was asleep in the other room, felt phenomenal. Alex finished his cigarette and the last of the wine. Despite the fact it was still early in the day, he took off his shoes and stretched out on the sofa. Feeling sleepy, he turned off the light closing his eyes. Quickly, he drifted off within seconds.

He was asleep for a short time when suddenly he felt soft hands gently caressing his day's growth of stubble. Noelle was leaning over him as he opened his eyes.

"Sweetheart, what's the matter? Are you okay?"

"Yes. I'm lonely," she whispered demurely. "I can't sleep without you next to me. Can you come into the bedroom and stay with me?"

Alex smiled. Without a single word, he lovingly scooped her up in his arms and carried her back to bed. Putting her under the warm covers, he slipped in beside her. Feeling the warmth of Noelle's body next to his felt comfortable. Within moments they fell asleep. They were home.

Chapter Five

Waking up to the brilliance of the morning light, which filtered in through the damask curtains, Alex stared at the beautiful woman sleeping peacefully beside him. Never before could he remember a time when having a gorgeous female in his bed hadn't resulted in passion and intimacy. However, this time, it was different. It was no longer about his needs but rather hers. She clung to him like an innocent child, scared and vulnerable. He could easily understand. Her past had been stolen due to the accident and the resulting amnesia. Yet, loving her made it easy for him to do the right thing. She trusted him.

Softly pulling her long curls away from her face, he gently kissed her on the forehead. Trying not to wake her, he quietly slipped out of bed. He needed coffee. Deciding the morning called for a proper breakfast, he walked into the kitchen. Unfortunately, finding his fridge empty, perhaps she was right. They might possibly starve. Alex laughed at the very notion. Brewing a pot of coffee, his usual morning routine of juice and oatmeal would have to take precedence over bacon and eggs.

Pouring two cups of coffee, he walked back to the bedroom. Sitting their hot beverages on the nightstand, he decided to wake the gorgeous girl sleeping peacefully in his bed.

"Good morning, Sweetheart," he lovingly whispered, kissing her awake.

Slowly opening her eyes, Noelle smiled. "Thank you for last night and bringing me to bed," she whispered, returning his kisses.

Pulling him down next to her, she playfully wrapped herself in his arms.

"I brought coffee."

"Coffee can wait. I just want to lay here in your arms. Surviving the accident and having you in my life has made me realize how lucky I am to be alive. I feel like I'm living in a dream," Noelle smiled, snuggling against his warm body. "The other guy involved in the accident didn't make it. Did you know? Perhaps, I was given a second chance because there's something that I'm supposed to do with my life?"

"Noelle, I'm sorry. Those are deep thoughts. I assure you, you're not living in a dream. Let me help you face reality. Remember how you said we might starve because you're not a great cook. Well, it just so happens you're stuck with oatmeal, coffee, or juice this morning," he grinned.

"Alex, I'm pouring out my inner feelings to you, and you want to talk about breakfast."

Tightly clenching her hand into a fist, she was just about to make him regret his words by jabbing him playfully in his upper arm. Suddenly, as if by instinct, Alex grabbed her hand, quickly preventing her assault. Pulling her closer, he kissed her with intense passion. Suddenly, she felt an invasion of warmth spread throughout her petite body.

"Alex, that's not fair."

"Really," he winked, giving her another quick kiss on the forehead. "Sweetheart, I'm a guy. We usually have only two things on our minds. One is food, and I'll let you guess the other," he teased wickedly.

"Oh, let me guess, sexy sports cars?" she questioned impishly.

He loved her feisty spirit and tenacity. It had only been their first night together, and he was already going to miss her.

"I think our coffee is cold. Would you like me to pour you another?"

"No. It's fine."

"At work, my coffee invariably gets cold before I can finish it. Do you feel well enough to have dinner with Trevor and Becky later tonight?" Alex questioned.

"Yes. Unless you've changed your mind."

"No. I would never hear the end of it from Trevor if we didn't show up. If it weren't for him, I probably would have given up on my aspirations of becoming a doctor. We went to medical school together, and his motivation and drive kept me from throwing in the towel several times."

"Sounds like he was significant in your career. I can't wait to meet him. I really like Becky."

"Why don't we get dressed, and I'll take you out for breakfast. Aren't you starved?

"No. Actually, I'm fine. I'd rather stay in and have a bowl of oatmeal. You did mention you had oatmeal, right?"

"Yes. Are you sure?"

"Yes. I love oatmeal," Noelle mentioned nonchalantly. "Oh my gosh, Alex, I remember. I love oatmeal. I remembered," she screamed excitedly, sitting up in bed. "Can you even believe it? I remembered oatmeal."

"Wow. You did," Alex smiled.

"What do you think? Do you think I'll get all of my memories back? What's going on? You're my doctor?" she questioned impatiently.

Alex loved the way she always invariably asked questions with other questions. He loved her childlike fascination and curiosity.

"Well, it's too early to know for sure. However, I've never seen anyone so excited over oatmeal," Alex laughed. "Do you remember anything else?"

"No. Should I?"

"Not necessarily. I was just curious. It's a great start."

"Alex, thank God you love oatmeal and that your fridge was empty. Do you know how much this means to me? Something as simple as oatmeal," she smiled.

"Yes. Sweetheart, I'm totally captivated by the fact we both share the love of oatmeal," he winked. "I think we better get up and get the day started. It's getting late. You do remember we've been invited to dinner later this evening?" he joked.

"That's not funny. This morning has gotten off to a great start. I'm so excited. Clothes, I have nothing to wear," she panicked.

"Oh, I'm not so sure about that. I think you look pretty darn sexy in my shirt. It's a great look for you."

"Really. Alex, I'm sorry, but you have no sense of style. You handed me a pair of camouflaged pants last night."

Quickly pulling her hair back, she reached for his hand.

"I'm starved. Let's eat. Afterward, I need you to take me to Edith's house to get my clothes."

"Geez, for someone who wasn't the least bit hungry a few minutes ago, you seem famished," he laughed. "Of course, I'll take you."

"Well, silly, that was before I remembered that I loved oatmeal, she laughed, giving him a quick, intense kiss.

"Sweetheart, another kiss like that, and I could easily forget about dinner. We could spend the entire day in bed. What do you think?"

"I think you better get dressed. We have to get my clothes. Besides, I'm anxious to meet your friends."

Stopping at Edith's later that morning, Noelle took her time sifting through clothes, shoes, and other necessities. Looking around the house, even her photos as a child didn't appear to trigger her memory. Then, walking over to the fireplace, she picked up her parents' wedding photo. Tears welled within her eyes for the parents she never knew.

"Noel, I gave you these diamond earrings on your twenty-first birthday. They always looked so lovely on you. Why don't you wear them?" Edith mentioned.

"Thank you," Noelle smiled, putting her arms around Edith.

After spending over an hour going through her closet, she was confident her wardrobe was complete. Saying their goodbyes, Noelle and Alex were finally on their way to dinner at Trevor and Becky's home. Remembering to purchase beer, Alex made a quick pit stop by the liquor store before arriving.

Ringing the doorbell, Noelle looked stunning in a pair of denim jeans and a navy blue sweater. Wearing her hair pulled back in a braid, it exposed the magnificent sparkling diamond earrings. With his arm tightly wrapped around her tiny waist, Alex looked handsome. He casually wore a pair of denim jeans and a blue sweatshirt, which depicted his favorite football team, the Seattle Seahawks. They appeared to a certain degree like Ken and Barbie.

"Come in. Glad you both could make it," Trevor greeted, taking the six-pack of beer that Alex was holding in his other hand. "Noelle, it's so nice to meet you finally. Alex has told me a lot about you. Have a seat. I'll let Becky know you're here."

"Wow, Alex, it appears they didn't use your decorator. Their apartment is gorgeous," Noelle smiled, taking a seat on their comfy leather sofa close to Alex.

Looking around their apartment, it was lavishly designed in modern décor and furnishings. The black leather sectional encased a wood coffee table that displayed unique carvings of elephants underneath its glass enclosure. Asian-inspired art was lit to enhance the walls. An ornamental palm and other greenery tastefully filled the room. It was exquisite.

"Trevor smiled as Becky walked in. Becky is from Manila. We met while I was working with an organization called Doctors Without Borders in the Philippines."

"It's nice to see you again. I must say Alex speaks highly of you and Trevor. In fact, he credits Trevor with his making it through medical school."

"Well, I'm not so sure that I can take credit for that accomplishment. Would either of you like something to drink?" Trevor questioned.

"Yes. I'll take a beer," Alex grinned. "Don't need a glass," he added. "Noelle seems partial to wine, especially the reds if you have it."

"Geez, Alex, I think I can speak for myself, " Noelle whispered, pinching him inconspicuously under his sweatshirt.

"Ouch," Alex quietly flinched, giving her an intense stare.

"That will teach you to let me speak for myself," she smugly corrected him.

"Why don't we take our drinks outside to the terrace," Trevor suggested.

"Noelle, would you like to accompany me into the kitchen?" Becky asked.

"Sure."

"You're apartment is beautiful."

"Thanks. I guess you've seen Alex's apartment?" Becky smiled.

"Yes. It certainly lacks ambiance," Noelle laughed.

"Oh, I know. I've repeatedly tried to let Alex know that I'd be happy to help him spruce it up a bit. He's a typical bachelor. If Trevor and I weren't married, I'm sure he would live no differently. Personally, I think it takes a woman's touch to make any place elegant and comfy."

"I totally agree. Is there anything I can do to help?"

"No. Just enjoy your wine. I've made a huge potato salad. It's the guy's favorite. Trevor is grilling steaks, and I've made one of my favorite recipes, baked salmon with herb seasoning. I've got everything else ready to eat as soon as he's done with the grill. How are you feeling? Trevor told me about the accident. I'm sorry to hear about your amnesia."

"Thank you. Actually, as of this morning, some of my memories seem to be returning."

"That's awesome. Hopefully, you'll recover all your memories."

"Yes. That's my goal. I did remember something as simple as my love for oatmeal, so that's a start."

Walking into the kitchen to grab two beers, Trevor paused. "Oh, I didn't mean to interrupt any girl talk," he laughed. "Oh, Babe, please don't let me forget the pitcher of peach slushies in the fridge."

"Trevor and his frozen concoctions. You would think he was a bartender in another life," Becky laughed.

As Trevor tended the steaks, Alex leaned against the balcony rail and lit a cigarette.

"Hey man, does Noelle know you smoke? Please take my advice and extinguish that thing before Becky sees it. You know how she feels about cigarettes."

"Trevor, I'm nervous. I still haven't told Noelle about my deployment."

"What? Are you crazy? Don't you leave in less than four days? What are you waiting for? This isn't good."

"I know. I guess it's just the chance of losing her." Taking one last draw on his cigarette, he hesitantly put it out, quickly hiding the cigarette remains in a trash can.

"I've got an awesome idea. It might just help with your dilemma. At least, it would be a great place to get away for the next three days.

I'll give you the keys to my parent's lake house on Summit Lake. You know the place, it's got a dock, boathouse, and my dad's speedboat. Not to mention, the location is breathtaking. You should drive up after dinner. In fact, if you'd like, I'll run inside and make the call. My parents have someone who looks after the place when they're not there. You remember, James, don't you? It should only take about three hours to drive up to the lake. The weather is amazingly warm this weekend. However, I'll tell James to make sure there is a stockpile of wood on hand for a nice fire tonight. It gets cold in the higher altitudes after dark. What do you think? Are you onboard?" Trevor grinned, totally pleased with himself for coming up with the idea.

"Well, if you're sure it wouldn't be an inconvenience?"

"Are you kidding? It will be perfect. My parents hardly go up anymore since my dad got out of the hospital. His emphysema has gotten much worse this past year. He's on oxygen twenty-fours a day now, and his mobility is minimal."

"Geez, Trevor, I sure hate to hear that."

"Oh, thanks. I think we all pretty much knew what to expect when my father's health deteriorated. That's another reason I continually nag you to stop smoking. Those things will kill you. But then again, you're a doctor, and I don't have to preach to the choir. You know I love you," Trevor smiled.

"I think the lake house is a great idea," Alex finally agreed. "Alright, go ahead and make the call. However, I want to keep it a secret. I don't want Noelle to know our destination until we arrive later tonight."

"Awesome, I'll sneak into the bedroom and make the call. What do you want on hand as far as food and snacks? Do you want to grill outside on the back deck overlooking the lake? Remember, there is only one restaurant nearby. It's a small place called The Country Kitchen. They serve a great breakfast. Also, I'll have James pick up a variety of prepared meals. You won't even have to cook unless either of you feels the need. I'm excited for you. Heck, next weekend, I might just take Becky. I need a break from the hospital. Enjoy some fresh mountain air, and put Dad's boat in the water. Okay, I'll be right back. Keep the grill going while I sneak inside," Trevor grinned.

Returning in only a few short minutes, Trevor was wearing a huge grin. "Great. It's all arranged. Consider it my going away gift. James said, not to worry about food or drinks. He'll take care of everything. Here are the keys. Don't lose them," Trevor teased.

"Wow. How can I ever thank you?" Alex acknowledged taking the keys as he twisted the top from another beer.

"Buddy, just enjoy yourself with that gorgeous girl of yours. I hope and pray everything goes well. Just remember, she's been through a lot."

"Thanks, Trevor, but I'm aware of that. Geez, I was the surgeon who operated on her when she was brought into the hospital."

"Wow. You're a doctor," Trevor teased lightheartedly. How in the world did someone like you get through medical school? Oh, I remember. You had a buddy," Trevor grinned, taking a huge sip of beer. "We should get the girls. The steaks are done, and I'm starved."

After dinner, everyone sat outside, enjoying Trevor's frozen slushies. As the evening got later, the darkened sky quickly filled with an abundance of twinkling stars.

"Well, I hate to end the evening, but I should get my patient home. Oops, I meant to say, my gorgeous girl. But, as her doctor, I'm afraid she needs a lot of rest," Alex winked, looking over at Trevor.

"Oh, we completely understand. It's been great having you both here. We look forward to doing it again," Trevor mentioned. How about a cup of coffee for the road?"

"Yes. I'll be right back," Becky agreed. Immediately she ran into the kitchen to pour them each a travel mug of coffee. Trevor had secretly disclosed their impending road trip to her without Noelle knowing.

Quickly returning, she handed them each a tall insulated cup of coffee.

"Thanks, Becky, but I really don't think it's necessary. We only live about two blocks away," Noelle laughed.

"Well, enjoy it anyways," Becky smiled.

"Good night. Talk with you tomorrow," Trevor grinned, seeing them to the door.

"Have a wonderful evening," he added coyly.

"Did I miss something? It felt as if they rushed us out of their apartment," Noelle explained, getting inside the Porsche.

After stopping for gas, Alex entered the freeway.

"Okay. What's going on? I know we didn't have to take the freeway to reach their apartment. Where are we going?" Noelle questioned curiously.

"Sweetheart, it's a surprise. Are you up for a little road trip this evening?" Alex winked.

"Well, maybe, if you tell me what's going on and where we're going."

Sitting back in her seat, she was puzzled. She had no idea tonight would include more than dinner with friends.

"Why don't you relax and take a nap. I've got this," Alex grinned. "I'll let you know when we arrive."

"Arrive, where?"

"I'm afraid your questions will get you nowhere. I love you. Suffice it to say, I don't think you will be disappointed. Trust me."

"Okay, Dr. Bennington, I trust you. I do feel a little tired. Maybe I will try to get a little sleep."

"Great, just what I wanted to hear. Close your eyes."

After driving for over two hours, the road leading up to Summit Lake was getting closer. Finally, after another hour, the road sign announced the off-ramp leading to their destination. They were almost there. Looking over at Noelle, she appeared to be sleeping.

Taking the next exit, Alex remembered the narrow two-lane road leading down to the shores of Summit Lake. He had spent many weekends here as a guest of Trevor's while attending medical school. Trevor was known for throwing outrageous, lavish parties at the lake house without his parent's knowledge. It would be the perfect environment to break the news. At least, he hoped the tranquility of the peaceful setting and fresh mountain air might help Noelle relax.

Turning into the short circular drive, they had finally arrived. The tall lanterns which hung on each side of the oversized oak doors were glowing. It made the house seem very warm and inviting. Apparently, James had left them on for their late arrival. Driving under the tall stone portico, Alex parked the car. Quickly getting out of the Porsche, he ran around the car and over to unlock the massive oak doors. Taking a glimpse inside, he noticed the fireplace and its glowing embers, which were still burning. A champagne bucket holding a bottle of champagne had been left sitting on the end of the massive stone hearth. James had not missed a thing.

Running back outside, he opened Noelle's car door. She was still sound asleep. Picking her up, he carried her inside. He noticed several decorative throw pillows on the floor in front of the fireplace and gently laid her down in front of the warm fire. Carefully removing her shoes, he tried not to wake her. Noticing a large quilted throw laying over a nearby leather sectional, he gently covered her. Amazingly, she had not awakened. Making another trip out to the car, he brought in one of her packed bags from Edith's and then returned to lock the car. Placing the bag inside by the front door, he would now be the one without clothes. Silently laughing, perhaps clothes would be optional this weekend. However, he knew the stunning young woman deep in sleep was a clothes hound. It was evident as nothing escaped her, not even camouflaged pajamas.

Deciding to see what was available in the fridge, he quietly walked into the kitchen. Without turning on a light, he looked inside. Wow, James did not disappoint. It was fully stocked with beer, wine, and water bottles. Not to mention the fact there was milk, juice, eggs, and bacon. James had done an unbelievable job of making sure they lacked for nothing. Checking the freezer, it contained steaks, salmon, and frozen entrees. Grabbing a beer, he twisted the cap from the bottle. Walking back into the living room, he looked around. The house had not changed in appearance. Massive wooden beams crisscrossed the vaulted ceilings, and enormous floor-to-ceiling windows encased the back of the living room. When exposed, the windows revealed the lake's beauty and the tall, rugged peaks of the surrounding terrain. The full moon was easily visible through the upper portion of the uncovered windows. Its brilliant rays cast a mesmerizing glow across the room. Alex gasped, looking down at the beauty of his life. Noelle's long blonde hair shimmered in the moonlight. Her striking angelic appearance took his breath away. He felt like the luckiest man on earth.

Sitting down on the sofa, he couldn't take his eyes off her as he quietly finished his beer. It was evident she was out for the night. He took off his shoes and laid down in front of the fireplace beside his beautiful apparition. Gently snuggling against her warm body, Alex gently pulled the large quilt over them and closed his eyes. He was tired from the long drive. It was only moments before sleep invaded his body.

Waking early the following day as sunlight streamed in through the vast vaulted windows, he rolled over, gently kissing her on her forehead. He prayed, not knowing what the day held for them as a couple. He could only hope that her love for him would be strong enough to endure what needed to be said.

Suddenly, Noelle slowly opened her eyes. Then, sitting up in amazement, she began to take in the surrounding beauty of the vast living room's décor and magnificence.

"Oh my gosh, Alex, where are we? This house is unbelievable. Who built this incredible place? Please tell me you own it," she laughed.

"Sorry, Sweetheart, I only wish. It belongs to Trevor's parents. It's pretty darn amazing, isn't it? He gave me the keys last night. Just wait until you see the house in its entirety. It has five bedrooms, a game room, and a kitchen that would easily be any chef's dream. Not to mention the fact, it also has a dock, a boathouse, and a fabulous deck for entertaining."

"Are Trevor and Becky driving up today?" Noelle questioned.

"Sweetheart, I'm afraid it's just us. Are you disappointed?"

"No. Not at all. It just seems odd they didn't come."

"Well, I believe they are coming up next weekend. Are you hungry?"

"Oatmeal, is it?" Noelle smiled, tossing back the quilt. "Wow, I must have been tired. I don't even remember arriving last night or walking in?" she laughed, standing up to stretch her long skinny legs. Then, walking over, she pulled back the heavy brocade drapes covering the massive windows. "Oh my Lord, Alex, this is spectacular. Look at this view. It's unbelievable. Wow, the lake is beautiful, and the mountains surrounding it looks like a painting. It's breathtaking," Noelle smiled, awestruck by the panoramic vista.

"Yes. Sweetheart, it's phenomenal. Now, back to the idea of

breakfast," Alex laughed, walking up behind her. Putting his arms around her, she remained fixated on the view.

"Breakfast?" Alex reiterated as he attempted to pull her away from her thoughts.

"Oh, I'm sorry. I was a bit captivated by the gorgeous scenery. What do we have?"

"I think it's more of an option. What would you like?"

"Well, yesterday, when you mentioned bacon and eggs, for a brief second, I'll have to admit it sounded delicious."

"Are you saying you'd like bacon and eggs?"

"Yes."

"Okay. I think you just set a world record for the longest thoughts regarding breakfast," Alex winked. "I'll cook. If you want to change, I placed one of your bags by the front door. The downstairs bathroom and shower are just around the corner if you want to freshen up."

"Thanks. Where are your clothes?"

"Well, the funny thing is, I didn't bring any. This trip wasn't exactly planned," Alex replied loudly from the kitchen.

"Wow, you don't have any clothes? Maybe, I might have something you'd like. But, of course, I don't really have a lot of camouflaged outfits," Noelle laughed.

"You're never going to let me live that one down, are you?" he questioned from the kitchen.

"No."

"How do you want your eggs?"

"Over easy with toast, please. I'm going to take a shower. I'll be out soon."

"Would you like a cup of coffee before you take your shower?"

"Thanks. Coffee actually sounds great, just a little milk, no sugar."

"I'll bring it to you. Just a minute."

Knocking on the bathroom door, Noelle didn't answer. So finally, hearing the water from the shower, Alex decided to open the door and leave it sitting on the vanity. Walking in, it was like a sauna. Steam filled every inch of the bathroom.

"Coffee?"

"Thanks, babe, just sit it on the vanity. Would you please hand me the hair clip? I want to pull my hair back."

"Okay."

Handing her the hair clip, he was set up like a naïve animal caught in a trap. Instantly, Noelle grabbed his hand, pulling him into the shower.

"Oh, babe, I'm soaking wet. You're going to be sorry. It's on," Alex exclaimed. "I've got nothing to lose and nothing to wear."

Grabbing her in his arms, he pulled her close to his chest.

"I love you. You're crazy," he whispered.

"Shush, don't talk. I love you too," she whispered, pulling his soaked sweatshirt over his head.

For the next few minutes, even the hot steam coming from the shower felt cold compared to the heated passion that transpired between them. It was unexpected. Yet, neither of them dared to stop, totally giving in to the moment.

"Wow, sweetheart, I'll bring you coffee every morning," he winked, reaching for a towel. Then, tying it around his waist, he grabbed another towel for her.

"I love you. Please don't ever leave me," Noelle begged, tightly wrapping her arms around him. She was holding on to him with every ounce of her being.

Where had that come from? There was no possible way she could know why they were there or the fact he was about to be deployed. It was uncanny, almost as if she could read his mind.

"Babe, don't worry," he slowly hesitated. He hated himself at this very moment. How could he ever tell her? She trusted him, and he felt sick.

"Alex, when you dry off, I have an extra robe. It's large and has a belt. I think you might be able to wear it while we dry your clothes. I'm starved. Are you going to finish cooking breakfast?" she asked, wrapping her wet hair in a towel.

"Yes. You're lucky I hadn't turned on the stove earlier. We might possibly have burned this gorgeous place to the ground," Alex grinned.

"You're silly. Let me grab my extra bathrobe for you while I dry your clothes."

Returning to the bathroom, she handed him a pink flowery housecoat.

"Really, Sweetheart, you expect me to wear this?" he freaked. "It's pink, and worse yet, it has flowers on it.

"You're being ridiculous. There's no one here other than us. So who is going to see you? What other choice do you have? Oh yeah, let me think," she laughed. "You might possibly splatter hot grease all over your naked body, or worse yet, you might burn, your, you know," she hesitated.

"Burn my, what?" he persisted.

"You know? Your man's part."

"Sweetheart, I'm a physician. The male anatomy does have proper names," Alex teased wickedly, trying to keep a straight face.

He loved her naïve innocence. Even though moments earlier, in the shower, it hadn't appeared as prevalent.

"Okay. Give me the robe. I'll try it on, but this never leaves this house. Do you understand? If this ever gets back to Trevor, he'll never let me live it down. You do understand, right?" he reiterated.

"Yes. But I don't see why you're making such a big deal out of it."

Handing him the pink flowery robe, it barely fit. However, he could wrap it around his waist and wear it while cooking breakfast or until his clothes were dried.

Standing in the kitchen wearing a pink floral housecoat, he could quickly feel his virility diminishing. Yet, he was willing to make Noelle happy, even if it meant wearing a floral housecoat.

Finally, after enjoying a leisurely breakfast and not burning his private parts, he heard the dryer's signal indicating his clothes were dried.

"Sweetheart, we have the whole day to ourselves. What would you like to do?" he questioned, finally walking out of the bathroom in his clothes.

"Would it sound crazy if I said I just wanted to stay in and watch old movies and snuggle with you on the couch?" she asked tentatively.

"I'll have to honestly admit, considering the fact we're staying on a lake with such spectacular surroundings, it does sound a bit crazy.

But whose to say, if that's what you really want to do, then I guess I'm your guy."

Taking her hand, he led her into the living room. He knew he would easily do anything she asked as long as it meant the two of them were together. He knew later that evening, he was possibly going to hurt her in such a way that she might never be able to forgive him. Yet, he craved every second with her. Whatever they did today meant nothing to him, only the fact they were together.

"Thanks. Why don't we start a fire in the fireplace and pop some popcorn?" Noelle eagerly suggested.

"Sounds wonderful. Why don't you pop the popcorn, and I'll get the fire started and open a bottle of wine."

"Okay, that sounds fair to me," she agreed. "I'll do the popcorn."

After starting a roaring fire in the fireplace, he tossed more large pillows from the sectional onto the floor. Now, the only thing missing was a bottle of wine, glasses, and the television's controller to list available movies. Returning from the kitchen with their drinks, they were set to enjoy a movie marathon.

Walking in with a large bowl of popcorn, Noelle closed the heavy drapes and sat down on the floor in front of the fireplace. She looked sexy, wearing a black pair of palazzo pants and a black cropped shirt made of lace, which exposed her tiny midriff. Her long hair was swept upward in the back and held in place with a silver clasp. She looked ravishing. He was going to have a hard time focusing on the movies.

"Do you think you could possibly find some old classic movies?" she asked.

"Yes. Possibly. Let me check. I found the *Wizard of Oz* and *Gone With the Wind,* but I'm not sure I can sit through *Gone With the Wind.*"

"Great. It looks like the *Wizard of Oz,*" Noelle smiled.

Pulling her close to him, they watched not only the *Wizard of Oz* but *Casablanca, Roman Holiday,* and *China Town.* It was genuinely a marathon of older movies. The selection had not mattered to him, only the fact she was next to him. The day had flown, as they had only stopped to make hoagies, hot chocolate, and take a couple of bathroom breaks. Snuggling together on the comfy pillows in front of the warm roaring fire, it felt amazing. Actually, the day had turned out to be perfect even though he had not thought so at the beginning.

"Sweetheart, there's a full moon tonight, and in the mountains on a clear night, there's an incredible display of brilliant stars. Why don't we make a thermos of hot chocolate and go down to the lake? The night air will be refreshing, and it will be the perfect ending to a perfect day," he suggested. He had to get everything off his chest. It was killing him. He had to know if she would be strong enough to handle his unexpected news. After all, it was his reason for bringing her to the lake house.

"Yes. That sounds wonderful. I think we could use some fresh air. Why don't you make the hot chocolate, and I'll change into something warmer? I'll look for one of the jackets I packed at Edith's house earlier this morning."

Rummaging through her bags, she found what she was looking for in a pair of jeans and a white sweater. Then, pulling out a beige cable knit scarf with a matching stocking cap, she was all set for an evening under the stars.

"Wow. You look beautiful," Alex whistled. "I've got the thermos and two cups. Would you rather have coffee instead of hot chocolate?"

"No. I'd rather have the hot chocolate."

Hurriedly, she returned accessorized with her beige scarf and matching stocking cap. She looked stunning.

"Okay. I guess we have everything," Alex winked, grabbing the thermos of hot chocolate and cups. "Let me turn on the outdoor porch lights."

Opening the door, he took her hand. Leading her down the cobblestone path towards the lake, he put his arm around her, pulling her close. Alex flipped another switch, reaching the dock, illuminating hundreds of twinkling white lights. The entire pier and sun deck brilliantly glowed under the dark sky, giving it the appearance of floating above the lake.

"Wow, Alex, this is gorgeous. Trevor's parents have really put a lot of effort into making this property absolutely perfect," Noelle mentioned walking along the dock.

"Yes. I'll have to admit, Trevor and I've had some amazing parties out here in the summer."

Reaching the spacious deck, Alex held her as they took in the beauty of the lake at night under the stars. The water appeared to sparkle as it reflected the light radiating from the full moon.

"This is magical."

"Yes. It's magnificent. Let's take a seat on the bench, and I'll open our thermos of hot chocolate."

Sitting down, the smell of steaming cocoa, along with the invigorating night air, was hypnotic. Smoke rose from their cups as Alex filled them with the hot beverage.

"Alex, look up. I've never seen so many stars. Have you ever seen anything so exquisite in all your life?" Noelle questioned with child-like wonder and fascination.

"Yes. I'm sitting next to her," Alex smiled.

"Awe, that's so sweet. You've made me blush."

"Sweetheart, do you even know how much I love you? If it were possible, I'd pull down all these stars and tie them with a bow just for you," Alex remarked, taking her hand.

"Alex, you're shaking. What's wrong? Are you cold?"

"Noelle, I've brought you here for a specific reason."

"What's going on? What are you trying to tell me?" she questioned, not knowing if she wanted to hear the answer.

"Babe, I need you to be strong. There's something I have to tell you?"

"For heaven's sake, get on with it. You're making me nervous."

"Noelle, my unit is being deployed for a year. I'm in the reserves, and I leave in three days."

"I know," she cried, surrendering to her emotions.

"How is that even possible? There's no conceivable way you could possibly know?"

"Well, I overheard a conversation between two nurses aids as they were moving me out of ICU. It appeared one of the girl's brothers was being deployed. They mentioned your name and the fact you belonged to the same unit, but they didn't specify when? Then earlier last night, while I was in Becky's kitchen, I asked her to tell me what she knew.

She didn't want to say anything at first. She was afraid of Trevor finding out that she'd told me. I'm sorry. I just had to know. I was so distraught in the car last night. You have no idea. I couldn't talk, so I pretended to be asleep."

"You're joking. Right?" Alex questioned, not believing a word she'd spoken. He was in shock.

"No. I knew. After talking with Becky, I was devastated?" she cried, wiping her tears with the back of her hand.

"Why didn't you say something?"

"I knew you would tell me in your own time and in your way. Babe, I love you so much, but I don't know how I'm going to get through this. Really, I don't. I'm not as strong as you think, and it's just a few weeks until Christmas."

"Sweetheart, I know. I'm truly sorry. Noelle, you're a lot stronger than you know? You have no idea how worried I've been over telling you. I was afraid I was going to lose you. Seriously, after everything you've been through, I was actually terrified of telling you. I was afraid you might not be able to cope with the fact I was leaving and that you would rid me of your life as a way of dealing with everything. But, truthfully, I wouldn't have blamed you for doing it either."

"Alex, I'm sorry. I didn't mean to make you worry. I had no idea those were your thoughts. Is it really for an entire year?"

"Yes, but we can get through this. I promise. I'll call you every day if it's possible."

Deep in thought, Noelle got up from the bench and slowly walked to the edge of the deck. Gazing into the dark starlit sky, she futilely tried to hold back the myriad of tears which gently rolled down her face. "What should I do? Do I move back in with Edith or stay in your apartment," she asked. She was confused in regards to the direction of her life. She was at a crossroads.

"Sweetheart, I love you. You do what makes you feel comfortable. Honestly, I'd love it if you stayed at our apartment. But, under the circumstances, if you feel more relaxed staying with Edith, I have no problem with that," Alex lovingly suggested attempting to wipe her tears with his hand.

Pulling her tight against his chest, he'd never loved her more than at this very moment. "Noelle, I wished that I could take away your tears and hold you here forever, never letting you go," he whispered, kissing her moist face. "You know we are not the first couple on earth having to deal with this."

"I don't care," she cried. "Alex, listen, I know you're just trying to make me feel better, but frankly, I don't care about other people right now. Look around. Do you see other people, or do you just see us?" she cried, burying her head into his chest.

"Sweetheart, of course, I just see us. I get it. Noelle, really, I do. Please don't cry."

Holding her tight in his arms under a canopy of twinkling stars, Alex kissed her with intensity. It gave her goosebumps as twinges of excitement raced throughout her body. But unfortunately, the full moon's romantic ambiance, along with the reflection of the tiny lights dancing on the water, was barely noticed due to her overwhelming sadness.

"Alex, let's walk back to the house."

Turning out the lights, he put his arm around her. Then, leading her back toward the house, he stopped. Scooping her into his arms, he carried her the rest of the way.

Walking inside, he gently laid her down in front of the fireplace.

"Sweetheart, please don't cry. I love you. We have a few days left before I leave. I say we stay here until I have to go back to the apartment and pack. You're not getting out of my sight."

For the next two days, they cried together and laughed together. They watched movies, stayed up late, and shared lengthy talks about what their lives would be like after the deployment. They discussed marriage, children, and their dreams of grandchildren and old age. But, most importantly, they simply took advantage of every possible moment, held each other, and shared their feelings. Then as with all good things, it was time to leave. After hurriedly cleaning the house, it was time to pack. Leaving behind only the imprints of two people who were madly in love, they drove away. Hopefully, someday they would be invited back.

Arriving back at the apartment, there was now less than twenty-four hours before fate would separate them for twelve lonely months.

Waking early, Alex wanted to be the first one to get up. But, remaining in bed for a few covetous moments, he simply stared at the love of his life. He just needed to watch her breath, to know that she truly belonged to him. Letting her linger in bed for a few seconds longer in a state of bliss was all that he could do for her. Soon, she would face the agony of watching him leave. Quickly, he showered and shaved. Finally, putting on his military uniform, it was time to wake sleeping beauty.

"Sweetheart, it's time to get up. We have to go," he whispered. Kissing her awake, she slowly opened her eyes. Then, taking his hand, she gently pulled him down to the bed.

"Noelle, I'm dressed. We can't possibly start anything we can't finish," he smiled, kissing her on the forehead.

"Wow, Major Bennington, I must say you look rather handsome, and your cologne smells divine," she smiled, sitting up in bed.

"Sweetheart, while I have your attention, there are a few things we need to discuss really quick," he smiled, sitting down on the bed. "Here is your set of keys to the Porsche. Please try not to wreck it. Also, here are your keys to the apartment. I've left you enough money in our joint account to make a few furniture purchases. Just don't go overboard. I know this place needs a makeover, and I trust you'll do a great job. Now get dressed. I have to be at the base in less than an hour. I'm going to make us a cup of coffee and wait for you in the living room. Please, don't take long. We don't have much time."

Quickly getting up, Noelle raced into the bathroom to get dressed. Deciding to wear a little black dress with a jacket and heels, she accessorized with a strand of white pearls and matching earrings. Finally, sweeping back her long hair with a clasp, applying makeup, and spraying a hint of her favorite perfume, Noelle was ready. She wanted his last memories of her to be unforgettable. Walking out to the living room, she stopped dead in her tracks. Sitting on the coffee table was a huge bouquet of red roses, which Alex had delivered to the apartment.

"Alex, those are stunning," she exclaimed.

"Sweetheart, they're nothing compared to you," he winked, dropping down on one knee.

"Alex, what's going on?" Noelle gasped, anticipating his next move.

"Noelle, will you marry me?" Alex asked, opening a little black box revealing a single sparkling three-carat diamond ring he purchased after learning about his deployment.

"Are you serious?" she screamed.

"Yes. I believe I am," Alex winked. "I've never been more serious in my entire life."

"Yes. Yes. A thousand times, yes. Of course," she exclaimed with tears filling her eyes.

He placed the ring on her left hand and held her in his arms, kissing her passionately.

"Well, I guess that was my last official act before I turn everything over to you. Are you ready to go?"

Admiring the brilliant diamond on her ring finger, she was speechless, not having heard a word he'd spoken.

"Sweetheart, we have to go? I'm sorry."

Riding with him out to the base, she was in shock. She was engaged. She had to call Edith and Becky. For a brief second, she let herself forget the man of her life was about to leave for twelve long months.

Arriving at the flight line, Alex parked the Porsche.

"Noelle, please be careful with the car. Don't drive fast. You do remember how to get back to the apartment, right?" he questioned.

There was already a large group of people gathered to say goodbye to their loved ones as they approached the flight line. Quickly, pulling her aside, Alex held her one last time. Then, pausing briefly to kiss her passionately, Alex didn't mind having an audience. It was an impressive loving gesture. But, unfortunately, their kiss would have to carry him for months.

"Babe, I love you. See you in a few months," Alex smiled with a wink.

"Oh, Major Bennington, I love you more. I'll be here. Waiting," Noelle smiled tearfully.

Watching as he walked out of sight to board the enormous cargo plane, a river of tears continually flowed down her cheeks. Wiping her eyes, shared feelings of sadness and loss was obviously being felt by other spouses and family members. Observing their emotions reflected the stark reality and heartbreak that's, unfortunately, shared by military families.

Somberly, Noelle watched as the huge aircraft slowly made its way down to the end of the runway, stopping momentarily to turn around. Quickly gaining in speed, the massive cargo plane sped past those left behind. Lifting skyward, the plane dipped its wings in a final salute to the loved ones remaining on the tarmac. Wiping her eyes, muffled cries from women and children filled the air. Turning around, it was time to go home. Finding some solace in the other women sharing the same heartache, she walked away.

Staring at her ring, it was time to plan a wedding. Perhaps, Alex had left her with the only thing he could, the promise of a life together. Not having any more recollections of her past, it was time to focus on the future. Walking toward the Porsche, she smiled.

Chapter Six

Rubbing her eyes, she felt exhausted. Without Alex, Noelle had experienced a grueling, sleepless night. She had never felt so alone. Pulling the covers over her head, Noelle felt hopelessly lost. If only she could go back to sleep and wake up twelve months into the future. However, knowing there was no possible chance of that, she sat up. Looking around was all the encouragement she needed. The apartment begged to be redecorated and refurnished. But, first things first, she needed a hot shower and coffee to get the day started. Just as she was about to get into the shower, the phone on the nightstand rang.

"Good morning, Sweetheart. How are you?" Alex inquired.

"Lonely. I miss you."

"I only have a few seconds to talk. I arrived at the base this morning, and I'm being transferred closer to the skirmish. Apparently, there's a need for doctors closer to the war effort. So I'm not sure when I'll get to call again. I love you."

"Oh, Alex, I love you too."

Before she could even demand that he be careful, the connection was lost. Knowing he was being transferred into harm's way sent chills down her spine. This was not what she wanted to hear.

Walking into the kitchen, she needed something to calm her nerves. Looking through the cabinets, she found a bottle of Jack Daniels. It was almost empty. Reaching for a glass, enough remained for at least two shots. Pouring herself a small amount, she winced, quickly downing the strong drink. She had never acquired a taste for hard liquor. Taking her glass, along with the bottle, she walked into the living room. She could never have known this bottle, and Alex had spent time together when he'd been suddenly hit with the shocking news of his impending deployment. Deciding there was no reason to leave even the smallest amount of whiskey behind, she downed a final shot. Still wearing her nightgown, Noelle laid her head back on the sofa. This wasn't the way she had planned to start her day. However, feeling the warm, soothing effect of the alcohol as it coursed through her veins helped calm her frayed nerves. Beginning to feel drowsy, she closed her eyes. Even though it was early morning, sleep began to invade her petite body. She'd only been napping for a short time when the phone rang once again.

"Noelle, I'm calling to check on you. How are you doing?" Edith questioned.

"Well, to be honest, I had just fallen asleep on the sofa. I didn't sleep at all last night. Alex called this morning. He made it to the base in Italy, but he's been transferred closer to the war effort. I'm so worried about him."

"Oh honey, he hasn't even been gone forty-eight hours. Please don't do this to yourself. Alex is a grown man and a very responsible one at that. I'm sure he can take care of himself. However, I'm worried about you. Why don't you come over and spend the day with me? I'll cook dinner."

"Thanks, but I promised Alex I would redecorate the apartment, and there's no better time than today to get started. Besides, it will take my focus away from the fact he's gone. I'll call you later this week," Noelle suggested. "I love you."

"Honey, you can call me anytime, day or night. I love you too."

Over the next few weeks, Noelle visited every furniture store in Arlington, some more than once, as she made decisions on style, comfort, and, most importantly, affordability.

Not having received another call from Alex, she began to worry obsessively. She was not good at waiting. Still unable to sleep at night, she stayed up late, hanging drapes and adding her magic touch to each room.

After reaching her decisions on the furniture, the delivery trucks finally made their appearance. The apartment now reflected her gorgeous changes. Walking through each room, she felt proud of her accomplishments. Hopefully, Alex would feel the same when he came home. The freshly painted walls in the living room reflected a warm neutral color of beige. They showcased a dark brown microsuede sectional with a large square matching ottoman used as a coffee table. Tiffany lamps beautifully graced carved oak end tables. Finally, the entire apartment reflected her gorgeous touches throughout each room. However, despite her best efforts to bring a much-needed new décor to the apartment, she still felt hopelessly lost. It was time to focus on her needs.

Picking up the phone one afternoon, she called Becky. After a long conversation, Noelle decided her only recourse would be to finish her degree over the next twelve months. However, with memories of studying at the university still escaping her, she wasn't sure about her former decision to pursue journalism. The next day she scheduled an appointment with her college advisor, Professor Ames. He had been on staff for over twenty years as a senior advisor. He'd played a significant role in her journalism studies at the University in Arlington. Noelle had been a source of pride to him and other educators who had been involved with her studies. However, knowing of her recent accident, he was delighted she had decided to return. The appointment was set. She would meet him the following day and hopefully get the guidance she was seeking.

"Good morning, Noelle. It's good to see you. Come in. I must say you had us all worried. The accounts of the accident in the Arlington Gazette were horrifying."

"Good morning, Professor Ames. Thanks for seeing me. I know. The driver of the truck was killed instantly. I apologize if I seem a bit disoriented. The accident resulted in my having amnesia, and most of my memory hasn't returned."

"I'm sorry. Thankfully you've otherwise recovered. How can I help you this morning?"

"I would like to continue my studies. However, I'm unsure where to begin, not having any recollections of my past studies. To be honest, I'm not sure it's even journalism that still has my interest."

"Well, I must say you do present somewhat of a challenge. I can't say that I've actually experienced amnesia. However, it happened to one of my students. But don't worry, someone with your high grades and intellect should have no problem. I guess what concerns me the most is your question about pursuing journalism. Do you feel drawn towards a different major?"

"That's just it. I'm baffled. However, Humanitarian Studies seem to interest me at present. The accident has given me a reason to rethink my degree program. I feel as if I'm being given a second chance in life and more than ever compelled to make my life count. Does that even make sense?"

"Definitely. It sounds as if the accident was a life-changing experience. I'm so glad you came in today. If this deviation from journalism truly interests you, our university is beginning our next overseas study program next month. Consider it fate. You could easily become a part of our new team. I'm on the committee to finalize our choice of students. Our Humanitarian Department is going to send aid in the areas of food, medical treatments, and other services to those who live in economically or environmentally deprived countries. The team of students leaving next month will be working in the Philippines. Is this something in which you might be interested? If so, I'll put your name at the top of my list."

"To be honest, leaving the country certainly wasn't on my mind when I walked into your office. However, I think the timing couldn't be better. I'd like to take tonight to think it over. Then, can I give you a call in the morning?"

"Yes. Tomorrow is fine. We'll just need to get you registered. If you decide this is what you're looking for, I'll put you in contact with

Doctor Edward Thomas. He's overseeing this semester of our overseas programs. I think you'll fit in great. It was nice seeing you. Let me know," Professor Ames explained, seeing her to the door. Noticing the brilliant ring on her left hand, he paused. "Who's the lucky young man?"

"Doctor Alex Bennington, he's on staff at Methodist. However, he's recently been deployed for the next year with the reserves."

"Congratulations. I'm sorry to hear about your fiance's deployment. However, it sounds like this could be a great opportunity for you. Talk with you tomorrow."

Driving back to the apartment, she had to call Becky. What a coincidence. Becky was born and raised in the Philippines. She could easily give input on what to expect if she were to sign up for the overseas program. This could easily keep her busy for months while Alex was away on deployment.

Unlocking the door, she raced over to the phone. Becky answered, and another long conversation between the girls ensued. It now appeared they would continue their conversation over dinner later that night at Becky's apartment. Trying to stay busy, Noelle listened intently for an incoming phone call from Alex. The hours passed slowly. It seemed safe to say that he wouldn't call this afternoon. The idea of not hearing from him was overwhelming. How could he expect her to wait for months by the phone? No one could possibly live this way, especially her. Not even the idea of planning their wedding excited her. What if God forbid something happened, and he didn't make it home. Looking down at her ring, tears slowly ran down her cheeks. She was so close to having the man of her dreams permanently in her life. Unfortunately, twelve long months were standing in the way. Looking down at the clock, it was almost 6:30 p.m. She would have just enough time to stop at the florist to pick up flowers before dinner at 7:00 p.m.

Hearing the doorbell, Trevor answered the door.

"Hey, Noelle, come in. I heard you're possibly going to the Philippines. How does something like that happen so fast?" he questioned, taking the bouquet of pink roses.

"Well, I'll explain over dinner. Where's Becky?"

"Oh, she just ran into the bedroom to change."

"Wow. Something smells delicious."

"Oh, that would be chicken adobo. Have a seat. Becky will be right out. By the way, have you heard from Alex?"

"Only once, when he arrived in Italy. He's been transferred closer to the war effort. I'm really worried."

"Oh, don't worry about him. Believe me, Alex can take care of himself. He isn't stupid."

"Geez, Trevor, I never said he was stupid. You certainly don't have to be stupid to be killed or injured."

"I'm sorry, the wrong choice of words. I never meant to imply that Alex was stupid. I'm certain he'll be just fine."

Catching sight of Becky as she walked out of the bedroom, she saved him from his embarrassing slip of the tongue.

"Hey, Noelle, you look pretty in your red cardigan. Thanks for the beautiful roses," Becky smiled, walking into the living room. "I hope you like chicken adobo."

"I'm sure that I'll love it. It smells delicious."

"Why don't we go into the dining room. Everything is ready to eat. Trevor, why don't you pour the iced tea. I'll get the warming trays."

Enjoying a sumptuous dinner of chicken adobo, along with rice, their topic of conversation quickly became Becky's native country. Ending their meal with dessert, Maja Blanca, coconut pudding, the meal was exemplary.

"Why don't we have coffee in the living room?" Becky suggested.

"Honey, why don't you and Noelle go in and sit down. I'll get the coffee," Trevor smiled. "I'm sure you both still have lots to talk about."

After hours of debating the pros and cons of taking the overseas assignment with the university, it was beginning to get late.

"Sorry, ladies, I think I'm turning in for the evening. I have an early call at the hospital in the morning. Noelle, whatever you decide, I'm sure Becky will agree with me that you have both our blessings. Not that you need it, but we love you and support you. However, as I told you earlier, I'm not sure Alex will agree. Your leaving might just freak him out."

"I know. That does concern me. Thanks, Trevor, for supporting me. It means a lot. I understand that you and Alex are close, but I'm doing this for me. I appreciate the offer to look after the apartment and the car. I know I can depend on you both. Good night."

"So, are you going to the Philippines?" Becky inquired with a curious demeanor after much discussion.

"Yes. I'm calling Professor Ames in the morning. More than anything, I feel the need to give back, and you've made the country sound exciting and fascinating. In fact, I can't wait."

"What about Alex?"

"Well, I don't see how he enters into the equation. He's on the other side of the world and will be gone for a year. He's doing his thing. I think it's time I get on with my life. I do love him, and God willing, when he returns, we'll be married. He hasn't even called me this week. How do you think that makes me feel? I can't possibly sit by the phone for twelve months, now can I?"

"Noelle, speaking of Alex, I didn't mean to hit a nerve. But, how could I not support you? After all, it's my native country. I think you'll do a wonderful job. Trust me, I think it's the right decision, and as you said, you can't possibly spend the next twelve months sitting by the phone. Not that you need it, but as Trevor mentioned, you have my blessings as well."

"Thanks, Becky. I know that I can count on you. Thanks for dinner. It was delicious. You've both been a tremendous help," Noelle smiled, noting the time on her watch. "I'll call you tomorrow."

"Please, don't worry about a thing. It's all going to work out. Call me tomorrow."

Arriving back at the apartment, Noelle ran to check for messages on the phone. There was none. Falling hopelessly into bed, she had never missed Alex more than at this very moment. How could fate have brought him into her life, only to pull him away? Burying her head into a soft pillow, memories of Alex consumed her. Once again unable to sleep, a myriad of tears flowed onto the moist pillow, keeping her awake. Finally, after restless hours of tossing and turning, she fell asleep.

The following day the phone on the nightstand instantly woke her. Her heart raced with the hope of it being Alex. Hurriedly, reaching for the receiver, the voice on the other end immediately sent tingles of excitement throughout her petite body.

"Hey, Sweetheart, how are you? God, I've missed you. Sorry, it's taken me so long to get back to you."

"Alex, I've missed you so much. You have no earthly idea. I love you."

"I love you too. Trust me. Life without you is the hardest thing I've ever done. Sorry, I don't have long to talk. Did you give the apartment a feminine touch? How's the Porsche?"

"Alex, really, you're worried about your car?"

"Sweetheart, you took that out of context. Sorry. What's my girl been up to besides redecorating?"

"Nothing. I had dinner last night with Becky and Trevor."

"Great. Noelle, if you should need anything while I'm away, don't hesitate to give them a call. Babe, I have to make this short. Since arriving, things have been very hectic, and we're short on doctors. I love you, never forget that. Talk to you soon."

"Love you more."

Before she could even utter another word, their conversation ended. She had not been given the remotest chance of discussing her relocating to the Philippines. Maybe it was for the best. She was sure he didn't need another distraction or worry, considering he'd just been transferred closer to the war effort. Sitting up in bed, she smiled. Hearing his voice soothed her rattled nerves. Now, she needed coffee to get the day started. It was going to be a busy day for her as well. First, she would meet with Professor Ames, letting him know of her decision to join the team. Next, she would register for the program and get a list of things that would be required. Afterward, she needed to obtain a passport. Finally, if time permitted, she would stop by Edith's and let her know of her impending overseas travel. Somewhat worried over Edith's initial concerns, she was determined not to let that affect her decision.

The following month appeared to race by as she celebrated Christmas without Alex. She never even bothered to put a Christmas tree as she hurriedly ran around, checking every box on her to-do list. Finally, after weeks of preparation and receiving her passport, it was time to leave. Confident that Trevor and Becky would take care of things while she was away, it only left saying goodbye to Edith. The day before she left seemed like the perfect time. Driving over, Noelle felt guilt for leaving Edith at her age. However, she needed to take this opportunity to further her degree program. More than that, Noelle felt the urgent desire to give back. After the accident, she knew that life could tragically be taken away in an instant. Noelle was determined to make her second chance at life count. Parking in front of Edith's tiny house, she took a deep breath.

"Noelle. Come in. Honey, it's so good to see you," Edith smiled, giving her a huge hug. Noelle could smell the savory aroma of braised pot roast with vegetables. It was heavenly. Even without prior memories of the relatively inexpensive dish, she knew it had to be her absolute favorite. Edith knew her love for this particular recipe and prepared it, especially for her."

"Wow. Do I smell pot roast?"

"Of course. I couldn't let my beautiful girl leave without having my pot roast."

"Edith, I love you. I'm going to miss you and your sumptuous home-cooked meals."

"Honey, sit down. I'll get us a glass of iced tea."

Watching as Edith walked into the kitchen, it appeared her frail frame and humped back ravaged by years of arthritis were more prevalent than ever. Noelle's heart ached for the woman who'd spent her retirement years making sure that she lacked for none of the basic necessities in life. Unfortunately, the accident and resulting amnesia had robbed her of the precious memories she had of her grandmother and their time together. However, it was evident the love shared between them could never be wiped away. Edith returned with their iced tea and sat down on the sofa next to Noelle, taking her hand.

"Noelle, I want you to know that I love you enough to let you go.

There's a big world out there just waiting for you to discover it. But, Honey, don't think I'm not going to miss you. You have no idea how your leaving is going to affect me. However, I'm an older woman now, and your life is still very much ahead of you. What does Alex think about your leaving? I really like that young man. I know he loves you."

"Well, I haven't exactly told him yet."

Seeing Edith's expression, Noelle paused to take a sip of tea. Noting the surprised look on Edith's face, she knew she would definitely have something to say about her not telling him.

"Noelle, you love Alex, and he loves you, right? So do you think it was a good idea not to tell him?"

"Well, it wasn't the fact that I didn't love him or want him to know, but rather him worrying."

"Honey, do you truly believe it's realistic to think he isn't going to find out. Noelle, you're naïve. Do you really want him to hear from someone other than you? Baby, I love you, but you have to tell him. God rest his soul. Your grandpa and I were married for many years. We never kept secrets, at least nothing as important as this. You've got to tell him."

"I guess you're right. I knew there was no way he could ever change my mind about going, and I knew he would try. So I didn't want him to be upset or worry."

"Noelle, Alex is stronger than you think. For heaven's sake, the young man is a doctor and a major in the reserves. I don't think he's gotten this far in life without coping with unexpected things that he can't change. Now, no more said about this, I hear the oven timer. The pot roast is done. Are you ready to eat?"

"I'm starved. I love you, Grandma. How will I ever manage without you when I leave?" Noelle smiled, wrapping her arms around the only mother she'd ever known.

"Oh, Honey, I'm sure you'll do just fine. I raised a smart, beautiful young woman. Your mother would be so proud. Now, let's get in the kitchen before we both start crying. I promised myself no tears today."

For the remaining few hours, Edith reminisced over their early years together. She hoped sharing recollections from their past relationship would somehow unlock Noelle's memories. Memories that were now hidden deep within the recesses of Noelle's mind and were stolen due to her ongoing amnesia. She hoped it might somehow trigger a response that would restore her memory. Their in-depth conversation continued until the early hours of the morning. Finally, they stopped to enjoy Edith's favorite recipe for banana pudding.

"Thank you for making your special pot roast and the banana pudding. You're the best. I love you so much," Noelle smiled, trying to hold back tears. "I've arranged for a taxi to pick me up early in the morning, and it's getting late. I'll call you when I get the chance. Please don't worry. I love you, and yes, I will try to get in touch with Alex." Tightly wrapping her arms around her loving grandmother, Noelle said goodbye to the person who'd lovingly raised her since birth. "Remember, no tears."

"Honey, I love you. Please take good care of yourself. Call Alex."

On the drive home, Edith's last words, "Call Alex," resonated in her ears. She promised herself that she would make the call regardless of how their conversation went.

Arriving back at the apartment, she anxiously looked up his emergency contact information. Deciding to change clothes, she would make the call from the bedroom. She had everything ready to go for the next day. Her bags were already packed and sitting by the front door. There was nothing left to do except get a good night's sleep. However, that would now depend on his reaction. Finding the number, she sat back on the bed in her pajamas and made the call. Unexpectedly, the phone was answered after the first ring.

"Good morning 60th Combat Hospital Support, Captain Daniels."

"I'm trying to reach Major Bennington."

"I think you're in luck. I just saw Major Bennington walk out of the operating room. Who's calling?"

"Noelle Carrington."

"Please, hold for a moment."

"Hey doc, I think it's your fiance."

"Are you sure?" Alex yelled, running for the phone.

"Yes."

"Thanks."

"Hello," Alex panicked. She'd never called his emergency number.

"Sweetheart, what's wrong?" he asked impatiently without waiting to hear her voice.

"Alex, nothing is wrong. I just needed to talk with you. That's all. How are you?"

"Sweetheart, I'm fine. I just got out of surgery. Are you sure everything is okay? Did you wreck the car?"

"Alex, you and that stupid car. No. I didn't wreck the car," Noelle laughed. "Can't a girl just call her fiance to tell him that she loves him?"

"Absolutely. I love you too, but I know you too well. What's up? You've caught me at a good time. I have a few minutes to talk. What's going on?"

"Well, I'm leaving tomorrow, and I wanted to talk with you."

"Sweetheart, did you say leaving? Noelle, what the hell is going on?"

"Yes. Alex, calm down. Don't be crazy."

"Noelle, you're the one making me crazy. Where are you going?"

"I'm leaving tomorrow morning with a team of students from the university. I'm going to the Philippines on a Humanitarian Studies program."

"Damn, Babe, I don't remember our discussing anything about your leaving. Did you say the Philippines? Why are you doing this? Wasn't decorating the apartment enough? Can't you just find a job in Arlington without having to go halfway around the world? Did Becky or Trevor talk you into going?" he ranted endlessly.

"Wow, Alex, let me think for a second. Oh yeah, aren't you somewhere on the other side of the world. I don't remember our discussing it or being given a chance to talk you into staying in Arlington."

"Noelle, that isn't fair. You knew I was in the reserves. I wasn't given a choice. Can't you simply wait for me to finish this deployment? Please, just wait for me. We'll figure this out when I get home. You've never been out of Arlington. Do you have any idea what life will be like in another country?"

"Yes. I talked with Becky and Trevor."

"Oh my God, that's what I thought. Noelle, please, don't tell me they had anything to do with this. I'll kill Trevor. What about the apartment? What about my car?"

"Geez, Alex, really, you're more worried about your stupid Porsche and the apartment. I can't believe it. I should have known. I was hoping you would understand. I knew it was a mistake to call, but you know what, I promised Edith that I would. So, there, you have it. I called. I love you. I have to go," Noelle remarked curtly. "We'll be in touch," she exclaimed, ending the call.

"Noelle, I love you. But, wait. Please, don't hang up. Damn," Alex yelled, slamming the phone against the wall.

"Doc is everything alright. You seem upset," Captain Daniels inquired.

"Hell no, everything isn't alright. Do you have any cigarettes?"

"Yes. Here's a pack, or I should say what's left of one and my lighter. Do you want to step outside and talk?"

"No. I just need time to think. Thanks for the cigarettes. I owe you. Stop by later tonight, and we'll have a drink. I'll explain everything."

Walking outside the makeshift hospital, the early morning sky appeared red and angry as strong winds blew sand in from the desert. Alex turned away from the sandstorm as he cupped his hand, lighting a cigarette. He was perplexed. Why hadn't his proposal and putting a ring on her finger been enough? Why wasn't she satisfied with what they had together? For most girls, this would have easily carried them for the next twelve months. However, he knew Noelle was fragile. Surely, she was just confused. How could she possibly justify her reasons for leaving? They were engaged, and the fact she never discussed it with him made him furious. They were a team now, and he'd been totally left out of her decision. Didn't she know how hard it was for him to be away from her? Even though he was on the other side of the world, he still deserved to have a say in her decision. Worst of all, Alex now felt betrayed by his best friends, Trevor and Becky. Despite her determination, he would never stop loving her. However, his mind was reeling with thoughts of her leaving Arlington.

Hanging up, Noelle cried bitterly. She knew that calling him wasn't the right thing to do. She felt it with every ounce of her being, and she knew that he would never understand. However, she'd promised Edith, and a promise was a promise. After hearing his callous, vicious words, it was clearly evident that being engaged to him at this time was probably a huge mistake. Maybe their whirlwind romance had simply been just that a huge mistake. Maybe there was no such thing as love at first sight. She was utterly devastated. Nonetheless, she would always love him.

Waking the following day, she got up early. She needed to try and explain her reasons for leaving. Finding a pen and paper, she sat down at the kitchen table. Wiping tears from her eyes, she removed her exquisite diamond ring, laying it on the table.

"Alex, I honestly love you more than you know. The morning you proposed, you made me the happiest girl on earth. But, I feel like I'm at another crossroads. I'm not making this decision to hurt you. I'm simply doing this for myself. After the accident, I felt as if I'd been given a second chance in life—a chance to make my life count. Hopefully, you will understand. I love you. I will always love you. God willing, one day, our paths will cross again. Love Noelle."

Hours later, as the plane lifted into the air, she looked down at the small town of Arlington. It was early January, and she was leaving behind the only place she'd ever lived and the one person who had loved her since birth. But, more importantly, she was taking with her the love of a person who had given her life for the second time, Doctor Alex Bennington. He would always hold the keys to her heart forever despite his resistance to her leaving.

Chapter Seven

As the small plane began its approach into Cebu City in the Philippines, Noelle got her first glimpse of the small island where she would live and work for the next six months. It was vastly different than Manila, where they had stayed the previous night. Manila appeared modern, offering a microcosm of diversity in its population and culture. Cebu clearly reflected a degree of poverty that hadn't been visible in Manila.

Grabbing her carry-on bag from the small overhead bin, she hurriedly followed the other students down the steps of the aircraft. Standing on the tarmac, along with other students, the mid-day sun was scorching. Finally, a cool breeze swept across the surface of the asphalt. It felt refreshing as they waited for the bus, transporting them to Oslob, their final destination. It would be a grueling four-hour drive

"This is our bus," Doctor Thomas announced, watching the antiquated vehicle arrive. "Make sure you have everything before boarding. Don't leave anything behind. Trust me. We're not making a return trip to retrieve backpacks," he reiterated.

"Hi, I'm Trisha," the young girl smiled, quickly taking the seat next to Noelle. "I don't think we've met."

"I'm Noelle. It's nice to meet you. Sorry, I'm sure I haven't met everyone yet."

"Oh, I'm not actually a student. Eddie, or rather Doctor Thomas, I should say, is my uncle. I begged him to let me tag along. Of course, after my dad talked to him, he had to let me come. Have you ever been to the Philippines?" Trisha asked, appearing much younger than the other students. Taking a more in-depth look, she was obviously still in high school. Wearing her auburn hair in braids, she was dressed in denim overalls, an olive shirt, and sneakers. Her green shirt seemed to enhance the color of her green eyes. Her features were cute. However, she appeared immature to be facing such huge responsibilities.

"No. I've never been to the Philippines. However, my friend, Becky, was born and raised in Manila. She told me a lot about the country. I'm excited to experience it up close and personal. Is this your first trip?"

"It's my second. I have several friends who chose to stay behind after my first trip. I can't wait to see them when we arrive. I'm sure you're aware that our trip is to finalize the second stage of the building, which will house the Oslob orphanage once it's completed. We're going to help install a huge kitchen along with three indoor bathrooms. How are your plumbing skills?" Trisha laughed.

"Well, I can't say that I have any degree of confidence in that department. However, it sounds intriguing," Noelle yawned, stretching her arms.

"Have you always been interested in humanitarian programs?"

"No."

Noelle rested her head against the window. Intentionally, she didn't offer any further explanations. Hopefully, Chatty-Cathy would see the significance and give her some alone time. Closing her eyes, memories of Alex instantly flooded her mind. Maybe he'd been right. Perhaps this was a huge mistake. She missed him terribly. How could she have let their last conversation spiral out of control so quickly? She knew deep in her heart that she would always love him. However, it was too late for regrets. Too many things had been put into motion. She was on her way to Oslob. There was no turning back. She'd almost fallen asleep when suddenly, the rickety old bus hit a deep pothole jolting her awake. Immediately, she sat up, opening her eyes.

"Wow, that was scary," Trisha squealed. "Oh, I'm sorry, were you sleeping?"

"Not anymore. You're right. That was a bit terrifying."

Now that she was obviously awake, she'd most likely be asked a thousand questions before reaching Oslob.

"Have you always lived in Arlington?" Trisha inquired.

"Yes."

"Well, I've lived all over the world. My dad is a senior analyst with a pharmaceutical company."

"Great."

Geez, even giving short one-word answers, the questions kept coming.

"Wow. It's sweltering in here. Do you think your window will open?" Trisha complained.

"I'm not sure. It's really an old bus. But I'll try."

Struggling desperately, it gradually opened to Noelle's amazement. "Thanks."

Reaching for a book in her backpack, it was Noelle's only recourse for the remainder of the arduous journey. Hopefully, the fresh air flowing through the opened window would diminish her companion's need for further questions. Glancing at Trisha, she'd finally closed her eyes. It appeared to be working. Deciding to take her chances, she quietly put the book away. Sitting back in her seat, once again, she closed her eyes. Miraculously, Noelle managed to sleep for the duration of the trip. Hearing Doctor Thomas's loud voice, she instantly sat up, opening her eyes.

"Can I have your attention?" Doctor Thomas spoke loudly as he stood at the front of the bus. "We're only about fifteen minutes from reaching our destination. I want to take this time to go over a few things before we arrive. As you all know, our work here includes the last phase of construction for St. Lorenzo's Orphanage. You're fortunate. This trip is mostly indoor work. We're completing the kitchen and bathrooms. Right now, there is no indoor plumbing. However, the facilities have been provided outdoors. There is a makeshift shower with latrines. I'm sure most of you will find it rather primitive, but it will get the job done. The installation of bathrooms is our first priority. By the time we finish, you'll certainly appreciate the feel of warm water. There are two large rooms inside which have adequate bunks for sleeping. It may not offer you the comfort of home, but sleep won't be a problem when you get tired. The nuns who temporarily reside at St. Joseph's Rectory have prepared a generous meal for us this evening. Tomorrow morning, you'll meet with your assigned crew leaders. In closing, our objective isn't strictly the completion of the orphanage. You'll be working alongside the local sisters in schooling the younger children who live nearby. I'll explain more in detail tomorrow. For tonight, just relax and enjoy the local cuisine that the sisters have graciously prepared. Welcome to Oslob."

"Ya gotta love Uncle Eddie. He eats, sleeps, and savors every second that he's in the Philippines. He did two tours of duty in Vietnam. Afterward, he came home, finished his doctorate in humanities, and has taken students at the university on overseas field studies ever since. So you're completely safe under his command," Trisha laughed. "Trust me. He's all bark and no bite. I wouldn't be here otherwise. Do you want to bunk together?"

"I suppose. I don't see other offers pouring in," Noelle smiled.

"Great. It'll be fun. Did you remember to pack a flashlight? Uncle Eddie forgot to mention the fact there's no electricity at the moment."

"Wow, this could be a little more than I bargained for without lights. How will I ever see to apply my make-up?" Noelle laughed.

"Well, at least you've got a sense of humor. You're going to need it before we finish the next six months. Would you like a chocolate bar? I purchased a few candy bars from the hotel last night in Manila?"

"Yes. Does that even require an answer?"

Surprisingly enough, maybe sitting together on the bus had resulted in an unexpected friendship. Trisha was already offering chocolate. Perhaps, it was payment for her chatty disposition. Whatever the reason, it worked.

As the bus stopped in front of the building, which would soon house the orphanage, Noelle took a few minutes to take in the views from the bus window. They were sitting towards the back, and it was going to be a slow go getting everyone and their bags off the decrepit bus. There was no kidding herself. She definitely wasn't in Arlington anymore. However, it was remarkably beautiful, despite the degree of poverty surrounding them. The sun glistened off the brilliant turquoise waters. Tall, straight palms and palms that had curved due to trade winds lined the white sandy beach. Oslob appeared to be a perfect dichotomy. It was the essence of both beauty and poverty.

"Wow. I don't think I've ever seen anything so picturesque. Despite their dire circumstances, the residents of Oslob live in paradise," Noelle remarked.

"Yes, it's always been one of my favorite places. I've traveled extensively throughout the Philippines with my uncle. I much prefer the Philippines compared to Thailand or even Tahiti. So I guess you could say I'm partial to this part of the world."

"Well, I can't honestly say that I have anything to compare it with, but it's breathtaking."

"I don't mean to change the subject, but have you had the chance to get to know my uncle since you signed up for the program?"

"Not personally, nothing outside of a brief student-teacher encounter at the university."

"Why don't we go inside, pick out our bunk for tonight, store our bags, and then I'll introduce him to you," Trisha suggested.

"Sounds good."

At this point, Noelle felt far removed from Arlington and her past. Was she really entertaining the idea of becoming fast friends with a teenager? Trisha seemed like a friendly kid, but would she spend the next six months hanging out with someone still in high school? Surely, she was jetlagged and tired from the long journey. She'd come to Oslob to work, to make her life count, not have it feel like a continuous teenage girl's sleepover. She desperately needed a cup of coffee. However, looking around, there certainly wasn't a coffee shop in sight. Perhaps the nuns drank coffee. She could only hope by some off chance they had the means to make coffee.

Following close behind her young friend, they entered the dimly lit building. Most of the walls lacked sheetrock and insulation. It appeared the orphanage needed more than a kitchen and bathrooms. The floors still consisted of cement. There was no linoleum or tile. Looking around, there were very few windows, which gave the structure a dark foreboding presence. Rubbing her forehead, Noelle felt perplexed. It was visibly hard to imagine this place as her home for the next six months. If she saw even one roach or spider, she might take the next plane back to Arlington. Pausing for another moment to take in its complete lack of ambiance, she panicked. After redecorating Alex's apartment, maybe she didn't belong here after all. Perhaps her inner feelings towards changing the world and making a difference in life were complete utter foolishness. It was hard for her to admit that she'd possibly made a huge mistake. Whatever her reasons for coming here, it no longer mattered. She was here, and she was here as a result of her doings. Now, she would have to endure whatever the remaining months held. Stark reality set in. If she survived tonight with Chatty-Cathy sleeping above her, surely it would all be downhill afterward.

"Noelle, come outside. Uncle Eddie wants to meet you. I've told him all about you," Trisha mentioned. Then, grabbing her hand, Trisha literally pulled her outside.

Wow. Noelle couldn't believe her ears. What on earth had Trisha conceivable told him? Hopefully, she hadn't been the entire topic of their conversation on the bus ride. However, she had answered a lot of questions. Once again, in only a matter of minutes, she felt unreservedly foolish. Seeing Doctor Thomas in the distance, they walked over.

"Nice to meet you again. It's Noelle. Right? Trisha has told me a lot about you. Welcome to Oslob."

"Yes. Noelle Carrington."

"Please, just call me Eddie. No need to bother with formalities. We're all on a first-name basis. I like to keep it that way. Trust me. No one calls me Doctor Thomas in Oslob. We're all part of the same team."

His appearance was somewhat intimidating, and as a gentle breeze wafted past, the fragrance of his cologne was hypnotic. Surely, he was old enough to be her father. After a closer look, perhaps in his late forties, she guessed. However, his gray hair, steel blue eyes, and chiseled facial features made him very attractive for a man of his age. He was tall and exceptionally fit for someone in their forties. Wearing dark denim jeans with a gray tee-shirt depicting the university logo, his rugged, handsome appearance didn't seem to fit the norm for any doctor or professor she'd previously known. Surprisingly, after talking with him for only a few seconds, he seemed very down-to-earth and approachable.

"What brings you to Oslob? Please, don't say it's because you have an inner desire to change the world," he laughed. "Sorry, I always like to throw that out there. I find it's a great conversation starter for someone like myself who's earned a doctorate in humanities. I'm sure I'll discover all your reasons for being here before we're finished. We've got six months, and unfortunately, I find there's usually more to that question than I care to know."

Wow, had he literally just read her mind? Was it possibly true that most people crazy enough to fly halfway around the world to live under such torrid conditions were, in fact, just running from their problems? Again, she was at a loss for words.

"Well, after living in Arlington all my life, I figured it was time to see other parts of the world, and this program seemed like a great place to start," Noelle smiled.

"Great," he paused, questioning her candor. "We'll save that discussion for a later day. Trisha seems really impressed with you, and I know Professor Ames speaks highly of you. Sorry to hear about your recent accident. How's your amnesia? He mentioned the fact you'd suffered a loss of memory as a result of the trauma."

"Yes. Amnesia is a weird phenomenon. I'm not able to recall any of my memories, yet I completely know everything else."

"As long as you know how to use a wrench, a few power tools, along with a broom and dustpan, we're going to get along just fine. Sorry, there's no electricity for tonight. We're having generators brought in tomorrow. Trisha mentioned the fact you're bunking above her tonight. I must warn you, you might happen to see a few green lizards."

"You're joking. Right?"

"I'm afraid not. Surely, you're not frightened of harmless, tiny lizards?" Eddie laughed.

"Uncle Eddie, did you have to mention that on her first night here. So you do want her to stay, right?" Trisha laughed.

"Oh, lizards don't bother me. You did say they were small?" Noelle hesitantly questioned.

"Yes. Don't worry. My girl, Trisha, will redirect them to the outside if you see any. It appears that dinner has arrived," he smiled, noticing the arrival of a small truck. I need to let the other students know. Enjoy the local cuisine. Hope you didn't lose your appetite," he teased. "Talk with you later."

"What did you think of my uncle?"

"Oh, he seems very nice. Was he joking about the lizards?"

"Don't worry about that. He likes to tease the newbies. Let's go. I'm starved."

The sound of waves gently washing ashore could be heard in the distance as they sat on wooden benches under huge palm fronds. It was sumptuous to feast on lumpia with various dips, curry laksa, along with custard for dessert and hot tea. However, she would have much preferred a hot cup of coffee over tea. After meeting several other students, Trisha was somewhat disappointed that her friends were not arriving until the following day. As the hour got later, the wind blowing in from the ocean became cooler.

"I think we should turn in for the night. But, first, I'll show you where the outdoor facilities are located. Do you have your flashlight?" Trisha questioned.

"No. Should I have brought it?"

"Well, it's probably best to keep it with you. Especially when you're outdoors at night and need to use the bathroom. Don't worry. We'll be fine. I brought mine."

"Okay. Just follow behind me and stay close. Oh, watch out for cobras."

"What the heck? I'm not going."

"Suit yourself, but how long can you hold your pee?" Trisha laughed.

"Okay. I'm coming. Please, don't leave me," Noelle begged. Following close behind, she wasn't about to have a chance encounter with a snake, especially a cobra.

Reaching the latrines, they were located inside what appeared to be a run-down shanty. However, there was one thing missing, a roof.

"Really. We're going in there. It's dark. You've got to be kidding."

"Yes. We're really going inside, and don't worry, we have the flashlight."

Shining the flashlight as they entered, Noelle freaked out. There were only two holes in the ground.

"Oh, no, I'm not using those. Are you crazy? Where are the toilets?"

"Noelle, for heaven's sake, you're in a third-world country. Those are the toilets, at least for this remote area. We're not in Manila. Do you have to pee or not? This is your last chance," Trisha laughed.

"Alright. I just don't like the idea of trying to squat over those stinky things."

"I'm afraid you'll have to get used to it unless you can completely install the bathrooms tomorrow."

"Just for the record, I didn't sign up for this."

"Noelle, you're too funny. Uncle Eddie said you looked out of your element."

"What? He said that, did he?" Noelle grinned. She would show him. How dare he question her abilities or reasons for coming to Oslob.

"I guess we're both done here. Let's get back to the bunkhouse. Follow me. I've got the light. Please, watch where you step."

Reaching the building with their flashlight in hand, it was time to turn in for the night. All eight of the other bunk beds held sleeping students. Theirs was the only open bunk in the room. Quitely, climbing into bed, Noelle pulled the smelly blanket up to her shoulders and closed her eyes. How was she ever supposed to get any sleep? The mere thought of a lizard possibly crawling across her in the middle of the night made her cringe. However, she was tired, and even the horrible idea of lizards wasn't enough to keep her awake. She had been in Oslob for almost twenty-four hours, yet Alex was still on her mind. Feeling sleepy, she wondered how his day had gone. Did he have latrines or lizards in his part of the world? Noelle's heart ached for Alex as she drifted off to sleep.

Undisclosed Black Ops Headquarters

"Major Bennington, we've got inbound casualties," Captain Rhonda Smith shouted. "A Black Hawk is coming in hot with six wounded on board. Two of the injured are missing limbs. They're only a few minutes out from the base."

"I'll scrub and meet you in surgery."

It appeared the rest of his morning would be spent in the operating room. It wasn't exactly what he needed after receiving the earlier call from Noel. He needed a stiff drink. However, that would have to wait. He was still on duty for the next six hours. Performing surgery would keep him busy and unable to process the reason for Noelle's call. He worked well under pressure, and this morning would be no different.

"Captain Smith, check the blood supply. I don't need any shortages this morning," Alex yelled in her direction as she ran down the corridor.

"Don't worry. I'm on it."

Racing through double doors, she hurried to ensure enough exam rooms were open and adequately stocked to evaluate the less critically injured. Captain Smith had been at the forward operations base for over four months. She was a seasoned professional. Her vast knowledge as a surgical nurse left no doubt that those who worked alongside her were dependable and able to handle any situation. In her mid-thirties, she was African-American, short with a medium build, and always wore her dark hair pulled back into a bun. Rhonda was gorgeous. However, she left no doubt among the nurses who worked under her command that she expected perfection.

"Doc, what's your preference this morning? You feel like a little Steven Tyler and Aerosmith?" Sergeant Ramirez questioned, seeing Alex walk into the operating room.

"Sounds good."

"Great. It was my first choice, as well. We've got you covered this morning. Doc, you just save our boys. I'll provide the music."

"That's my reason for being here. It's not exactly Club Med."

Everyone loved working with Alex. He was one of the better, if not the finest, trauma surgeon within his reserve unit. He had a natural way of bringing out the best in those around him. Any soldier coming in as a casualty of the war effort could consider themselves lucky to wind up on his operating table if you could call a casualty lucky.

After hours of being in surgery, he'd finally seen his last patient. They were all hopefully recovering in the ICU Unit. As always, he knew he'd done his very best. They were in God's hands after they left his operating room. Walking out of the operating room, he removed his surgical mask. Throwing it into a hazardous waste bin next to the door, he needed a cigarette. Quickly cleaning up, he went to the doctor's lounge to retrieve his smokes. His shift was practically up at this point, and he was tired. However, more importantly, there was a bottle in his tent, calling his name. Walking outside, he would enjoy at least one cigarette before leaving the hospital.

"Great job," Captain Smith acknowledged with a smile, passing him in the hallway. "I'd say those were some lucky young men."

"Thanks. Let's hope their luck holds them through the night."

Alex knew the next twenty-four hours of their recovery would be crucial. The worst part of being a surgeon was doing your damn best and still losing someone to unforeseen complications.

The horrendous winds had finally abated as Alex stepped outside the hospital's back door, and the clear evening sky revealed thousands of sparkling stars. Pausing for a moment to take in the wonder of it all, thoughts of Noelle and their few days at the lake house instantly came to mind. God, what he'd give to relive it all again, except perhaps omitting the part where he had to explain the details of his deployment. He was tired and missing the best thing which had ever happened to him. Resting his foot against the back of the building, he lit a cigarette.

"I thought I'd find you out here," Captain Daniels grinned as he opened the back door. "Can I bum a cigarette and lighter?"

"Hey, Craig, not a problem. Are you off duty?"

"I will be in about ten minutes," Craig answered, lighting his cigarette. "What about that drink you promised earlier?"

"You must have read my mind. I have a bottle waiting for us. Why don't we run over to the mess tent and pick up something to eat. Then we'll knock off a bottle or two."

"Great. It sounds like a plan. I'm dying to hear the details regarding that earlier phone call."

"Oh, you would. Let's get out of here. It's been a long day," Alex smiled, stamping out his cigarette butt.

"Okay, Doc, after you."

Later that evening, after picking up a large pizza loaded with everything imaginable, they made a pit stop by the Class Six Store to pick up another bottle of Jack Daniels. Then, taking their prized possessions with them, they headed over to Alex's tent.

"Geez, Alex, don't you ever clean up," Craig teased, clearing a spot on a card table for them to eat. "I swear you have the most disorganized tent at Club Med."

"Hey, man, open that bottle. Did you come over to complain or drink?"

"Okay, dear, anything else."

"Yeah, here are two glasses. Fill them."

Finding two paper plates, Alex opened the pizza box.

"Wow. The pizza is incredible," Craig smiled, stuffing his mouth with a large slice.

"Yep, not bad at all, considering our location."

Alex's thoughts instantly flashed back to the morning Noelle had moved into his apartment, and he'd bought pizza at Geovany's. There was no getting away from her. Memories of Noelle haunted him day and night, even in the middle of nowhere.

"Here's to another day at Club Med," Alex toasted, tossing back a huge gulp of Jack Daniels.

"I'll drink to that. How many days do we have left in paradise?"

"I guess around three hundred and fifty. Too many to think about."

"Okay, are you ever going to tell me what happened between you and Noelle this morning? Something seems a bit off-kilter for two people who recently got engaged. Watching you slam that receiver against the wall was a bit intimidating.

Taking several sips of Jack Daniels, Alex sat back in his chair. "Who are you, my therapist?" Finally, throwing back his entire drink in one long continuous gulp, he reached for the bottle.

"Oh, sweetheart, who do you need me to be tonight? I'm yours," Craig teased in a girlish voice finishing the last of his Jack Daniels.

"Knock it off, and pour yourself another drink."

Craig was a few years younger than Alex and easily the life of any party. He was tall, blonde, extremely handsome, with an athlete's physique. He graduated from the Air Force Academy and chose a career path that took him away from Nebraska and his parent's farm. Craig worked in management and logistics at the hospital. It was a job of importance. However, he often referred to his position as the role of a pencil pusher.

"What do you want to know?"

"Everything. I want to know everything," Craig mentioned pouring himself another glass of Jack Daniels. I've got all night and no place to go."

"Well, Noelle was brought into the hospital in Arlington, where I'm on staff. She'd been in a horrible car accident, a head-on collision. By all accounts, she shouldn't have survived. The other person died on impact. Guess it wasn't her time. Thank God," Alex paused, taking a long slow, sip of his drink. "I was working the late shift that night, and being the only trauma surgeon, as expected, I was called to the emergency room. Except for a small laceration on her forehead, you'd never known at first sight that she'd been involved in an accident. She was gorgeous. To be honest, she took my breath away. However, I suspected her injuries were far more severe than her outward appearance indicated. After a quick initial exam, her blood pressure was almost non-existent. Once I got her into the operating room, I found she had a ruptured spleen. However, worse than that, her brain began to swell—nothing unexpected after a severe auto accident. I had to induce a coma and get her started on diuretics. Amazingly overnight, with the help of the diuretics, she made an almost miraculous recovery. I'm telling you that girl had a lot of help from above. I've never seen anyone recover as quickly as she did," Alex explained, taking another drink. "The next day, I was paged to her room in ICU. She was screaming and giving the nurses a hard time. Apparently, she'd come out of the coma with no recollection of the accident, and her memory was impaired. In fact, she didn't even remember her grandmother, who was in the room. Noelle was hysterical. The only way I got her to calm down was by asking her grandmother to leave the room. That was hard because her grandmother was visibly upset and concerned."

"Damn, that had to be really hard on Noelle as well as her grandmother."

"They were both having a difficult time," Alex added. Then, taking another slow sip of Jack Daniels, he reached for a cigarette.

"So, she had amnesia?" Craig asked, stuffing another slice of pizza in his mouth.

"Yes. Most of Noelle's memory has never returned. However, weirdly, I think it's what connected us the most initially. I somehow became the one person she trusted and relied on for information regarding her past. I asked numerous questions when Edith, her grandmother came to the hospital. It was just easier for me to relay everything. She didn't trust Edith because she really didn't know or remember her. In fact, she was extremely intimidated to go home with Edith the day she was released, so I suggested she stay with me."

"Wow, Buddy, I'm sure you did. How did that go?" Slouching back in his chair, Craig poured himself another drink. He was more than curious to hear the rest of the story.

"It's not as you think. We were totally in love. Do you believe in love at first sight?" Alex inquired, reaching for the bottle of Jack Daniels.

"I'm not sure. All I can say is that it's never happened to me. But then again, I guess anything's possible," Craig grinned, savoring the flavor of a long, slow sip.

"I would have questioned the real possibilities of that before meeting Noelle. But, trust me, it happens. It happened to us. As I said, Noelle moved in with me. I couldn't have been more excited to get on with the story. Things were great. However, just a few days before she moved in, I received news of my deployment. I was selfish. I wanted her with me every minute before I left. I thought if she knew, she might decide to stay with Edith. I worried Noelle was too fragile to handle something of this significance so early into our relationship," Alex continued, tossing back another drink.

On the other hand, there wasn't a damn thing I could do about it. I really didn't know how to break the news to her. I sweated bullets over that one. I was so afraid she would leave and simply want out of our relationship. Trevor, a good friend of mine, who happens to be a doctor on staff where I work, invited us over for dinner. Privately, I told him my worries about breaking the news to Noelle, and he came up with the perfect solution. His parents own a beautiful house on Summit Lake. He gave me the keys and made arrangements for us to drive up that night. It gave us all the privacy we needed, plus a chance for me to figure out a way to tell her. The weekend was incredible. However, the weirdest thing was when I decided to tell her. She told me she already knew. I was totally shocked. She had kept the fact that she knew from me the whole time. Noelle said she was waiting for me to bring it up first. It seems she overheard some of the hospital staff discussing the fact I was leaving, and then she put Becky, Trevor's wife, on the spot by questioning her. Of course, Becky being the sweet person she is, told her everything," Alex paused. Downing the remainder of his drink, he quickly poured himself another glass.

"Doc, don't you think you should slow down on those?" Craig teased, watching as Alex continually threw back shots of Jack Daniels.

"Really, Craig, pass me the cigarettes and lighter." Stopping briefly to light a cigarette, Alex sprawled back in his chair. Taking another sip of Jack Daniels, he stared at Craig. "Can I get on with the details?"

"By all means."

"The few days at the lake house were phenomenal. Noelle was full of surprises. She suggested we spend an entire day watching old movies. I wasn't keen on wasting an entire day indoors, but I easily went along with anything she suggested. As I said, our few days at the lake house were amazing. Afterward, we drove back to the apartment, and the morning before I left, I proposed. Thank God, she said *yes*. I didn't want to leave without knowing for sure we had a future together," Alex continued lighting another cigarette. Sitting up for a moment, he hesitated before pouring Craig another glass of Jack Daniels. "Are you going to help me kill these two bottles?"

"Pour away. You don't see me stopping. Do you?"

Filling their glasses, Alex sat back, savoring another long, slow sip.

"Here's where I don't understand women. Noelle wanted to redecorate my apartment. It certainly needed a woman's touch. I left her enough money to buy new furniture and redecorate it in any style she preferred. I own a new Porsche. I gave her the keys. I'll have to admit, maybe I cringed a little turning over those keys, but she needed transportation. So, now, she has a stunning three-carat diamond ring on her left hand, a beautifully decorated apartment, drives a new Porsche, money in the bank, and she isn't happy. What the hell? What woman on earth wouldn't be ecstatic?" Alex frowned, reaching for another cigarette. "She's going to the Philippines. Can you even believe it, the Philippines? She's going over with her humanities class at the university. Noelle feels like she needs to give back because she survived the accident and miraculously was given a second chance at life. What's worse, she was so mad at me when she called for not understanding her aspirations to go overseas. I'm not sure we're even still engaged. I'm really freaking out," Alex explained, rubbing his forehead.

"Well, if I can finally interject, I'm sure she's still in love with you. However, it sounds like she may be a bit confused. Is there anyone in Arlington she could go to for advice?"

"Yes, and that's another thing that's got me steamed. My best friend, Trevor, and his wife, Becky, whom I mentioned earlier, have evidently gone along with her crazy idea. Trevor will have to answer to me for not stopping Noel when I get back, and I was the one who told her to go to them for help while I was on deployment. A lot of good that did," Alex vented, lighting another cigarette.

"Alex, I'm certainly no expert on women. I'm obviously still single. But one thing comes to mind, just because you put a ring on someone's finger doesn't mean you own them. You're right. It sounds like she might have been a little fragile due to the accident and amnesia. Damn, that in itself would be a lot for anyone to deal with. The fact she relied on you for so many things and you're being deployed so soon had to be unnerving. Just give her a little time. Who knows, maybe she didn't go," Craig suggested looking down at his watch. "Wow, it's early morning. I have to go, some of us have to be at work on time tomorrow. Thanks for the pizza and Jack Daniels. Don't worry. I'm sure it will all work out," Craig commiserated, pushing back his chair. "I'll see you tomorrow."

"Thanks for being such a good listener. I owe you. I'll be in later tomorrow."

Falling onto his cot, thoughts of Noelle still lingered. Whatever she decided, wherever she went, he would find her as soon as his deployment ended. There was no way he would ever give up on their being together.

As he was going to sleep, Noelle was beginning another day.

Chapter Eight

"Noelle, grab your backpack. The bus is almost here. We're going to visit the children's home in Oslob. It houses some of the students who will later be relocated to the orphanage once it's finished," Trisha explained.

"Okay, be right with you. Wow, I can't say that I've ever worked with young children before, but I'm looking forward to meeting them."

"Oh, you'll fall in love with their sweet little faces. Everyone does. I can't wait to see Ian. He's ten, and I love that little boy. I've always thought Uncle Eddie should adopt him."

Waiting for the bus, Noelle took the opportunity to find out more about Doctor Thomas or Eddie, as he asked everyone to call him. After all, it appeared he doubted her reasons for being there and her abilities.

"You mentioned Eddie. He never married?"

"No. My dad, Brian, says he's married to his career. When Uncle Eddie came back from Viet Nam, he focused on getting his doctorate. He's been in a few relationships, but nothing which ever led to marriage. I've never understood that part of his life. He's handsome, smart, and has a gregarious personality. But, of course, I could be partial. After all, he is my uncle," Trisha smiled.

"You're right. It's hard to imagine someone like your Uncle Eddie having never married."

Watching as the antiquated bus made another appearance, Noelle gasped.

"Geez, is this our only mode of transportation?"

"I'm afraid so, but don't worry about that ole rattletrap. It never fails to get us where we're going. It might not appear new and shiny, but we've been using it for years."

After only two attempts, Noelle took a seat in the first row and opened the window.

"Thanks. It always smells musty in this old bus. We could use some fresh air."

It was only a short ride. The bus followed the shore's natural curves as it made its way along the narrow single-track road. Finally, stopping in front of a dilapidated bungalow, children ran out to meet them. As kids surrounded the bus, Trisha caught sight of Ian.

"Oh my gosh, I see Ian. He's gotten so much taller. Just look at him."

Poking her head through the open window, Trisha waved to the young boy, calling out his name.

"Ian, Ian, over here," Trisha screamed. "Do you see him? He's the taller one in the group. He's waving his hands."

"Yes. I see him," Noelle gasped.

To her astonishment, Ian resembled Alex. It was uncanny. How do you possibly come halfway around the world and find anyone who remotely resembles someone from back home? Noelle was mesmerized by the little boy's appearance. Their darker skin tones were almost identical, and they both shared the same texture and shade of shiny black hair and facial features. Noelle was instantly drawn to Ian. How was it even possible that Alex, born and raised in Greece, closely resembled this remarkable little boy in the Philippines.

"Wow, he totally reminds me of someone."

"Oh yeah. Who would that be?"

"Well, without having to answer a lot of questions, why don't we just save that discussion for later tonight."

"Okay, but I'm going to hold you to it. My curiosity is killing me."

Walking towards the front of the bus, Jimmy Hodges, the group leader for the day, made a few announcements before everyone got out of their seats.

"Welcome to Oslob's Children's Home," Jimmy began. "It's a temporary shelter for the children who will soon be relocated to the new orphanage once it's completed. Hopefully, and God willing, we'll finish everything during this trip. We're here to spend quality time with these awesome kids and help with their continued education. Needless to say, I'm sure you'll easily fall in love with their beautiful smiling faces. I certainly have. I've been coming to Oslob for many years, and my most enjoyable reason for coming are these children. We will divide the children into groups, so hopefully, each child can experience a one-on-one connection with you today. You'll find supplies inside. Sisters Agnus and Rose will give you specific instructions regarding each child. I'm afraid all the children are not on the same level concerning their educational needs. The sisters will inform you which children require more help. Enjoy your day. Oh, before I forget, lunch will be provided at noon. Have a wonderful day."

Jimmy Hodges was a former Marine. He always looked forward to his yearly trips to Oslob. A longtime friend of Eddie's, Jimmy paid his share of expenses. Owning a large construction company in St. Louis, he always felt it was his way of giving back. Tall and thin, his tan, rugged, good looks made it quickly apparent that he spent a lot of time outdoors. Wearing a dark blue flannel shirt and a pair of worn denim jeans significantly brought out the color of his baby blue eyes and short blonde hair. Eddie always relied on him to keep a keen eye on Trisha making sure she was safe at all times. However, more importantly, the fact he was knowledgeable in construction made him a valuable asset.

"Noelle, hurry, grab your backpack and let's go. It's been over a year. I can't wait to see Ian. I love that little guy."

Watching as Trisha got off the bus, Ian immediately rushed over to give her a huge hug. Putting his arms tight around her waist, it was evident how much he'd missed her. His facial expressions were priceless. It was easy to see how thrilled Ian was to see her.

"I missed you. I'm so glad you're here. Where's Eddie? Did he come?"

Ian asked, desperately clinging to Trisha's hand. He wasn't about to let her out of his sight.

"Oh, Ian, I've missed you too. Sorry, Eddie isn't coming today. He's waiting on some generators to be delivered," Trisha answered quickly, embracing the young boy. "Ian, this is my friend, Noelle. She's going to help with school today. How are you doing with math? Still having problems?"

"Maybe? She's pretty," Ian blushed, staring at Noelle.

"Well, I think you're handsome too," Noelle smiled. "I look forward to working with you today."

"Why don't we go inside. I know Jimmy said we would be divided into groups, but we're working with Ian. There are some advantages of having Uncle Eddie in charge," Trisha laughed. "Besides, Uncle Eddie and Jimmy are friends. They've known each other for years. I'll introduce you later."

Walking inside the dark, run-down shanty, Noelle's heart broke for the young children. They lacked so many basic needs that children in America took for granted. Taking a closer look at Ian, she became emotional. She desperately tried to hide the tears that instantly welled within her eyes. It was evident these kids had never known a different standard of living. Yet, they appeared extremely happy despite being surrounded by squalor. Looking around, she felt such compassion for each smiling face and was blessed to offer help, even if it happened to be in the area of math. She couldn't fathom the idea that most of these young children hadn't found a permanent home, and she entertained thoughts of one day returning to adopt Ian.

After spending the morning hours teaching the essential elements of math, reading, and literature, Jimmy felt the kids would benefit from an hour of outdoor activities. It appeared playing soccer was one of their favorite past times. Dividing them into two groups, a competitive game ensued. Noelle loved being part of Ian's team. She relished every minute she spent with him. The fact he reminded her of Alex, Ian represented the very essence of a future child they might have had if their relationship had endured. Watching as Ian vigorously moved the ball through the large group of children towards their goal, she yelled. She felt inspired and drawn to his compulsion for winning. Now more than ever, she knew she was where she was supposed to be. Although Alex didn't understand her desire to try and make even the slightest difference in the world, Ian confirmed she had made the right decision. She smiled, knowing deep within her heart she would always love Alex. However, she also knew that remaining in Arlington for the next twelve months without him would have suffocated her.

On the bus ride back to their accommodations, it appeared Trisha was determined to make good on her promise of wanting to know more about the person which Ian resembled.

"Okay. What gives? I saw the way you interacted with Ian today. You mentioned earlier that he reminded you of someone. Apparently, it's someone of importance in your life."

"If you must know, Ian has an uncanny resemblance to someone with whom I recently became engaged. I loved him very much. Actually, I still do. However, we were hit with an unexpected dilemma early into our relationship. I felt as if I was at a crossroads in my life, so I chose to leave. It's a long story, too long for a short bus ride. Perhaps later tonight, I'll fill you in on the details. But, you know, if I ever come back to Oslob in the future, I would adopt Ian."

"Wow. That would be awesome. But, I want to know more about you," Trisha inquired, pressing for answers. "So, you were recently engaged."

"Yes. My fiance, Alex, is on a year-long deployment. Please, no more questions. I really don't feel like reliving all the details right now."

"Alright, if you insist, we'll save it for later. But, I'm not letting you off the hook so easily."

"Thanks," Noelle smiled, laying her head against the window.

Today had been great meeting Ian and the children. However, surprisingly enough, it had been emotionally draining on the other hand. It brought her face to face with her decisions. Even though she finally knew her decision to come overseas with the university was the right thing to do, it did nothing to make up for the giant hole she felt in her heart. The one place in her heart that only Alex could ever fill. She felt torn. To make matters even worse, she had now befriended

Trisha, a young teenager, whom she felt obligated to divulge her whole life history or at least what she could remember of it.

Arriving back at the orphanage, she was ready to eat and turn in early. It had been a long day. However, unexpectedly, it appeared someone wanted to chat—someone she couldn't exactly turn down.

"Noelle, how was your day?" Eddie asked, walking over. "Trisha just mentioned that you met Ian. He's a unique little guy. Isn't he? I have to say, for me, he's the quintessence of why I continue to make these trips. I have a couple of sandwiches and some soft drinks. Why don't we walk down to the beach? I want to know more about your reasons for deciding to join us in Oslob. I love getting to know my students and what motivates them. Besides, Trisha really likes you."

"Okay. If you're offering food and drink, I certainly won't turn you down." How could she possibly say no to the Field Director, Dr. Edward Thomas?

"Great. Follow me. I hope you like egg salad. It seems to be the menu for tonight. The nuns who cook for us are good, but they're definitely not chefs. It seems we're at their mercy regarding meals and what they have on hand to work with. However, last night the lumpia was delicious."

"Egg salad sounds wonderful. I'm starved."

"It certainly takes a lot of energy to keep up with those young kids. Sometimes I regret not having married and raising a family. However, I feel the kids in Oslob are mine and consider it an honor to come over every year," Eddie smiled.

Noticing a massive outcropping of rocks near the shore, Eddie reached down for Noelle's hand. Then, firmly grasping her hand, he led her over to one of the more enormous boulders, which sat only a few feet above the shore.

"Would you like to sit here, or do you feel daring? The view from the top is incredible."

"What's good food without an awesome view," Noelle agreed.

"Great. Please be careful. I don't want you to slip."

Eddie assisted her up the gigantic slippery boulders. Finally, reaching the top, she gasped.

"Wow. This is unbelievable. It looks like a painting,"

Numerous tiny islands dotted the horizon. They were covered in lush greenery, which consisted of tropical palms and set amid a backdrop of turquoise water. It was paradise. Fishermen standing in their outrigger boats could be seen casting nets into the clear, greenish-blue waters.

"I thought you would appreciate the view from the top. Sit down. I'll get our food and drinks. Like I said before, I have to apologize for dinner tonight. But, I suppose, beggars can't be choosers. I'll have to check with the nuns. They might be low on supplies. I'll have someone make a grocery run into Cebu City tomorrow."

"No apologies needed. I'm quite happy with egg salad. Especially when it comes with such a spectacular view."

"So, what really brought you to Oslob? I'm always more curious with my older students?" Eddie inquired, taking a drink. "I always find with the younger students, it's more often than not, just simply the idea of getting away from home for the first time and their parents."

He had wasted no time. Eddie and Trisha were much alike. Their curiosity to know everything was a shared trait. Looking over at Eddie, Noelle smiled. For an older gentleman, he was rather sophisticated and handsome. His gray hair gave him a distinguished sexy appearance, and his charming disposition easily compelled her to tell him everything. However, feeling a slight attraction towards him, Noelle felt an urgent need to establish boundaries.

"Trisha mentioned the fact you served in Vietnam. My father, Ben, also served in Vietnam. Unfortunately, he was killed before I was born. I've never talked with anyone from my father's generation. What made you enlist, and what was it like over there? I'm really curious," Noelle inquired, pulling her windswept hair away from her face.

"Well, since you asked that war was hell in a nutshell. I was young, just out of college. Like most young men of that era, we all felt obligated to support our country. I wasn't enlisted. I was a second lieutenant in the Air Force, never drafted. However, most young men during that time were drafted. Looking back, I think our country should have never entered that war. We lost so many brave young men and women in Vietnam. Sorry for your loss. That's truly unfortunate. Now, let's get back to you and your reasons for being in Oslob," Eddie smiled, changing the subject.

"Thanks for taking the time to answer my questions. I've always wanted to talk with someone of your generation—especially someone who served in Vietnam. Concerning what you said earlier about your younger students, I think you're right," Noelle remarked, once again trying to pull long strands of her blonde hair away from her eyes. "The cool breeze feels refreshing."

"Yes. It feels great. I much prefer sitting outside to sitting in my hot, cramped office with no windows. Not to change the subject once again, but I have to say my niece is totally fascinated with you. The way you interacted with Ian today left quite an impression," Eddie smiled, finishing his sandwich. "Trisha said Ian reminded you of someone back home."

Geez, not only did they share related traits of curiosity, but it was also evident they confided in each other.

"Yes, Trisha's correct. It was bizarre. Now that you've mentioned Ian, perhaps, this would be a good place to start. Ian resembled my former fiance. Their similarities are amazing," she paused, taking a sip of soda. "My fiance was born in Athens. He came over to the states when he was a young boy."

"I take it your breakup was recent."

"Yes."

"I guess that explains a lot. Running away is always the easiest way out of any relationship."

"Eddie, you've totally misread me and my reasons for being here. Things are not that black and white. Trust me. It's way more complicated."

"The wind is picking up. Would you like my jacket? Evenings can be somewhat chilly." Gently covering Noelle with his jacket, he took the liberty to sit closer.

"Thank you."

"Okay. I get it. You're not running from anyone or anything. So, why are you here?"

"I'll be brief. Do you believe in love at first sight?"

"Well, I suppose. However, I've never given it much thought. Though, I'm sure the possibility exists."

"When I woke from the medically induced coma, as you know, I could not remember anything from my past. However, the doctor who operated on me was one of the first persons I saw besides my grandmother, who I, unfortunately, didn't remember. There was something so serenely comforting about him. To be honest, I was mesmerized. I guess the fact he was extremely handsome didn't hurt either. Thank God the feelings were mutual on his part as well. To make a long story short, we fell in love almost immediately. Let me digress. I told you a few minutes ago that I lost my dad in Vietnam. Well, what I didn't tell you was the fact that I also lost my mother, Cindy, that same year. She died giving birth to me on Christmas Eve. Unfortunately, she had breast cancer, and the tragic news of my father being killed in Vietnam hit her hard. She barely managed to carry me to term before cancer took her life. My grandmother, without hesitation, took me in and raised me despite the fact she was retired and on her own after my grandfather passed," Noelle paused to take a drink.

"As I mentioned, I had no memory of her after the accident. So, it left me with no one that I could honestly trust except Doctor Bennington. We not only fell in love, but he became a significant person in my life. To keep this short, we moved in together. However, before I left the hospital, he received orders. He's was being deployed for twelve months, and he chose not to tell me. He was afraid that I wouldn't be able to handle the news and would simply want to leave as a way of dealing with everything. The odd thing was that I already knew. I overheard a conversation between hospital staff. They mentioned the fact he was leaving," Noelle continued taking another sip of her drink.

"Later, I questioned his friend without him knowing, and she verified everything. To get on with things, he proposed the morning before he left. At the time, I couldn't have been more ecstatic. He left me everything, his apartment, and enough money to completely redecorate it, plus his Porsche. As good as life seemed at the time, I felt something was missing. Getting back to the accident, I'm truly convinced that I had a near-death experience. That experience is why I'm here. I saw and felt the real peace and joy of being in a heavenly realm. However, I was told that I couldn't stay, that I had to come back. I know that I was given a second chance in life. Once you have experienced something that real, it's truly life-changing. To make a long story short, that's basically my reason for being in Oslob. I remember you mentioned that everyone always tells you they want to change the world. Well, that's not exactly true for me. Though I would like to help make it a better place for children like Ian, who deserve so much more."

"Why would Alex have a problem with you coming over to Oslob, especially taking into consideration he was deployed for twelve months? I'm not sure that I understand? You were engaged, and he still loves you. Right?"

"Well, to be honest, I'm not really sure. We got into an argument over the phone. I was afraid Alex might have a problem with the idea that I didn't seem happy after everything he'd done for me. I felt like he owned me at that point. Does that make any sense? After the phone call, I left him a note along with my ring. I felt like I was at a crossroads in my life. Everything happened so fast, sometimes I look around, and I can't believe that I'm here."

"How do you feel about your decision? Do you still love him?"

"Today, after meeting Ian, I no longer doubted my reasons for coming. I'll always be in love with Alex, even if our relationship is over at this point. I'm still trying to understand it all. How is it even possible for two people to fall in love so effortlessly and then so quickly have their romance snuffed out like a candle?"

"That's a remarkable story. I want you to know that I love the fact you chose to come. I've heard all kinds of reasons and explanations for why people take time away from their lives to do humanitarian work. However, there's something different about you. I've never spoken with someone who had a near-death experience and felt they were given a second chance in life. I have to say that's commendable. I can't say that I've ever had that experience. However, seeing the poverty level among the children in Vietnam was why I came home and got a doctorate in humanities. I saw firsthand the ravages of war and its effect on children. It not only takes the lives of their parents, siblings, relatives, and friends, but for those who are lucky enough to survive, it totally devastates their existence. Thank you for deciding to come to Oslob. I'm sure you've made another friend today besides myself. Trisha said Ian fell in love with you. I've always felt if you change the life of even one child, you've changed the world. It's been wonderful talking with you. Unfortunately, it's getting late, and I've taken up way too much of your time. Hold onto my hand, and try not to fall. I'll walk you back."

How could she have ever misunderstood the honesty of Eddie's intentions? She felt like an idiot. It appeared his heart easily belonged to the children of Oslob. They were lucky to have him in their lives. His caring ways would soon result in a new orphanage with indoor plumbing and warm water.

Chapter Nine

The next day after breakfast, Eddie received an unexpected phone call from the office of Professor Ames. It appeared a 7.5 magnitude earthquake struck the Indonesian island of Sumatra, and the university was asked to send at least two students to help in a humanitarian effort. Eddie knew there was no need for a general meeting among his students other than to inform them of the disaster. He already knew the two people he would ask. He needed someone with hands-on experience, which meant Jimmy and one of his older students, Noelle. These two seemed the most qualified. There was no way he would let Trisha go without him, and the other students were much younger and required more supervision. Calling them into his make-shift office, he gave them the news.

"Ed, what's up? Why the urgent meeting?" Jimmy questioned in total confusion.

"Trisha said you wanted to speak with me," Noelle smiled curiously.

"Yes. Please, both of you, have a seat. I received a call from the office of Professor Ames at the University earlier this morning. It appears there's been an earthquake in Indonesia. Actually, it was a rather large quake. It registered 7.5 and has resulted in heavy casualties and extensive damage to the island of Sumatra. I'm being asked to send over at least two of my students to help in a humanitarian relief effort. It appears a lot of people are still either missing or presumed dead. They're most likely trapped under debris. I would like to send you both to Sumatra. Jimmy, I know you have invaluable skills in construction. Trust me. I'm desperately going to miss working alongside you on this project. Still, I feel your skills could better be used in Sumatra. Noelle, after talking with you last night, you seem to be a very grounded individual, and I know you would be a great asset. Most of the other students are much younger, and I feel they would need a lot of supervision. You both would be able to hit the ground running once you arrived. What are your thoughts? Could you be ready to leave as early as this afternoon?"

"Ed, I have no problems going to Sumatra. I can be ready as soon as you need. Although, I feel like I'll be leaving you in over your head with the installation of the bathrooms. I think my question would be, can you finish this project on your own?" Jimmy inquired.

"Eddie, I also have no problem in going to Sumatra," Noelle interjected. "As I said before, I feel like my whole purpose for coming to the Philippines is to give back. I'm sure that I could be more useful there. Would it be possible for you to have Professor Ames call my grandmother in Arlington and make her aware of my new location? I can be ready to leave at once."

"I appreciate the fact you both are willing to go on such short notice. I know that you'll be invaluable in the rescue and clean-up efforts. Jimmy, I will definitely miss your expertise in the field of plumbing. However, I'm sure your skills will be put to good use. I've arranged for the bus to pick you up at 2:00 p.m. this afternoon. You'll fly back to Manila and hopefully arrive in Sumatra early tomorrow morning. Jimmy and Noelle, I appreciate your willingness to take this assignment. I'll let you both go so you can start packing. If you have any questions, please feel free to ask. Oh, Noelle, I've already spoken with Trisha. I've made it quite clear that she isn't accompanying you to Sumatra. She wasn't exactly happy with my decision, but I'm sure you understand my reasons for not sending her. I always feel personally responsible for her when she accompanies me on overseas trips. Unfortunately, she's not prepared to handle such dire circumstances. Noelle, I apologize if she begs you to stay. I'm afraid she isn't happy with me at the moment."

"Eddie, that's not a problem. I completely understand your reasons for keeping Trisha here and under your careful supervision. I agree. The trauma and devastation would be too much for her to handle at her age. I'll talk with her before I leave."

"Thanks. You two get out of here. You only have a few hours before you leave. Oh, I almost forgot. The campus newspaper and the Arlington Gazette will feature an article on you and other locals being asked to help the earthquake victims. I'm sure you'll make us proud. Thanks again."

Even though Noelle had only been in Oslob for a few days, she readily agreed to take on a more serious commitment. Without hesitation about what her new role would entail, she stepped up to help. Quickly finding Trisha, Noelle explained her reasons for accompanying Jimmy to Sumatra. She certainly didn't owe her any explanations. However, she felt obligated to Eddie to patch up his niece's differences before leaving. At first, Trisha seemed obstinate in her hostility towards her uncle. Finally, Noelle was able to break down Trisha's barriers of anger and resentment towards him. Carefully explaining the horrific details of what life would be like in a country just ravished by destruction and death, Trisha began to understand her uncle's reasons. Packing her belongings, Noelle waited outside with Jimmy for the bus to arrive.

"Have you ever been to Indonesia?" Jimmy asked, putting his bags down.

"No. Have you?"

"Yes. After the Vietnam war was over, I visited the capital, Jakarta. It was a much-needed reprieve after the war. However, I haven't been back.

Noelle felt a brief moment of sadness, watching as the dilapidated bus made another appearance. She had enjoyed her short time in Oslob and the friendships she had made. Nonetheless, she was intrigued by thoughts of visiting another country and a chance to help the less fortunate people of Sumatra. Jimmy grabbed her bags and ushered her into a seat near the front of the bus. Opening the window, she waved to Trisha as the bus entered the dusty road to Cebu City.

"I'm grateful you decided to join me. Hopefully, we'll only be in Sumatra for a few short weeks. By the way, just call me James. I much prefer that over Jimmy. However, everyone insistently uses the name, Jimmy."

"Okay, James, that won't be a problem. Trisha mentioned that you and Eddie have been coming to the Philippines for several years."

"Yes, that's right. I guess the fact that we're both unattached makes it easy to break away from our work in the states and come over each year. So what's your story? Why are you here?"

"Well, it's rather complicated. To make a long story short, I was briefly engaged to someone back home. My fiance, Alex, belongs to a reserve unit. As fate would have it, his unit was activated for a twelve-month deployment. I think he felt that asking me to marry him would result in my playing the role of Susie Homemaker until he returned. After he left, I suddenly realized there was more to life than just sitting in an apartment. However, there's not a day that goes by that I don't think of him. I still love him."

"I'm sorry to hear that. Does your fiance know that you came over to Oslob with the university?"

"Yes. I tried to explain my reasons for signing up for the program during a phone call, but we just got into an argument. I haven't talked to Alex since our last phone conversation."

"Geez, that's unfortunate. Maybe after Alex returns, you'll be able to work things out."

"Oh, I'm not sure about those possibilities. I wrote Alex a note before I left and placed my engagement ring next to it. However, I can't think of anything that would make me happier than getting a second chance to make things right between us."

"Well, you never know. I suppose if it's truly meant for you to be together, somehow fate will intervene."

"Thanks, James. What a thoughtful thing to say. I only wish I shared your confidence."

The bus ride to Cebu City was long and exhausting. Finally, after several tedious hours, they reached Cebu and boarded their flight to Manila.

Finally, arriving in Southern Sumatra the following day, the devastation was beyond comprehension. There were no buildings that remained fully intact. Driving through small communities, it looked like a war zone. People were frantically trying to excavate ruins using their own hands as tools. They were desperate.

"Oh my God, this is unbelievable," Noelle exclaimed in sheer panic.

"Wow, you're right. I haven't seen destruction like this since the war in Vietnam. I'm so glad we came. However, these people will need heavy excavation equipment to get the job done correctly. Without it, this is going to be a daunting task. What worries me the most is that many people may be buried alive under all the debris. So the most crucial factor is timing," James explained, taking in the horror of their surroundings.

As their van came to a stop, an elderly gentleman ran up to meet them.

"Good morning, I'm Jack Townsend. I'm with the Red Cross. Thanks for coming. Please join those folks waiting in line. We simply need to get your names and the organization you're with. Then you'll be assigned to a group and given further instructions. As you can see, the survivors require food, water, shelter, and medical assistance. Right now, trying to get organized is a critical component of our efforts. We're going to need search and rescue crews. Also, we're in the process of setting up rows of tents to house those involved in the effort."

"Noelle, I'm going to work with the search and rescue teams. Would you rather stay here and help with the crucial aspects of housing the victims?" James inquired.

"No. I'm going with you. Timing is critical for anyone who might be trapped. There could be children buried under those demolished buildings."

"Okay, suit yourself. But, I'd feel more comfortable knowing you were in a safer area. Trust me, sifting through this rubble is going to be dangerous. If you were to get hurt, I'm not sure enough medical personnel is on-site to handle difficult injuries. Plus, you've had no sleep."

"I don't care. I'm coming," Noelle insisted.

"Alright, but if something happens, I'm not responsible."

After registering, James and Noelle were assigned to a rescue team.

Receiving hard hats and essential equipment, they followed their trusted team leader to a designated search area. A German Sheperd was brought over to sniff through the rubble about an hour later. It was only moments before the dog desperately began digging through the ruins.

"Over here," someone yelled desperately. "Hurry over here."

James and two other guys quickly removed bricks and broken masonry from the massive pile of rubble. Persistently sniffing the debris, the dog remained close to the excavation site.

"I see a hand. It's moving. Oh, my God, it's a child," one of the team members shouted. "Faster, you have to work faster."

Hurriedly, they moved everything that stood between them and the trapped child. Finally, a small bloody arm was exposed.

"Hang in there, we've got you," James screamed, pulling the child from beneath the rubble.

Miraculously, it appeared she was alive. However, it was apparent she might require surgery, despite her only visible superficial cuts and scrapes on her legs and arms. From outward appearances, she seemed fine. But, not wanting to take any chances, James yelled for a stretcher to carry the young girl to the waiting medics. Worried she might not have been alone when the earthquake struck, James and those around him frantically intensified their efforts. Moments later, the lifeless body of the child's mother was discovered. It appeared she had tried to shield her daughter from the crumbling building. As the mother's body was pulled from beneath the debris, Noelle's knee's buckled from beneath her petite frame, and her eyes moistened. She had been in Sumatra for only two short hours, and yet she'd already seen first hand the devastation an earthquake of this magnitude could inflict on a community.

Noticing the visual effects on Noelle, James walked over and put his arms around her.

"Are you okay? Why don't you take a break? You've been up all night. I think you should get some rest."

"I think you might be right. I feel a little dizzy."

"I'm going to walk Noelle over to the tent and get her some water. I'll be back in a few minutes," James explained to their team leader, Jason.

Jason Carter came over with the Red Cross organization in Hawaii.

He was an avid surfer. Coming from a prominent family, he was known for his humanitarian endeavors. However, Jason was the embodiment of a surfer. He was tall, with blonde cropped hair and sapphire blue eyes. His lean, tanned body made him extremely popular. Despite his wealth and striking physique, he always stepped up when the Red Cross became involved in natural disasters.

"Okay. Take a break. You've hit the ground running since you arrived," Jason suggested. "Get some water. You have to stay hydrated."

For the rest of the day, which was extremely hot and tiring, James worked diligently alongside the other team members. None of them dared stop their search efforts until later that night when a replacement team arrived. Finally, being completely exhausted, James found his way to the tents which housed the volunteers. Walking inside, Noelle was still asleep on the cot where he'd left her hours earlier. Apparently, she'd never woke up. Grabbing a blanket, he found an open cot and laid down. Then, laying his head on a pillow, he was out like a light bulb.

Their first day in Sumatra had been hectic but fulfilling. Little did Noel know that Alex was frantically calling everyone back in Arlington. He was desperate. She knew nothing of the risks he would soon take to find her.

Chapter Ten

Undisclosed Black Ops Headquarters

"Hey, Doc, how's your day going?" Sergeant Rameriz inquired. "Okay. How about yourself?"

"I guess I can't complain. I'll see you later in the operating room. Oh, Doc, I'm thinking the Beach Boys. Does that fit your mood today?"

"Sounds good."

Alex was searching for a phone. It appeared every telephone he walked past was in use. He needed to call Trevor. After talking with Craig, maybe he had been unfair to Noelle. He certainly didn't own her, and she had every right to pursue her education while he was deployed. Perhaps, this place was beginning to get to him. The fact the hospital was short on trauma surgeons kept him extremely busy. Finally, he noticed someone walking away from a nearby phone. Hurriedly running over, he called Trevor. The phone seemed to ring forever.

"Hello," Trevor finally answered.

"Trevor, this is Alex."

"Alex, what the hell? Do you know what time it is? Some of us are still sleeping," Trevor vented.

"I don't give a damn about your sleep. Do you understand?"

"What's going on? Is everything okay?"

"No. I understand you talked Noelle into going to the Philippines. Are you crazy? I thought I could trust you? I even told her she could rely on you and Becky while I was gone. I must have been insane for trusting you. Noelle wasn't well enough to take on such a commitment. She's still suffering from amnesia."

"Damn, Alex, it's way too early in the morning to be having this discussion. First of all, neither Becky nor I talked Noelle into going anywhere, especially the Philippines. Buddy, you better get your facts straight. She came to us and basically informed us of her decision to go. We simply gave her our blessing. She only came over to talk with Becky to learn more about the Philippines. Becky was born and raised there. Did you expect her not to recommend Noelle going? You've got this all wrong. This was completely Noelle's decision. I think you better talk to your fiance. However, just saying, I don't think she would have ever been happy remaining in the apartment after you left, especially for twelve months."

"Trevor, I still don't give a damn regarding your explanations. She's gone, and I have no way to contact her. Can you even imagine how I feel? What if Becky left the country and you had no way to get in touch with her. Do you have a phone number where I can reach Noelle?"

"No, but someone at the university or Professor Ames's office should have a way to contact her. Have you tried calling Edith, her grandmother? Maybe she's heard from her."

"Trevor, you better hope to God she has. If I can't locate Noel, I'll never speak to you again. You got that, buddy. I'm pissed at you and Becky. I feel you've both let me down. Do you understand?"

"Alex, this whole conversation is ridiculous. I'm hanging up. Do you remember me giving you the keys to the lake house that night? I would have done anything to seal your chances with Noelle. Becky and I considered you both our dearest friends. You better get your facts straight before you start accusing us. Damn. Do you understand?" With that being said, Trevor hung up the phone.

Wow, maybe he'd been too hard on Trevor, Alex thought. After all, he had given him the keys to his parent's lake house. Hopefully, Edith would know something. She would be his next call. However, there was no way he could wake her up in the middle of the night. He would call her after he finished his last surgical procedure. It was scheduled for 5:00 p.m. Perhaps, after he cleaned up and got a bite to eat, it would be early morning in the states, and Edith would be awake.

After five hours of complicated surgeries, Alex was mentally and physically exhausted. Nonetheless, he would let nothing stand in his way of trying to find Noelle. Changing out of his scrubs, he walked outside to enjoy a cigarette. The evening sky was a massive canopy of twinkling stars. As a cool breeze gently blew in from the desert, he felt a cold chill. Worried about Noelle, he had no way to know that she was in Sumatra. Quickly finishing his cigarette, he hurried back inside the hospital, hoping to find an available phone. Luck would be on his side. Not only did he find a phone which wasn't being used, but Edith answered on the first ring.

"Hello."

"Good morning, Edith. This is Alex Bennington. How are you?"

"Oh, Alex, it's so good to hear your voice. I'm fine. How are you?"

"Well, I've been better. Edith, the reason for my call this morning is to ask about Noelle. Do you know where she's at or how to contact her?"

"Sweetheart, I'm so glad you called. I received a phone call from the university yesterday. I believe his last name was Ames. He's a professor at the university, and he called to inform me that Noelle was being sent to Sumatra. She had been working with the Humanities Program in Oslob in the Philippines. I think it's on the island of Cebu. Did you hear about the earthquake that struck Indonesia? Well, I guess she volunteered to fly to Sumatra to help in a humanitarian relief effort. Although, I have to say that I'm a little worried about her."

"Oh, my God, Edith, did you say she went to Sumatra?"

"Yes."

"Do you have a phone number or a way to contact her?"

"No. Honey, I'm afraid that I don't. Why? Is there something wrong?"

"Well, I haven't been able to contact her. She called me a few days ago, and I'm worried she might be upset with me. I wasn't thrilled over the idea of her going to the Philippines."

"Oh, Honey, don't worry. I'm sure she's fine. Professor Ames mentioned the fact she would have no way to contact me. I guess the earthquake did a lot of damage. But, I'm sure if she gets a chance, she will call you."

"Well, Edith, if you hear from her, will you please have her call me. She has my emergency phone number where she can reach me. It was good to speak with you. Take care of yourself."

"Thanks, Sweetheart, I will. Take good care of yourself as well. If I hear from Noelle, I will certainly tell her to call you. Please, don't worry."

"Thanks, Edith."

Hanging up the phone, Alex was more worried than ever about Noelle. Maybe he could understand her reasons for helping in Oslob, but her decision to go to Sumatra was crazy. There was probably no clean water or available housing. Why had he been so vehemently against her desire to go to the Philippines? Now she was in Sumatra, where the dangers were overwhelming. He should have been more understanding. Now, their stupid argument would cost him a lot of sleepless nights. He loved Noelle. He would never stop loving her. He desperately needed to get to Sumatra. For a short second, he almost contemplated going AWOL, absent without leave. However, that would be utter stupidity. He couldn't jeopardize his career if they were to have a future together.

Walking up the narrow hallway, Craig noticed Alex hanging up the phone.

"Hey, Doc, you seem to live on the phone these days. Is everything alright?"

"No. It appears Noelle left the Philippines and went to Sumatra to help the earthquake victims. Can you believe it? After being hit with a 7.5 magnitude earthquake, I'm sure Sumatra and the surrounding communities are a complete disaster area. Edith, her grandmother, said she went with a humanitarian relief effort connected with the University. I'm really worried about her. There's probably no clean drinking water or other services. Diseases can be spread rapidly under those circumstances, and to make matters worse, there is no way anyone can contact her."

"Buddy, I hate to say it, but I think you've got to wait this out. I'm sure Noelle is fine. From everything you've told me about her, she seems like a smart, intelligent woman. She'll be fine. I'm sure she'll be a lot of help in the clean-up efforts."

"Well, that does nothing in regards to my worrying about her."

"I'm sorry that I can't be of more help. You just need to relax and know that she can take care of herself. Aren't you off duty? Why don't we go over to the Class Six Store and pick up another bottle? I think we obliterated the other two. Alex, come on, you can't do this to yourself. Do you feel like a game of pool at the rec center?"

"No. I'm exhausted from the earlier surgeries. However, having a few drinks sounds like a great idea. Let's get out of here. Why don't we go over to your place?"

"Sounds good. Your place is a pig's pen. I know these tents aren't the Taj Mahal, but they are home," Craig mentioned.

"Enough with your Suzy Homemaker lecture. Let's get out of here. I need a cigarette."

Walking over to the Class Six Store, Alex was consumed by thoughts of getting to Sumatra. He was desperate to see Noelle. There had to be a way to find her. Once he made his mind up to do something, usually there was little anyone could do to change it. However, considering he was deployed to a Black Ops unit, it would demand serious logistics.

Entering Craig's tent, Alex had to admit it was well organized for a tight, cramped space.

"Come in. Mi Casa Es Su Casa," Craig grinned.

"Whatever. Get some glasses. I've got the bottle of Jack Daniels."

Craig poured them each a drink, watching as Alex downed his drink in one swallow. Then, reaching for his smokes and a lighter, he leaned back in his chair. Lighting a cigarette, he slowly inhaled, taking a deep breath.

"Wow, that's just what the doctor ordered," Alex laughed.

Pouring himself another stiff drink, he slowly exhaled the smoke from his cigarette.

"Geez, Alex, that's disgusting. Hasn't anyone ever told you how bad those things are for you?"

"Oh, wow, Craig, another lecture. You were smoking like a chimney the other night. Isn't that like the pot calling the kettle black?"

"Wow, Doc, I love your sarcastic remarks," Craig smirked, pouring himself another drink.

"Damn, that woman is driving me crazy. I have to find her," Alex remarked, pouring himself another drink. "Man, it's a good thing we bought two bottles of Jack Daniels. We've already killed this one. Craig, what do you think Colonel Williams would do if I asked for a few days to go to Sumatra?"

"Alex, are you serious? You're either drunk or crazy. Maybe both," Craig laughed, pouring himself another shot of whiskey.

"What can Colonel Williams do? Throw me out of his office? It's not like that hasn't happened before." Lighting another cigarette, Alex once again leaned back in his chair.

"Hell, man, you are desperate."

Lounging back in his chair, Craig starred at Alex. He was certain Alex had gone entirely bonkers.

"Oh, you have no idea."

"I just hope she's worth it. Considering the fact you're the best damn trauma surgeon Colonel Williams has at Club Med, it might just work. I can't wait to hear how this turns out. Here's to you and Noelle," Craig toasted.

"Thanks, Craig, I'll drink to that," Alex grinned, taking a huge sip. "Well, it appears we've almost killed another bottle. I think it's time for me to turn in while I can still walk. Thanks for letting me vent. I'll throw in a good word for you tomorrow in Colonel William's office,' Alex laughed, pushing his chair back from the table as he grabbed his cigarettes.

"Oh, hell, no. You're on your own tomorrow. You leave me out of this. I may only be a Captain, but I love those silver bars. Good luck."

"Thanks. Talk with you tomorrow."

Walking back to his tent, Alex fell onto his cot the second he entered. Grabbing a blanket, he was out for the night. It appeared that Jack Daniels effortlessly released him from his worries. Tomorrow he would take his chances in the Colonel's office.

Waking up with a splitting headache the following day, he grabbed two aspirin and a bottle of water. Looking down at his watch, it was almost 6:00 a.m. Quickly getting dressed, he wanted to stop by the Colonel's office before making his morning rounds. Deciding to drink some orange juice, he sat down and lit a cigarette. It was a short reprieve before he jumped off the deep end, so to speak. He couldn't be sure of the Colonel's mood this morning or how he might react when approached with the question of asking for leave. On the other hand, maybe the fact a trauma surgeon would be helpful in Sumatra might work in his favor. Nevertheless, he was willing to take his chances. Putting out his cigarette, he walked over to the hospital.

First, he needed to ensure the Colonel was in his office and available.

"Good morning, sir. Could I possibly have a few minutes of your time?" Alex smiled.

"Major Bennington, come in and have a seat. What's on your mind? Would you like a cup of coffee?"

"No, sir, but thanks for asking."

"What can I do for you?"

Pouring himself another cup of coffee, Colonel Williams stared at the young Major contemplating the reason for his impromptu visit.

"Is there any chance that I could ask for leave? I understand the serious component of our commitment to the troops. However, it seems I have an emergency and need to get to Sumatra."

"Hasn't there been a horrific earthquake in Indonesia?"

"Yes. That's part of the reason I'm asking for leave."

"Do you have relatives there?"

"Yes. My fiance, Noelle, has just arrived in Sumatra as part of a humanitarian relief program. Unfortunately, no one has been able to contact her. I'm worried about her safety. Also, I would like to offer my expertise as a trauma surgeon while there. I'm sure I could be of help to some of the casualties."

"Well, Major Bennington, as incredulous as this might sound. I'm glad you stopped by my office. Normally, there wouldn't be a chance in hell that I would let you go. However, there might be something you could do for me. Earlier this morning, I received a phone call from General McFarland. His daughter, Amanda, was in a horrific car crash in Hawaii. She's in serious condition and will require immediate surgery on both legs. There's a chance she might never walk again. However, the doctors are waiting to see if she survives the next twenty-four hours before operating. She's on life support at this time. Major Bennington, I don't have to remind you that you're the best damn trauma surgeon I've ever had under my command. I've seen you do the impossible. Knowing your extensive expertise in orthopedics, I'd like to recommend your impeccable skills as a surgeon to Frank," Colonel Williams remarked, pouring himself another cup of coffee. "I've always considered our incoming casualties to be extremely fortunate to make it to our hospital and into your operating room. Frank and I go way back. We've served together in several wartime theaters during my career. I'm sure he would be relieved to know someone of your caliber could be available to perform the surgery on his daughter. If you agree, I can have you out of here this morning. In return for your cooperation, I'll agree to your taking a few days afterward. As unbelievable as this seems, I guess this is your lucky day. Let me remind you, normally, I would never entertain thoughts of letting my most talented surgeon leave during deployment of this importance. However, I feel I owe it to General McFarland. Are you onboard?"

"Yes, sir. I would consider it an honor. Also, I would like permission to offer my services as a surgeon to the casualties in Sumatra. I can be ready to leave at a moment's notice. Thank you for stating your strong beliefs in my abilities as a trauma surgeon. I won't let you down. Please inform General McFarland that I would consider it a privilege to give any medical assistance to ensure his daughter walks again. Thank you."

"I'll have a temporary replacement flown in from Germany to cover for your absence. I'll make the call to Frank."

"Thanks, sir. I won't let either you or General McFarland down."

"Oh, Major Bennington, before you go, I'll have someone notify you when your flight leaves. Good luck. I'll be waiting for an outstanding report from Frank. I'm counting on you. Please, don't let me down. You're dismissed."

Walking out of Colonel Williams's office, Alex now more than ever believed in miracles. Craig would have a hard time believing the outcome of the meeting. Heck, he wasn't sure he even believed what had just happened. Walking down to Craig's office, he couldn't wait to give him the unbelievable news.

"Hey Craig, do you have a minute. I just left Colonel Williams's office."

"Well, it appears you're still in one piece," Craig smiled. "Have a seat."

"I'm on my way to Sumatra."

"How the hell did that happen?" Craig exclaimed, totally astonished by the news.

Lounging back in his chair, Craig couldn't wait to hear what had just transpired in the Colonel's office.

"All I have to do is make sure General McFarland's daughter walks again," Alex laughed, taking a seat.

"Damn, that's a pretty tall order. I hate to tell you, but you're not God. But, for heaven's sake, Alex, how could you ever agree to something like that? I truly hope that girl of yours is worth it. Your whole career could be on the line. Are you crazy? Wait, don't answer that. I think I determined last night you've completely gone bonkers."

"Don't be silly. I've got this. It's what I do for a living."

"What? Play God?"

"Geez, Craig, I never said I was God. However, I do have certain skills. Now, you're the one being ridiculous."

"Alex, do I have to remind you, this is General McFarland's daughter we're talking about. Have you ever stopped to consider the consequences of what might happen if the surgery isn't successful? Your whole career could go down the drain."

"Damn, buddy, have a little faith. The word on the streets here at Club Med is that I'm a damn good trauma surgeon. Actually, I'll recount Colonel Williams' exact words this morning. It went something like this, "Alex, you're the best damn trauma surgeon that I've had under my command.""

"Well, I wouldn't be too anxious to run out and buy the general's daughter a pair of Nike running shoes if you catch my drift."

"Hell, Craig, that's a low blow. Oh, she'll be running all right.

Trust me. She's my ticket to finding Noelle. You'll see. I'm out of here in a few hours. I've got to go, but I'll think about you when I arrive in Hawaii. Oh, that's right. You'll still be here at Club Med in the middle of the desert," Alex grinned, walking to the door.

"Good luck with the surgery. Tell that cute girl of yours that I said, "hello."

"Will do, Buddy. See you when I get back."

Closing Craig's office door, Alex made a mad dash to his tent. He needed to pack. He was anxious to find Noelle. Fortunately, he didn't have long to wait before news of his impending departure arrived. Now, only a few hours of surgery stood between him and the love of his life.

"Sir," the young Sergeant saluted. "I'm here to drive you out to the flight line. I believe a C-141 transport just landed. It's going to be a quick turnaround. Are you ready to leave, and do you have more than one bag?"

"Yes. I'm ready. However, there's just the one duffle bag sitting next to the cot."

"I've got it," Sergeant Guthry mentioned picking up the bag. "Heard you're on your way to Hawaii."

"Yes. That's right."

It only took a few minutes to drive out to the flight line. Alex was anxious to be on his way. Parking next to the enormous military aircraft, Sergeant Guthry sat the duffel on the tarmac.

"Sir, have a nice flight. Enjoy Hawaii."

"Thanks."

Alex found it amusing everyone assumed his destination was Hawaii. Little did they know it was Sumatra. He couldn't wait to feel the warm embrace of Noelle's body against his. It simply didn't matter the price he had to pay for seeing the love of his life. It was insignificant.

"Good morning, sir," the young officer saluted. "I'll take your duffel. We're just waiting for another passenger, Captain. Harris. You're welcome to board the aircraft. We're ready for takeoff as soon as she arrives."

"Thanks."

Climbing aboard the huge cargo plane, Alex took a seat along the interior wall of the aircraft. It was minimal seating at best. The long rows of gray canvas seats definitely weren't first class. However, he was excited to be aboard regardless of his comfort level.

"Sir, I think you might need this," Lieutenant Hoffman smiled, handing him a pair of noise-reducing headphones. "You'll find blankets scattered behind the canvas seats if you get too cold. Captain Harris just arrived. We'll be airborne in a few minutes."

"Thanks."

"Oh, I forgot to inform you. We'll be making a stop in the Philippines and Okinawa. We're fully loaded with food items for the embassy commissaries. I'm afraid you're in for quite a long haul this morning. However, we will get you to Hawaii," Lieutenant Hoffman smiled. "We have prepared box meals. Make yourself as comfortable as possible. I'll keep you informed of our location."

Looking around the vast steel-gray structure, it had a foreboding appearance. Huge wooden pallets covered in cellophane were strapped into bolts on the floor. The pallets contained food items destined for military commissaries. Sparsely scattered small circular windows left the aircraft's interior dimly lit and gave little chance of viewing outside. It definitely wasn't a commercial flight or first-class accommodations. However, he was thrilled to be getting a hop to Hawaii. Maybe he would get a commercial flight later to Sumatra.

Finally, a young woman, he assumed, was Captain Harris entered the aircraft, taking a seat across from him. Hearing the loud whine of the engines, the gigantic plane slowly rolled towards the runway. Within minutes the transport climbed steadily, reaching its cruising altitude. Tomorrow he would be in Hawaii. Then, hopefully, soon after, Sumatra.

Reaching Hawaii the following evening, he immediately checked into billeting at Hickham Air Force Base. The next day, he went to the hospital to meet General McFarland and his family. The General was delighted that he had taken time away from his duties to ensure his daughter had the best possible chance to walk again. The fact his daughter was well enough to be taken off life support meant Alex could proceed with the surgery the following morning.

Performing surgery the next day, it couldn't have gone better. After putting a couple of pins in her legs and replacing one knee, it not only assured that Amanda would walk again but run as well. She was indeed a lucky young woman, and despite Craig's rude joke, she would need those Nike running shoes.

After being in Hawaii for a few days, Alex was excited to be on his way to the airport. Finally, he was on his way to Indonesia. Arriving in Jakarta in less than twenty-four hours, he would catch Lampung's flight to southern Sumatra. Afterward, it would only be a matter of elimination to find which community she had been assigned.

Boarding the plane, Alex found his seat and made himself comfortable for the long flight. Reclining his seat, he closed his eyes. Thoughts of Noelle consumed him. Hopefully, tomorrow, he would be holding the only girl who had ever mattered to him. There was no way for Noelle to know that he would soon be in Sumatra. Unexpectedly, she was about to receive the surprise of her life.

Chapter Eleven

Indonesia

Arriving in Jakarta, Alex was exhausted from the long flight. However, he continued his journey, boarding a flight to Bandar Lampung in southern Sumatra without any thoughts of staying overnight. Upon reaching his destination, he would begin the arduous task of finding Noelle. It appeared the most devastating damage from the earthquake was near Bintuhan. It was a small community located near the coast of western Sumatra. It would be a great place to start. Hopefully, with a bit of luck, he would find Noelle.

Boarding the small plane, it was completely filled with passengers. Searching for a place to sit, Alex noticed an open seat near the back of the aircraft and settled in for the short flight. Looking around, perhaps some of the passengers belonged to humanitarian relief organizations. Somewhat curious, he decided to ask the young woman sitting next to him. Amazingly, as fate would have it, she belonged to Doctors Without Borders. During their brief conversation, Alex discovered a high probability that Noelle could be in Bintuhan and that they desperately needed doctors. Not only was he close to finding her, but he also could put his expertise as a surgeon to excellent use. Reclining his seat, Alex was relieved, knowing his chances of finding Noelle in the small coastal community were extremely good.

Arriving in Bintuhan, Alex followed directions the young woman had given him to a small outpost, which housed operations for search and rescue efforts. However, the effects of the long trip and no sleep were beginning to take their toll. Getting some much-needed rest was paramount at the moment. Finding Noelle would have to wait until morning. The most important fact was that he'd finally made it to Bintuhan. Tomorrow, he would begin his search.

Checking in with the local Red Cross efforts, Alex, without hesitation, offered his vast experience and knowledge as a trauma surgeon. He was immediately made aware many casualties were waiting to have either arms or legs reset. Without hesitation, Alex agreed to perform the surgeries the following day. Now, with a bit of luck, the only thing standing between him and Noelle was a good night's sleep and a few surgeries. Walking over to one of the large tents which housed sleeping volunteers, Alex quickly found an open cot. Finding a musky blanket neatly folded at the end of one of the beds, he pulled the covers up to his chest and buried his head in the pillow. Hopefully, tomorrow, he would be reunited with Noelle. Drifting off to sleep, she was the last thing on his mind.

Waking early the next morning, it appeared sleep had eluded him for the most part. The noisy rotation of volunteers during the night had kept him awake. First, however, he needed to get dressed and find his way to the small temporary building that housed the hospital. He'd committed himself to perform several surgeries, and the sooner they were completed, the sooner he could continue his search for her.

Walking over to the hospital, he looked for Noelle. Unfortunately, he passed no one who came close to fitting her description. Somewhat disappointed, he was directed to the physician's lounge as he entered the makeshift medical facility. Pouring himself a cup of coffee, he discovered an assortment of muffins made available to the staff. After taking a few minutes to enjoy a hot cup of coffee along with a cinnamon muffin, he changed into a pair of green surgical scrubs.

Finally, after spending five hours in surgery, he was ready for a long-overdue break. Quickly tossing his surgical mask into a nearby waste bin, he hurriedly walked out of the operating room. Noelle consumed his every thought. Surely, she had to be in Bintuhan. He couldn't imagine coming all this way only to leave without finding her. Whispering a short prayer, he asked for divine help in locating the love of his life. Without his knowing, his prayers were about to be answered most unexpectedly.

Continuing his brisk walk down the dim, narrow hallway, he was anxious to change out of his green scrubs and finally begin his long-awaited search. Suddenly, out of nowhere, Alex heard a familiar voice. Stopping at the door to the physician's lounge, he turned around. Flashing him one of her silly smiles, Noelle walked towards him.

"Doctor Bennington, can I help you out of your scrubs?"

He was speechless. How did Noelle know he was in Bintuhan? How did she know he was performing surgeries this morning. It didn't matter. None of it mattered. She was simply there, and he was ecstatic.

"Oh, my God, Sweetheart, you're here," Alex exclaimed, scooping her up in his arms. Then, holding her tight against his chest, he spun her around. He never wanted to let her go. "Babe, how in the name of heaven's did you know I was here?"

"Stop talking and kiss me," Noelle smiled.

Pulling her closer, Alex kissed her with such passion it left her breathless. Melting helplessly into his arms, the magic of his kiss sent tingles of excitement throughout her petite body.

"Wow, Sweetheart, did you miss me?" Alex whispered.

"Alex, that's not fair. Did you miss me?"

"Babe, I'm here. Does that answer your question?" he winked, kissing her once more.

"Noelle, get your things. I'm taking you to Thailand for a few days."

Looking down at her left hand, he noticed her engagement ring was missing.

"What the hell? Noelle, you're not wearing your engagement ring," he panicked.

"Alex, did you stop in the states at the apartment before coming here?"

"No. Why?"

"Well, I sort of left the ring at the apartment along with a note."

"Sweetheart, what are you saying? Are you saying we're no longer engaged?" His breath hitched, and his heart stopped.

"No. Babe, I was confused. After you left, I simply felt like my life had no meaning. You have no idea what it was like living without you. I was devastated and missed you more than you could ever imagine. I found myself lost without you. Alex, I love you. I'm so sorry. Can you ever forgive me?" Noelle begged with tears in her eyes.

"Oh my God, Sweetheart, I love you. I'll always love you. Let's get out of here. You can explain it all later. Just one thing, how did you know that I was here?"

"Well, the little girl you operated on this morning, Isabella, is a friend of mine. James pulled her small body from beneath a pile of rubble a few days ago. She lost her entire family in the earthquake. So I've become her surrogate mother. One of the medics told me she was finally having surgery today. We've been waiting for an orthopedic surgeon to arrive. I inquired about her doctor this morning, and I almost fainted when they referenced your last name and that you arrived late last night. Babe, this is a small community. I knew it was you. However, I wish I had known last night when you arrived," Noelle smiled.

"Oh, I think that was for the best. Sweetheart, had I found you last night, one thing is for certain, I wouldn't have been doing any surgeries this morning. Babe, trust me on that one," Alex laughed, pulling her into his arms.

Finding James, it appeared that he easily understood her need to get away for a few days with Alex. Likewise, he felt Noelle deserved a few days respite from Bintuhan and the surrounding devastation caused by the earthquake. After packing, she checked on Isabella, assuring her that she would soon return, then excitedly accompanied Alex to the airport. Finally, leaving Jakarta, they were on their way to Thailand, specifically the island of Phuket.

Later that afternoon, arriving in Bangkok, Alex arranged for them to stay in a luxurious five-star resort while in Phuket. Now, only a boat ride stood between them and their lavish accommodations.

Unfortunately, the seas were unexpectedly rough. After a few hours of being on the boat, it was evident Noelle was getting seasick. Bouts of vomiting sent her racing to the bathroom.

"Geez, Sweetheart, I feel bad that I recommended taking a boat to Phuket. I could have arranged a different mode of travel had I known," Alex apologized, wiping Noelle's face with a wet towel.

"Oh, it's not your fault. Who knew?"

Laying her head on Alex's shoulder, she looked forward to arriving at their destination more than ever. Noticing her level of discomfort, Alex decided to check the small store on board the boat for medications. It appeared they carried Dramamine, a medicine that helps motion sickness. Quickly, giving her one of the small tablets, he hoped to ease her symptoms. It seemed the medication was effective. However, she was rather sleepy for the remainder of their trip. Arriving in Phuket, Noelle was still out. He carried her off the boat and put her in the limo for the short ride to the resort.

Arriving at their destination, the Phuket Bay Villas, it was exquisite. As the limo parked under the portico, it resembled a Buddhist Temple with its tall, gold triangular roof. Sparkling water fountains surrounded by lush greenery encased the circular entrance. Thankfully, Noelle had somewhat recovered. She managed, with Alex's help to walk inside the lobby. Receiving room keys, the concierge carried their luggage outside to a waiting golf cart and drove them down to the beach and their private villa. It had magnificent views of the Bay of Phuket. Still, somewhat under the effect of the Dramamine, she was rather tired and sleepy. Pulling back the luxurious satin duvet, Alex lovingly put her to bed. She was out for the night. Pouring himself a stiff drink, Alex walked outside to the patio. Sitting down to finish his drink, he lit a cigarette. It had been a long, grueling journey, yet he smiled, knowing that he was finally reunited with the love of his life. Finishing his drink, he put out his cigarette. Walking inside, he stripped down to his briefs and slipped into bed. Feeling the warmth of her slender body next to his, he gently kissed her good night. Tomorrow held the promise of a new day.

Waking first, Noelle stared at the handsome young doctor who still slept so peacefully. How could she have ever said such hurtful things to him during their last phone conversation? Looking down at her left hand, it felt naked. How could she have ever removed her gorgeous engagement ring? She must have suffered a moment of insanity. Noelle had never loved him more. Leaning over, she began kissing him awake. She craved every second of the time they would have together in Phuket.

Slowly opening his eyes, Alex smiled.

"Sweetheart, I love you," he softly whispered, returning her kisses. "What do you want to do today?"

"Babe, really, is that even a question," she smiled. "You should know me by now."

"What? Spend the day watching vintage movies?" he teased.

"No, Doctor Bennington, I've got you right where I want you for the rest of the day." Then, playfully pulling the covers over their heads, Noelle laughed mischievously.

"Wow, my kind of girl," he softly whispered.

For the remainder of the day, they stayed in bed. Exactly, as Noelle had wished, it was easy loving Noelle. He'd waited his entire life for someone with whom he felt such a strong connection. But, now that fate had reunited them, he wasn't about to waste a moment.

Later, ordering room service, they enjoyed dinner in bed. The whole day was spent as only lovers would except for a brief moment of insanity on his part when he dared question the condition of his Porsche. Immediately, she hit him with a pillow and raced for the bathroom. Chasing after her, he caught her just before she locked the door, scooping her into his arms. He laughed, carrying her back to bed as Noelle yelled every obscenity known to man regarding his car.

"Really, babe, it's just a car."

Apologizing, he lightheartedly held her against her will until she finally came to her senses and began laughing. "I'm sorry. I don't know what it is with you and that car," he confessed.

"Maybe it's the fact that sometimes I feel as if you love your stupid Porsche more than me," she vented. "Okay, you're forgiven. I didn't mean to lose it like that. The Porsche is in the garage at the apartment, and Trevor has the keys," Noelle grinned.

"Trevor," Alex yelled. "Did you say, Trevor?"

"Now, look, who's getting steamed? I thought he was your best friend?"

"Noelle, why in the hell does he have the keys to my Porsche?"

"Alex, your car is simply in the garage for safekeeping. I'm sure that Trevor isn't driving it. However, I felt it was best to leave the apartment and car keys with him."

"Well, Trevor isn't exactly on my friend's list at the moment. He agreed with you leaving the country without even calling me. He had to know that I wouldn't have approved of your going to the Philippines, at least not at that time. Heck, we were engaged, and I was never consulted. No one bothered to call and ask how I felt."

"Oh, you poor baby," Noelle laughed. "I'm truly sorry that I didn't discuss my plans with you. I was afraid you might be upset, and I felt it was something I had to do. I was going crazy in the apartment without you. I loved redecorating and purchasing new furniture, but after that, I became extremely bored."

"We'll discuss that later. Go put on your bathing suit. I think we could use some fresh air. The beaches in Phuket are gorgeous. I think we should go swimming."

"Okay, that sounds like fun. The beaches in the Philippines were beautiful too, but I never had the chance to enjoy them. So instead, I kept busy working with the children, who would be moving into the new orphanage. Later, I'll tell you about Ian, one of the little boys. He so reminded me of you."

"Well, I'm sure he was smart and handsome."

"Geez, you're conceited," she laughed, tossing another pillow at him as she jumped off the bed.

Searching through her bags, Noelle found her swimsuit. Walking into the bathroom, she glanced in the mirror and contemplated the idea of wearing her hair in braids. Then, deciding it was worth the effort and the few extra minutes it would take, she pulled back her long blonde curls weaving her long locks into braids. Afterward, quickly spritzing on her favorite fragrance and changing into her bikini, she was finally ready to enjoy the afternoon in the warm turquoise waters surrounding Phuket.

Captivated by the sight of Noelle walking out of the bathroom, Alex's heart stopped. He was totally mesmerized by her appearance. She looked stunning. Noelle's slender, sculpted figure, and her blonde braids, totally complimented the sexy black bikini. She took his breath away, making him easily forget their earlier argument over the Porsche.

"Wow, Sweetheart, you're gorgeous. Maybe you were right. We should spend the day indoors," he winked, wickedly pulling her into his arms.

"Don't be silly. I didn't braid my hair to stay indoors. Now, put on your swimsuit. We're going swimming."

"Okay, if you insist, but I can certainly think of better things to do than swim."

"Babe, get changed and grab some towels. I'll get the sunscreen," Noelle laughed, searching for her sunglasses.

Walking out of the bathroom, Alex playfully modeled his black swim trunks.

"Geez, Babe, you don't look half bad yourself," Noelle whistled.

Putting his arm around her, they walked down to the pristine beach. Laying their towels on a giant rock that jutted out of the water, Alex took the opportunity to rub sunscreen on Noelle's body. Getting a bit carried away with the process, she stopped his advances. Grabbing his hands, she pulled him into the warm turquoise water. Like two spirited kids at play, Alex eagerly followed her away from the shore and further out into the sparkling, calm waters of the bay. Suddenly, without warning, she stepped into a hole on the ocean floor, instantly sinking underneath the water. Reacting quickly, Alex grabbed Noelle, immediately bringing her up. However, she panicked as he pulled her from the depths.

"Are you okay?" Alex remarked, glimpsing her terrified expression.

Freaking out, Noelle choked as she desperately tried to clear her throat. Finally able to breathe, she gasped for air.

"Wow. That was scary," she coughed, barely able to talk.

"Sweetheart, are you sure you're alright?"

"Yes. I think so."

Picking Noelle up in his arms, he carried her back to shore.

"Babe, do you know how to swim?"

"No. Why?" she asked, clinging to him like a terrified child.

"Well, for one thing, the way you were pulling me further out, I assumed you could swim. But, Sweetheart, when you're in unfamiliar water, there's always a slight chance you could step in a hole or be pulled out over your head. So I'll teach you how to swim."

"Not today. That was terrifying."

"Sweetheart, you're funny. Why don't we relax in the hot tub? I'll get us a drink. Doctor's orders, I'll be right back," Alex winked, sitting Noelle inside the warm swirling water.

Tying a towel around his waist, Alex walked inside the villa. Popping the cork on a bottle of champagne, he grabbed two glasses. Alex took the champagne and glasses outside and stepped into the hot tub sitting close to Noelle. Pouring them a drink, he quickly kissed her and handed her a glass of the sparkling beverage.

"Here's to your saving me for the second time," Noelle toasted. "Thanks for always being there. I love you."

"Sweetheart, I love you too."

"Alex, let's get married. I don't want to wait," Noelle blurted out with tears in her eyes. Snuggling into his arms, she waited pensively for his reply.

"Where did that come from?"

"Well, earlier, I think my life flashed before my eyes. Then, for a moment, I thought I might drown."

"Noelle, I'd marry you today, tomorrow, or right now, for that matter. However, we're not exactly in the states. I think you owe it to Edith to wait until my deployment is over."

Taking their glasses, he set them on the edge of the hot tub. Pulling Noelle into his arms, he kissed her. The intensity of his kiss, combined with the effects of the alcohol and warm water, made her feel as if she was melting into his arms. She loved him with every ounce of her being. The fact he was simply there each time she'd encountered a life-threatening crisis was unimaginable. She never wanted to live without him. However, thoughts of him returning to Aviano sent rivers of tears flowing down her cheeks.

"Babe, what's wrong?" he asked, gently wiping her face with the back of his hand.

"Alex, I know you have to go back to Aviano. We only have a few days together. What am I going to do?"

"Sweetheart, you're stronger than you think. I love you. Please, don't think about it, not tonight, and not while we're together. Promise me."

He reached for a towel and lifted her out of the warm water and into his arms. Carrying her inside, he would erase any further thoughts of his deployment from her mind.

"I love you. Let's take this party inside," Alex suggested.

The next morning, Alex slowly opened his eyes. Staring at the love of his life, she still slept peacefully. Gently pulling back strands of her long blonde curls, he softly kissed her awake. She'd easily stolen his heart the first time he saw her. Thoughts of leaving her again were killing him. However, he had to be strong for her for the remainder of their time in Phuket.

"Babe, I'm going to get a shower and order room service. Go back to sleep. I'll wake you when breakfast comes."

"Okay, thanks," Noelle whispered, barely audible as she snuggled under the covers.

Walking into the bathroom, Alex opened the glass shower door and turned on the warm water. Closing his eyes, he lathered his hair with shampoo. Suddenly, he felt her hands softly caressing his back. Turning around, he smiled.

"Wow, Sweetheart, I thought you had fallen asleep," Alex laughed. "Here's the shampoo."

He knew she was going to make it extremely hard for him to leave her again.

After their unexpected rendezvous in the shower, Alex called room service. He ordered lots of coffee along with oatmeal, eggs, bacon, and hash browns. He was starved. Today he planned to take Noelle by helicopter to Ko Tapu, Phang Nga Bay, where James Bond filmed *Man with the Golden Gun* in 1974.

Hearing a knock at the door indicated the arrival of breakfast. Deciding to eat outside on the patio, Noel wrapped her damp hair in a towel. Lifting the silver tops from the serving dishes, she smiled, discovering oatmeal.

"Wow, Alex, you remembered how much I love oatmeal."

"Sweetheart, we both share a love for oatmeal. As an intern, I lived off oatmeal, juice, and coffee every morning."

Taking a sip of coffee, Noelle had a lot of questions.

"Alex, you never told me how you managed to leave Aviano or how you knew where to find me.

"Well, to start, I called Trevor and then Edith. That'll be the last time I ever call Trevor. He was no help at all. In fact, I'm pissed at him," Alex paused, taking a sip of coffee.

"Stop right there. You've got this all wrong about Trevor. Seriously, neither he nor Becky had anything to do with me going to the Philippines. I signed up with the university to take the trip with the Humanities Class. Becky cooked dinner for me one evening and answered questions about the Philippines. To be honest, I had already made up my mind. However, they did give me their blessing when they knew I was going and agreed to check on the apartment and the Porsche. I know you and Trevor have been good friends since medical school. I hope that doesn't change. Trust me, Trevor did nothing wrong, and I definitely don't want to be the reason you're both mad at each other. You have to make things right between you and him. At least, think about it. I know you'll do the right thing," Noelle smiled, stirring a spoonful of sugar into her oatmeal. "Continue. I want to know more about how you managed to get leave."

"Alright, I'll think about talking with Trevor. It wasn't exactly easy getting away from the base. However, I'll have to admit I got lucky, real lucky. Usually, no one leaves a deployment unless it's perhaps a family emergency. I told Craig that I would simply walk into Colonel Williams's office and ask for a few days' leave. I'm sure he thought I'd lost my mind," Alex smirked, pouring himself another cup of coffee.

"Who's Craig?"

"Oh, he works at the hospital in administration. We're drinking buddies. Some nights after our shift ends at the hospital, we stop at the Class Six Store. Trust me. There's not a lot to do on the base. He's a nice guy. Hopefully, one day you can meet him. Anyway, getting back to Colonel Williams, I stopped by his office early one morning. It must have been a divine appointment. He wasn't busy, and it just so happened he'd received an earlier phone call, which made what I was about to ask him possible. Unfortunately, General McFarland's daughter had just been injured in an auto accident in Hawaii. Fortunately for me, General McFarland and Colonel Williams are good friends. The Colonel had been impressed with my abilities as a trauma surgeon, and he knew that I specialized in orthopedics. So, when I asked for a few days of leave, knowing you had been sent to Sumatra to work with a humanitarian relief effort, he offered me a deal. A deal I couldn't turn down," Alex smiled.

"Oh yeah, what kind of deal?" Noelle asked curiously.

"Well, Sweetheart, the chance to find you. All I had to do was make sure that General McFarland's daughter could walk again."

"What? Are you kidding? You're not God. You do know that, right?" She was shocked at the degree of risk Alex undertook to find her.

"That's funny. That's what Craig said. Well, to get back to my story, his daughter had severely injured her legs in the accident. It was doubtful that she might ever walk again. So, of course, Colonel Williams recommended that I fly over to Hawaii and perform the surgery. As I said, he was aware of my performances in the operating room with our troops. He said he had faith that I could easily do the job. In fact, he insisted that I go to Hawaii if General McFarland agreed. Naturally, McFarland agreed after hearing the Colonel's recommendations. So, that was it. I flew to Hawaii and performed the surgery in exchange for leave time. Thank God the surgery was easier than I expected. She simply needed pins put in her legs and a knee replacement. She made it through surgery just fine. As a result, she will be able to walk and run. Can you believe it?"

"Alex, that's unbelievable. I'm so proud of you," Noelle remarked, getting up to kiss her handsome doctor. "I'm scared to ask, but what would have happened if the surgery hadn't been a success?"

"Well, I don't even want to think about it. Needless to say, my career would probably have been over. Who knows for sure," Alex frowned, taking another sip of coffee.

"Alex, how did you know that I was in Sumatra, especially Bintuhan?"

"Oh, I called Edith. Professor Ames called her and informed her that you had volunteered to go to Sumatra to help the earthquake victims. Landing in Jakarta, it seemed a lot of the efforts were centered around Bintuhan. Catching a flight to Bandar Lampung, one of the passengers, a young lady sitting next to me, came over to work with Doctors Without Borders. It just so happened she was on her way to Bintuhan. I had a strong hunch you were there. Sweetheart, don't worry, I'll always find you. You're not getting away from me that easy," Alex winked.

"Babe, I love you. The world's a big place," Noelle teased, walking over to sit on his lap. "Doctor Bennington, do you even know how much I love you," she smiled, running her fingers through his silky dark hair. Then, removing the towel from her head, she kissed him passionately.

Wiping her moist eyes, his story was almost unbelievable. Never had anyone put their professional career on the line for her. Tears slowly trickled down her face as she looked down at her left hand. She hated that she had removed her engagement ring and left the note.

"Alex, I'm so sorry I put you through all of that. I can't believe I left my ring at the apartment," Noelle sobbed once more, looking down at her ringless finger.

"Sweetheart, it doesn't take a diamond ring to prove my love for you or the fact we're engaged. However, if you want, when we get back to Bangkok, we'll shop for another ring. Does that make you feel better?" he winked.

"Yes. Are you sure?"

"Trust me, I'm sure—no more crying. Finish your oatmeal. I have a special day planned. I think you'll like where we're going."

After breakfast, Alex suggested they go inside and get dressed.

"You might want to wear your swimsuit under your outerwear today."

"Are you implying that we're going swimming?" Noelle hesitated. "I'm not sure about getting back in the water again. I still feel nervous about the fact I almost drowned."

"Sweetheart, you didn't drown. I was right there to save you. I promise nothing will happen as long as you're with me. I didn't come all this way to lose you," Alex winked, giving her a quick kiss on the forehead. "Now, stop being silly. Let's get going. The car will be here soon."

Walking out of the bathroom, Noelle once again looked fabulous. Wearing a beige see-through lace tunic and denim shorts over her bikini and her blonde hair pulled back into a ponytail, she looked gorgeous. She was now sporting a tremendous tan compliments of their time in Phuket.

"Wow. Noelle, you're stunning."

Hearing a knock at the door, Alex quickly answered.

"Babe, our ride is here. I'll get our beach towels and a blanket. Oh, don't forget your sunglasses."

"Okay. Where are we going?" Noelle enthusiastically inquired, grabbing her glasses.

"It's a surprise," Alex smiled, closing the door.

Getting inside the limo, it was only a short ride out to the airport. But, as the limo parked next to a helicopter, Noelle became anxious.

"Alex, really, a helicopter. I've never been in one before. I'm not sure about this."

"Sweetheart, you're with me. You're completely safe."

Departing the limo, the driver handed them a small wicker picnic basket. It contained everything needed to spend an entire day on the gorgeous beaches of Phuket.

Noelle held tightly to Alex as the helicopter lifted high into the air. Turning sharply in the direction of Ao Phang Nga National Park, James Bond Island, it was a quick flight. The pilot gave them a bird's eye view of the iconic, vertical rock formations that towered upward from Phang Nga Bay's turquoise green waters. It was breathtaking. However, Alex had arranged for them to spend the entire day away from tourists on a less visible portion of the island. Landing on an isolated, narrow strip of sandy beach, the pilot reminded them of their pickup time. Helping her down from the helicopter, Alex took the picnic basket. Then, quickly leading her away from the aircraft as it readied for departure, they walked towards a small frond-covered palapa. It provided the idyllic setting for spending an entire day alone on the beautiful beaches.

"Alex, what if he forgets to pick us up?" Noelle worried.

"Sweetheart, I don't think you have to worry about that. The tourist agency doesn't make money by dumping vacationers and not retrieving them each evening. Look around. Do you see stranded tourists everywhere?" Alex laughed. "Change into your swimsuit. I'll pour us a glass of champagne."

Spreading out a blanket under the open-air palapa, Alex reached inside the wicker basket for two glasses. It contained enough champagne, cold cuts for sandwiches, assorted fruits, and cheese to last the entire day. Popping the cork from the champagne, Alex poured them each a sparkling drink.

"Here's to an unforgettable day," Alex toasted.

"Thanks. I'll drink to that. I could never have envisioned us being together in this remarkable place. The day you left for deployment, I felt like my whole world had ended."

"Sweetheart, I don't want you ever to feel that way again. You're never getting away from me. Do you understand?" he winked, giving her a quick kiss. "Drink up. I have something to show you."

Quickly finishing their champagne, Alex grabbed her hand. Pulling her towards a clearing in the dense jungle, they came upon a small trail. Leaving the windswept beach, it immediately became humid and somewhat cooler as they retreated farther into the lush green foliage.

"Hold my hand, and follow me. It might get slippery, so don't fall."

Leading Noelle down a steep path, he had been assured it was only a short hike. However, it appeared a bit further than he'd expected. Trudging through the thick, tropical terrain, they soon found themselves stepping over small boulders and expansive Banyan tree roots.

"Alex, do you know where you're going? Please, don't get us lost,"

Noelle laughed, trying to balance herself as she stepped over the gigantic roots.

"I've never been here before, but I was assured it would be worth the hike. Guess we'll soon find out," Alex smiled, giving her a quick kiss.

"I'll take your word for it that you know where we're going."

"It should only be a little farther down this trail. So have a little faith."

Helping Noelle over a large boulder, Alex feared the trail might get more dangerous and challenging than he'd been informed. However, he was not about to let her know his concerns.

Suddenly, the thunderous sound of falling water could be heard in the distance. Picking up their pace, they were anxious to see what was up ahead. Then, barely visible through the canopy of trees, a spectacular waterfall appeared out of nowhere.

"Geez, babe, look up," Noelle gasped.

"Wow. That's spectacular."

Racing to get a closer look, they were amazed to find themselves standing at the bottom of a magnificent waterfall. A gorgeous rainbow was clearly visible in the mist of the water as it plummeted over two hundred feet into a large shimmering pool.

"Well, sweetheart, are you thinking what I'm thinking?" Alex smiled, wiping sweat from his forehead.

Before she even had a chance to answer, he scooped her up in his arms and carried her into the cool refreshing water. It felt invigorating after the long, arduous hike.

"Alex, there better not be any snakes in here," she cringed.

"Don't worry, I've got you," he laughed. "Sweetheart, can you believe it? We have this place all to ourselves."

Holding Noelle in his arms, he quickly dunked her under the clear, refreshing water. It felt relaxing. Pulling her closer into his chest, he held her tight. Energetically, Alex twirled their bodies around in the sparkling water, kissing her passionately. Totally captivated by the sudden intensity of his kiss and the surrounding ambiance, she felt giddy with excitement. Any lingering worries she had about the fact he would soon be leaving vanished. Completely captivated by the moment, it easily felt like they were the only two people on earth.

"Alex, this is truly paradise. It's gorgeous," Noelle whispered, taking in the beauty of the afternoon sun as it reflected off the swirling water.

"Sweetheart, why are you whispering?" he laughed. "I believe we're the only ones here," he winked with a kiss.

Out of nowhere, two wild monkeys walked down to the edge of the pool.

"Wow. I guess I was wrong about us being the only ones here," Alex laughed, catching sight of the timid monkeys. They appeared curious but harmless. Noelle cringed, totally freaked out at the mere sight of them. Then, screaming at the top of her lungs, she clung to Alex.

"Geez, Noelle, you scared the living hell out of me. Seriously, Sweetheart, you're afraid of those little guys," Alex laughed. "You almost gave me a heart attack. However, I must admit they don't seem bothered by your craziness."

"Alex, I hope they leave. I'm not getting out of the water while they are sitting so close to us," she insisted.

"Well, Babe, I'm not sure about you, but I have a helicopter to catch later this evening. They're harmless. I bet they simply came down to see who was playing in their pool. Trust me. If we ignore them, I'm sure they'll eventually leave."

"I want to go back to the beach."

"Really, I thought you loved it here."

"Alex, don't tease me. It's gorgeous, but I'm scared, and I'm getting hungry."

"Okay. But your friends are still staring at you. Are you sure?" he laughed curiously.

"Yes. Can you throw something at the monkeys or make them move?"

"Sweetheart, we're standing in the middle of a pool. What do you suggest that I throw at them? Besides, they've done nothing to us. Just stay close to me. I'm sure they won't bother us."

As Alex slowly walked towards the edge of the water, one of the monkeys let out a loud, terrifying howl.

"Oh, my God," Noelle screamed. "Alex, stop. Please, don't get out of the water. What if he's calling his friends?" she panicked.

"Well, I'm afraid we could be in a whole heap of trouble," Alex laughed.

"Alex, this isn't funny. Aren't you scared?"

"No. We'll be fine. However, if I say run, you better run," Alex laughed. He loved teasing Noelle. However, she never appreciated being the target of his mindless sense of humor.

Taking her hand, he slowly led Noelle out of the water and directly passed them. Fortunately, the monkeys made no sounds. They simply remained still and curious. Not daring to look back, she gripped Alex's hand like a vice as they carefully hurried down the trail and out of sight. He desperately wanted to yell run for the fun of it. However, his amusement wasn't worth the risk of seeing her get hurt.

Finally, arriving back at the palapa, Noelle collapsed on the blanket.

"Okay, Sweetheart, let me pour you another glass of champagne. I think it'll calm your nerves. Doctor's orders," he winked, handing her a glass of the sparkling beverage. "Try these. They're delicious," Alex mentioned giving her a small cluster of grapes. "I'll make sandwiches." Staring at the love of his life as she rested on the blanket in her black bikini, Alex smiled. He'd never loved her more, even if she did have an unusual fear of wild monkeys.

Later after eating, they relaxed on the blanket. Listening to the tranquil sound of waves gently washing ashore, thoughts of their future became the topic of discussion.

"Sweetheart, we've never discussed children. But, you do want children, right?" Alex questioned.

"More than you know. I never had siblings. How does an even dozen sound?" Noelle laughed.

"I might need an extra job to support a crew of that size. However, having a large family sounds intriguing."

"What are your thoughts on adoption?"

"Well, I can't say that I've ever given it much thought, but if the right child came along, I wouldn't rule it out."

"Alex, the little boy, Ian, the one which I said reminded me of you at the orphanage in Oslob. Well, it was bizarre, but I instantly felt a connection to him. He was so sweet and kind. Everyone loved him. I think it would be great if we were able to adopt him. He deserves so much more in life than growing up without a family of his own. If it were possible, would you ever consider adopting him?"

"Sweetheart, if this is something you're serious about, I'd love to meet him. If he reminds you of me, then he must be a great kid," Alex teased. "However, I think we should get married first."

"Babe, I love you. How did I ever get so lucky?"

Lovingly caressing his face, she gently rubbed her hands through his day's growth of stubble. She'd never been more in love. She knew that he would do anything to make her happy.

Pulling her into his arms, Alex gently kissed her. He knew that Noelle had a huge heart and would make a wonderful mother.

"Wow. I had no idea when we started this conversation it might end with a possible adoption."

"Alex, I can't wait to marry you and start our life together. I feel as if we're already a family. Do you even know how much I love you?" she smiled, smothering him with kisses.

Discussing their future together, Noelle couldn't have been happier. However, as hard as she tried, thoughts of him leaving still plagued her mind. Massaging his back, she tried to put on a brave face. Wiping her moist eyes, she hoped Alex wouldn't sense her worries. However, that was not to be the case. He knew her too well. He easily felt her concerns and uncertainties.

"Sweetheart, let's go swimming." Then, turning over, he grabbed her hand, pulling her up from the blanket.

"Alex, I'm not sure about getting back in the water. I almost drowned."

"Noel, trust me, nothing is going to happen."

Taking her hand, he pulled her to the edge of the sparkling, clear turquoise water.

"Babe, hop on my back. Don't worry. You're safe with me." Slowly, he carried her out through the incoming waves. "See, this isn't so bad."

"Okay, maybe you're right, but don't let me fall," she warned.

"Noelle, you're acting like a frightened child."

"Well, maybe I am," she smiled.

Suddenly, out of nowhere, a huge wave knocked them over. Noelle screamed.

"Sweetheart, stand up. It's not that deep," he laughed, pulling her up.

Taking his hand, she playfully tugged him back down into the warm water. Amazingly, she'd lost her inhibitions about drowning. Putting her arms around his neck, she kissed him passionately.

"Wow, what a brave little girl," he laughed.

"Alex, don't tease me. I almost drowned. I was truly petrified."

"Whatever, Babe, I was right beside you. Trust me. There was no chance of you drowning."

As the next wave gently rolled over them, they caught sight of a giant green sea turtle slowly swimming past them. The giant turtle seemed unaware of their presence. However, Noelle screamed at the mere sight of the sea creature.

"Alex, did you see that?" she yelled, completely terrified. "Geez, it was huge."

"Yes. It's just a harmless sea turtle."

"I'm getting out of here," Noelle gasped. "I'm not staying in here with that huge thing swimming around us."

"Sweetheart, the turtle was harmless. Trust me. It isn't going to hurt you. Heck, it was probably swimming away from you."

"I don't care. I've had enough of the crazy wildlife around here. I'm going back to the palapa."

"Okay, wait. I'll join you," Alex laughed.

Slowly, hand in hand, they leisurely strolled along the warm, sandy shores of the beach. Discussing future wedding plans and a honeymoon, Alex suggested meeting in Paris when his deployment ended. Noelle loved his suggestion. She'd had enough of the exotic beaches. She'd never been to Europe, so the idea fascinated her.

Continuing their walk back towards the Palapa, she found herself once again becoming emotional. Trying to hide her tears, she knew she had less than forty-eight hours with him. Their amazing time together was almost over, and she wasn't ready for it to end. She would never be ready. Trying to choke back tears, she became reticent. Finally, sensing her anxieties, Alex stopped, pulling her closer to his chest. Staring into her gorgeous blue eyes, he gently kissed the tears from her face. His heart ached for her. He knew that being separated from her once again would be hard.

"Sweetheart, you can't do this to yourself. You have to know by now how much I love you. How many doctors do you know would take on a difficult surgery for a General's daughter? Especially knowing that whether she ever walked solely depended on their skills as a surgeon. I could have easily been demoted if that had not gone well. Trust me. I'm totally crazy in love with you," he winked, pulling her into his arms.

"Alex, I know. I've never doubted your love for me. It's just the fact that I hate being alone when you leave. You have no idea what I go through."

"Noelle, this deployment might not be as long as we originally expected. Why don't you go back to Missouri and stay with Edith? Sweetheart, I know your heart for helping the earthquake victims and the children in Oslob, but have you ever considered what Edith might be going through. Babe, she isn't getting any younger. You mean the world to her, don't you think she misses you. Wouldn't you like to make what time she has left the best? I'm so proud of you for deciding to finish your degree and stepping up to join the humanitarian program at the university. However, maybe you should consider going home. Noelle, please don't misunderstand what I'm trying to say. I would never tell you to go home or demand that you do, but it might make life easier for Edith. I'm sure she would love nothing more than taking care of you while I'm away. What do you think?"

"Alex, you make it sound as if I'm weak and need someone to take care of me. That's not true."

"Sweetheart, that's not what I meant. I know you're a strong, determined young woman. Just look at you. You're absolutely stunning. You simply take my breath away," Alex winked, giving her a quick kiss.

"Awe, Babe, that's so sweet. I'll think about it. I do love you more than you could ever know. I've waited my entire life for someone, and never in a million years did I ever expect it to be someone as wonderful as you."

"Awe, that's sweet," Alex reiterated.

"Alex, are you mocking me? How dare you when I just poured my heart out to you."

"Noelle, lighten up. This whole conversation is getting way too serious."

Pulling her even closer, he kissed her.

"Now, does that make things better?"

Looking down at her, he smiled. "That's my girl. We're going to get through this deployment. One day, we'll look back at our adventures and laugh. I think we should get back to the palapa. Hopefully, our ride didn't forget us. I'd hate to spend a night on these beaches. I'm sure the jungle is teeming with all sorts of scary, wild animals," he teased, trying to deter her thoughts away from the fact he would soon be leaving.

"Alex, that's not funny."

As the evening sun began to set, they witnessed the most incredible sunset. Vivid hues of orange, pinks and purple covered the vastness of the evening sky. Its brilliance was magnificent.

Alex poured the remainder of the champagne into glasses.

"Here's a toast to our day on the beach."

"Here's to Paris," Noelle toasted.

Suddenly, out of nowhere, sounds of the approaching helicopter could be heard in the distance.

"Well, sweetheart, it looks like our ride is here. Guess you won't have to worry about those wild creatures, after all."

Helping Noelle aboard the helicopter and into her seat, it soon lifted skyward. The evening sky was illuminated with an enormous display of twinkling stars. It was the perfect ending to a perfect day.

Arriving back at their villa, Alex jumped in the shower. He smiled, knowing within seconds that she would probably join him.

"Wow, Babe, you certainly don't disappoint," Alex laughed as she opened the shower door.

"Shush, no talking. Hand me the shampoo," Noelle giggled, stepping into the warm shower.

Later that night, as they lay in bed, Alex held her in his arms. Now, he was the one who had to bite his bottom lip to keep from becoming emotional. He wasn't about to let her see him cry. Grown men aren't supposed to cry, and besides, she seemed to be handling her emotions just fine at the moment. The last thing he wanted or needed was to make her emotional. She needed her rest. Tomorrow was going to be a difficult day. First, they would stop in Bangkok and shop for a ring as he'd promised. Next, he would fly with her to Jakarta. Once there, they would part ways saying goodbye. Finally, he would be returning to Aviano, and she would once again be on her way back to Bintuhan. Phuket had been more than he could've ever imagined. Feeling the warmth of her body next to him, he closed his eyes.

Chapter Twelve

Black Ops Headquarters

Arriving in Aviano, Alex quickly boarded a transport aircraft to his final destination, the forward black ops headquarters to which he'd been assigned. Once there, Alex made his way to his home away from home, a cramped camouflaged tent. Extremely tired and missing Noelle, he somehow managed to fall asleep on the hard, uncomfortable cot.

Early the following day, news of his return seemed to travel quickly. Trying to wake from his deep slumber, he heard someone calling his name. Sitting up, he recognized Craig's voice.

"Come in," Alex reluctantly answered.

"Hey, Buddy, heard you were back. I just had to walk over and find out for myself."

"Man, can't a guy get a little sleep around here?" Alex yawned, getting up from his cot.

"How was your trip?"

"Damn, Craig, really, couldn't this have waited until later tonight?"

"No. You're the one who should be well-rested. Remember, the rest of us remained at Club Med, working while you were in paradise. I heard the surgery went well. It seems as if you're a local hero around here."

"Really, is that what you've heard?" Alex grinned.

"It appears Colonel Williams is extremely relieved the surgery went well. In fact, to hear his side of it, you sound like a superhero. You should be proud of yourself. I can't believe you pulled it off. Congratulations."

"Geez, Craig, have a little faith. I do possess certain skills. Hand me that pack of cigarettes and a lighter," Alex smiled, getting dressed.

"I assume you found Noelle. How did that go?"

"To be honest, better than I ever expected. I found Noelle in a little coastal community called Bintuhan in southern Sumatra. It was simply a hunch. Bintuhan seemed to have experienced the worst of the devastation. On my flight from Jakarta to Bandar Lampung, as luck would have it, I sat next to a young lady who worked for Doctors Without Borders, and she was on her way to Bintuhan. I took it to be a sign that I was correct in assuming she was probably there."

"It sounds as if you had a little help from above."

"You're probably right. Looking back, it does seem like things unexplainably fell into place. During my conversation with the young lady on the plane, she informed me they were short on doctors, so I promised to do a couple of surgeries the following morning. It just happened that James, a friend of Noelle, had pulled a little girl, Isabella, from beneath some rubble. He literally saved her life. Unfortunately, she lost her entire family in the quake, and Noelle became her surrogate mom. Isabella had been placed on a waiting list for surgery. Noelle just happened to inquire about the doctor who would perform her surgery. Can you even imagine her surprise when my name was mentioned? Noelle said she almost fainted. Without a doubt, she knew it was me. She immediately rushed down to the surgical suite of the hospital. What are the odds?"

"Man, I'd definitely say you had a little help from above," Craig smiled. "What an unbelievable story."

"I was walking down to the doctor's lounge when she found me. I heard a familiar voice. Turning around, I got the surprise of my life. Noelle walked up, flashing one of her silly smiles. At that moment, it was worth everything I had to endure just to see her smiling face. I was ecstatic. I can't even begin to tell you how relieved I was to see her. Thank God she felt the same," Alex explained, taking a drag on his cigarette.

"Wow, that's incredible."

"Yep, it was darn amazing."

"So, what happened after that?"

"Geez, Craig, let's go eat breakfast. I'm starved. I'll explain all the details later tonight. But, first, we'll get a bottle of Jack Daniels, and then you can ask all the questions you want. Let's just say I took Noelle to Phuket, Thailand, and leave it at that right now," Alex grinned, putting out his cigarette.

"Really, Phuket?" Craig asked, totally surprised. "Wow, how lucky can one guy get? Does she have any available girlfriends?"

"No, I'm afraid you're out of luck. I can't wait for you to meet her. She's one of a kind. However, she's definitely afraid of monkeys and sea turtles. I'll explain that one later tonight," Alex laughed. "Let's go eat."

Craig couldn't believe how well the surgery had gone for the General's daughter walking to the mess tent. The fact that not only had Alex found Noelle but had also enjoyed a few days in Phuket was unbelievable. Craig felt envious. It seemed some guys had all the luck.

"Major Bennington," the Lieutenant saluted. "Colonel Williams would like to see you in his office.

"Thank you. I'll be right there."

"Craig, go ahead and eat breakfast. I'll catch up with you in a few minutes."

"Okay. He's probably going to give you the keys to Club Med," Craig smirked.

"Good morning, sir. I was told you wanted to see me," Alex saluted.

"Yes, Major Bennington, come in. Please have a seat. Well, son, you've made me extremely proud, but more than that, you've made General McFarland very grateful. His daughter, Amanda, will now walk and run without any problems. This procedure will be a huge milestone in your career. I don't have to tell you how thankful Frank and his entire family were that you flew over to Hawaii and saw them through some of their most difficult days. Major Bennington, it's truly an honor to have a physician with your credentials under my command. How did you find your fiance?"

"She was safe. Thank you for asking and allowing me to help General McFarland's daughter, Amanda. I must say, she's a courageous young lady."

"Major Bennington, you should know this will look outstanding in your military records. The rank of Lieutenant Colonel will easily be within your grasp. Son, you should be extremely proud of your success. Thank God you didn't let Frank or me down. I don't have to remind you of the repercussions had that happened. However, thanks to your impeccable skills as a surgeon, we'll never have to visit that discussion. Again, I just want to add my congratulations along with Franks. I'm sure you'll be receiving a letter of accolade from the General in your military record. You're replacement leaves for Ramstein, Germany, tomorrow. Our troops will be fortunate to have you back. Major Bennington, again my sincere appreciation for a job well done. You're dismissed."

"Thank you, Sir," Alex saluted.

Now, it was time to eat. He was starving. Plus, he couldn't wait to see Craig. Nothing like rubbing more of the rave compliments he'd just received from Colonel Williams into Craig's face. Poor Craig would now have to endure reminders of his rare accomplishments for the remainder of their deployment.

Walking into the mess tent, he quickly went through the chow line filling his plate with everything imaginable before taking a seat across from Craig.

"Okay, let's have it. Let me guess? Colonel Williams gave you the keys to the kingdom," Craig teased, taking a sip of coffee.

"Craig, knock it off. I can't help it if I have the extraordinary powers of a superhero. Isn't that what you called me earlier?" Alex laughed, shoveling scrambled eggs into his mouth. "Seriously, I just got extremely lucky. But, to be honest, there's only one thing on my mind right now, that's getting this deployment behind me and marrying that gorgeous girl of mine. I'm going to meet her in Paris as soon as we're out of here."

"Wow, seems like you've got it all worked out. Congratulations."

"Thanks. I had to purchase another engagement ring for Noelle in Bangkok. She left her ring in the states at our apartment along with a note, which, thankfully, she now regrets. I have to be honest for a moment. I thought she'd ditched me for good. When I saw that she wasn't wearing the ring I'd given her before I deployed, I panicked. Fortunately, we got everything straightened out, and I couldn't be happier."

Refilling his coffee, Alex ravenously finished his entire breakfast.

"Geez, you must have been starving," Craig laughed.

"What's your schedule like for today?" Alex inquired, finishing his coffee.

"Well, I just worked two days straight. So, today is a down day for me,"

"I don't have to be at the hospital until tomorrow morning. Why don't we play racquetball and work out at the gym? Then we'll head over to the Class Six Store and pick up some Jack Daniels and maybe a bottle of Jameson. Later we can grab a pizza and go back to the tent. Then I'll tell you all about Phuket."

"That sounds great. I haven't worked out in a few days. So I could use the exercise. But, of course, eating pizza afterward and drinking shots of Jameson might just blow the whole point of working out," Craig laughed.

"Really, Craig, you could live here at Club Med without drinking or eating pizza? This isn't Phuket. I'm afraid it's going to take a lot to keep me sane here, especially missing Noelle."

"Wow, you must really love that girl."

"Oh, you have no idea. Noelle's one in a million."

After spending the afternoon on the racquetball court and finally an hour in the gym, Alex and Craig stopped by the Class Six Store to pick up their drink choice for the evening. After picking up two large pizzas covered with everything imaginable, they were ready to spend the evening hours with their best friend, Jack Daniels, and a bottle of Jameson.

"Let's go over to my casa," Craig insisted.

"Sounds good. I won't argue with that."

Walking over to Craig's tent, he was anxious to hear all the specifics regarding Alex's trip. He seemed to live vicariously through the details of Alex's life.

"Would you like a plate?" Craig asked, grabbing two glasses and napkins as they walked in.

"Why? You have napkins. It's simply pizza, not a formal dinner. Just open the Jack Daniels and pour us a drink," Alex scoffed.

"Got it. Calm down. I think you need this more than I do," Craig frowned quickly, handing him a glass of whiskey.

"Sorry, guess I'm suffering from jet lag and the fact that I'm back in this hell hole," Alex apologized, taking a huge sip.

"Geez, Alex, at least you got away for a while. Most of us will never see the outside world until this deployment ends. I think you've been fortunate. Hell, you've spent the last few days in paradise with the girl of your dreams. I don't see how that gives you the right to be so angry," Craig mentioned handing him a large slice of pizza. "Here, eat this. Maybe it will help."

"Thanks, Mom. Do you have any more motherly advice?"

"Yeah, well, Buddy, I'm not your mother. Any more talk like that, and you can do your drinking by yourself. Got it," Craig scolded, taking a long, slow sip.

"Okay. I get it. I guess it's the fact that I miss Noelle terribly, and I truly don't want to be here."

"Really, Alex, I don't think any of us want to be here. However, no one forced us to sign up with the reserves, and we are committed to supporting our troops. I think they're fortunate to have a physician of your caliber. After all, you are a superhero, remember?" Craig joked.

"Alright, one more wisecrack about me being a superhero, and I'll take the Jack Daniels and Jameson over to my casa. Pass me the bottle. I need a refill."

"So, are you ever going to give me the details of your time in Phuket?"

"Geez, Craig, you act like a teenage girl insisting on specifics. So what do you want to know?" Alex laughed, lounging back in his chair, lighting a cigarette.

"Well, for starters, I've heard Phuket is amazing. Didn't they film one of the James Bond movies there?"

"Yes. *Man with the Golden Gun* and *Tomorrow Never Dies* were filmed on Khao Phing Kan, the James Bond Island. The turquoise-green waters surrounding the island are covered in towering limestone karsts. They're magnificent. They rise from the water in various heights and widths and are mostly covered in green vegetation. You can take a Longboat tour of the island or explore the numerous caves in a kayak. However, we simply chose to be taken to a private part of the island by helicopter on our second day in Phuket."

"That sounds romantic."

"Trust me. It was until we encountered two wild monkeys. We'd hiked into the jungle to check out a waterfall. The trek in was a little farther than I thought. It was hot and humid, so naturally, getting into the cool water seemed like the next logical step. It was gorgeous and romantic until the monkeys walked down to the edge of the waterfall to watch us. Noelle freaked out when one of them howled. She was afraid he might be calling his friends. I'll have to admit, it was a little intimidating, but I never made her aware of my concerns. Some of them can be mean and dangerous. However, we got lucky. Fortunately, they seemed uninterested and docile as we walked past them on our way back to the beach." Reaching for his pack of smokes, Alex lit another cigarette and poured himself another glass of JD.

"So, you were only in Phuket for three days?" Craig inquired, stuffing another slice of pizza into his mouth.

"Yes. The best three days of my life. I rented a villa on the beach. It was a five-star resort and came with all the amenities you could hope for, including a hot tub. The beaches were beautiful. However, the first day we went swimming Noelle playfully pulled me out a long way from the shore. Then unexpectedly, she stepped into a hole and suddenly plummeted under the water. Instinctively, I pulled her up, but she panicked. I think she inhaled a small amount of water because it took her a few seconds before she could take a deep breath or talk. I'll have to admit it was rather frightening, so I carried her back to the shore. I simply assumed she knew how to swim, but she didn't, making matters far worse. After that, she hesitated to go back into the water," Alex grinned, exhaling the smoke from his cigarette.

"Well, who wouldn't after that experience. Poor girl, no wonder she was scared to go back into the water."

"I know. I felt bad for Noelle, so I suggested enjoying the hot tub with a glass of champagne. I'll admit it was far better than swimming. I have to tell you that girl of mine can make a two-piece bikini look ravishing. She took my breath away," Alex grinned, quickly downing his drink. Holding his cigarette between his lips, he reached for the bottle. Pouring himself another tall one, he again lounged back in his chair, sliding the cigarette pack across the table to Craig.

"Thanks. It's a darn shame Noelle doesn't have a twin sister," Craig reiterated, pulling a cigarette from the pack.

"Oh, I bet you do," Alex grinned. "Noelle is definitely one of a kind. I've waited my entire life for someone like her. Thank God she happened to be brought into the emergency room at Methodist while I was on duty. I'd give everything I own to hold her in my arms. You have no idea how much I love and miss that girl," Alex smiled, taking another long, slow sip of Jack Daniels. Lighting another cigarette, it was clearly evident how much he missed Noelle. "God, I miss that girl."

"Geez, Buddy, I feel your pain. I just hope she appreciates what you went through to see her for those few days. You put your whole career on the line," Craig recapped, pouring himself another round.

"The risks never entered my mind. But, truthfully, I'd have done anything to have those few days with Noelle."

"Well, I'm just happy for you and Noelle that everything turned out as you'd hoped," Craig smiled, reaching for another slice of pizza. "What are your plans after the deployment is over?"

"For starters, she's going to meet me in Paris. My aunt has an apartment located on Rue Cler. It's not far from the Eiffel Tower. That will give us some time to get reacquainted, and I can't wait to show her the city. Afterward, we'll head back to Missouri and get married. You're definitely invited. Noelle also mentioned adopting one of the children from the orphanage in Oslob. A little boy named Ian. I guess he reminded her of me, so we've talked about adoption."

"It sounds like you've got your future all worked out. I'd love to be at your wedding. Just keep me posted on the date. I can't wait to meet Noelle," Craig added, lighting another cigarette.

"What are your plans after we leave Club Med?" Alex inquired.

"Well, to be honest, I've really not thought that far ahead yet. I suppose I'll head back to Nebraska and continue helping my dad on the farm. He's getting older, and it takes a lot to keep an operation of that size going. I'm trying to talk him into putting it on the market. He simply needs to liquidate everything and enjoy what years he has left. I really don't see myself remaining in Nebraska."

"Wow, I never envisioned you as a farmer."

"Really. Why?"

"I don't know. I guess I had you figured for a city boy, that's all."

"Trust me. Farming isn't an easy life, and it's definitely not for everyone."

"Geez, Craig, are you calling me a sissy because I don't live on a farm?" Alex laughed, almost falling out of his chair.

"No, not at all. I just meant it takes a lot of hard work and getting up each morning at the crack of dawn. I'm just ready for a change."

"Well, why don't you come down to Arlington? I can put in a good word for you at the hospital where I work. You'd be a great addition to their staff. It's a mid-size community hospital. Still, I think you would like it," Alex suggested pouring the last of the Jack Daniels into his glass.

"I'll give it some thought. Geez, we've finished both bottles, and it's still early."

"Early for you, maybe, but I'm beginning to feel tired. So I think I'll head back over to my casa and try to get some sleep. Give some thoughts about relocating to Arlington. I think it would be a great move. I'm going to bed," Alex yawned, putting out his cigarette.

"Okay, Buddy, I'll give it some thought. Glad to have you back. See you tomorrow."

Alex had been at Club Med for less than a day. However, he'd easily settled once again into his routine. He could only hope that Noelle had reached Bintuhan safely and that perhaps she would seriously consider going home to Arlington.

Chapter Thirteen

Arriving in Bandar Lampung, Noelle boarded a bus for the eight and half hour drive to Bintuhan. She was utterly exhausted and missing Alex when she arrived. It seemed the past three days had passed in a dizzy, romantic blur. Yet, once again, she found herself totally consumed with thoughts of Alex.

It was almost midnight when the bus made its final stop in Bintuhan. Checking on Isabella and talking to James would have to wait until morning. Hurriedly finding her way to the tent where she usually slept, her cot appeared open and available. Quickly throwing her bag underneath, she laid down. Pulling the musky blanket up to her chin, she said a short prayer for Alex's safe return to Aviano and Edith. Then she was out for the night. The following day she would meet with James.

Being awakened by the muffled sounds of her alarm clock, she rubbed her eyes. She didn't feel prepared to start the day, and she could have never been prepared for the unexpected news she was about to receive.

"Noelle, are you awake?" James whispered, leaning over her cot.

"Yes. Hey, James, what brings you here so early?"

Immediately sitting up, she sensed the urgency in his voice. The fact he never came over to see if she was awake gave her cause for alarm.

"Noelle, Eddie called last night for you. I guess Professor Ames was trying to reach you regarding Edith, your grandmother. I'm so sorry to give you such terrible news so early in the morning, but your grandmother has had a heart attack. She's at the Methodist Hospital in Arlington. Professor Ames said you should consider coming home. There's no need for you to return to Oslob. We can make arrangements for you to leave Jakarta this evening. I'm so sorry."

"Oh, my God, not Edith," Noelle panicked. "James, I want to leave as soon as possible. But, depending upon her health when I arrive, I may not return."

"That's completely understandable. However, you've truly been an invaluable asset to our Humanities Program. I sure hate to see you leave, but I know you have to go. I would do the same thing. I'll try to look you up the next time I'm in Arlington. The bus to Bandar Lampung will be leaving in about an hour. Do you think you can be ready?"

"Yes, there's really not much to do. I never unpacked last night when I arrived. First, however, I would like to say goodbye to Isabelle."

"Of course, she would definitely want to see you before you leave. Is there anything I can do?"

"No. Thank you. You've been a great friend. I've learned so much from you, Eddie, and even Trisha. Will you please give them my best when you return to Oslob?"

"Yes. Definitely. It was wonderful working with you—best wishes to you and your fiance. I look forward to getting an invite to your wedding. I've got to run over to the Red Cross tent and put in your paperwork. Take care."

"Thanks. You take care, as well. I'm sure going to miss you. As soon as Alex returns from his deployment and we have the chance to nail down a date, you'll get an invitation," Noelle smiled, giving him a huge hug.

How could this have happened? She worried. Edith seemed to be in good health when she left Arlington. However, she knew Edith wasn't getting any younger. The hardship of dealing with the auto accident and her resulting amnesia had left Edith a bit frail. It was uncanny how Alex had just encouraged her to return to Arlington and spend time with her. His words now seemed almost prophetic. Wiping tears from her eyes, Noelle looked for a tissue. Edith was the only family she had. She was the only mother she'd ever known, and she wasn't ready to lose her. She would never be prepared. Trying desperately to control her emotions, she sat down on the cot. How could this be happening? She had just spent the most memorable days with Alex in Phuket. It was sheer heaven. Now to be faced with the news about Edith, it seemed more than cruel. Burying her head into her pillow to muffle her cries, once again, she felt hopelessly lost. She needed Alex more than ever. Maybe she could contact him while she was in Jakarta. At least she had to try. Desperately attempting to regain her composure, Noelle wiped her face. She needed to say goodbye to Isabella and put on a brave front. There was no way she would let herself show any signs of emotional distress. Isabella had just lost her entire family and undergone surgery.

Leaving Isabella's hospital room, Noelle felt even more emotionally drained. She knew that Isabella's life would not be easy. However, Isabella did have the remaining humanitarian workers to take care of her. With a heavy heart, she walked outside to wait for the bus. The grueling eight-hour ride wasn't something she looked forward to. However, in this part of the world, it was the only mode of transportation available. The roads' treacherous conditions meant no chance of sleep as she'd, unfortunately, endured the previous night on the incoming bus ride. She would have only her thoughts to keep her company on the arduous journey back to Bandar Lampung. Just as she was about to board the bus, she once again heard a familiar voice.

"Have a safe trip. Don't worry about Isabella. I'll personally see to it that she has everything she needs. I sincerely hope you find your grandmother much improved. Take Care," James smiled, running up to the bus.

"Thank you. We'll be in touch," Noelle replied with the hint of a smile.

Enduring the rough, bumpy ride, she finally arrived in Bandar Lampung. Catching a small charter plane, she was now on her way to Jakarta.

Arriving at the international airport in Jakarta only a short time later, it appeared she would have an extended layover until later that evening.

Next, searching for a phone, she needed to call the hospital and check on Edith's condition. Afterward, she would attempt to contact Alex.

"Good afternoon, Methodist Hospital. How may I direct your call?"

"I'm calling to inquire about the condition of my grandmother, Edith Edwards. I was informed that she had a heart attack and was admitted to Methodist."

"Please hold. I'll transfer you to the ICU desk."

"ICU, this is Jodie."

"Oh, my gosh, Jodie, this is Noelle Carrington. I was informed that my grandmother was admitted to Methodist. Unfortunately, I think she had a heart attack. I'm so worried."

"Noelle, it's so good to hear your voice. Yes. She's been admitted. In fact, Doctor Reed is in with her right now. But, sweetheart, I'm afraid the news isn't good. Are you coming to the hospital?"

"Well, that's just it, I'm in Indonesia right now, but I'm on my way. Would it be possible for me to speak with Trevor?"

"Yes. Just a moment."

"Doctor Reed," a voice quickly answered.

"Trevor, oh my God, how's Edith?"

"Noelle, we've done everything possible. I'm afraid the damage to her heart was extensive. However, we have her on life support. How soon can you get here?"

"I'm in Jakarta. I can't possibly be there before tomorrow afternoon. I have several layovers. Trevor, you have to keep her alive until I get to the hospital. Do you hear me?" Noelle cried.

"Sweetheart, I'm not sure if I made myself clear. Edith isn't breathing on her own. However, we're keeping her on life support until you can get here. I'm so sorry. Since you're Edith's only relative, I'm afraid you may have to make a hard decision. Noelle, I want you to know that we did everything possible. I'm truly sorry. Would you like for me to get in touch with Alex?"

"Yes. I'm not sure that I'll be able to reach Alex. Oh, Trevor, I can't believe this. I never got to say goodbye," Noelle cried. "I would have never left Arlington had I even suspected something like this might happen. She just saw me through the worst days of my life. Now, I'm not there for her. Trevor, I'm totally devastated. Isn't there anything you can do?"

"Noelle, trust me, I made sure she received the best care possible. However, by the time she arrived at Methodist, the damage from the heart attack was irreversible. Don't worry about the time it will take you to get here. I'm afraid there's nothing more we can do. Noelle, I'll have Becky pick you up from the airport. Just call the apartment and give her your flight schedule and arrival time. Sweetheart, I'll call Alex. Becky and I love you. Just know that we're both here for you. Hang in there, and please don't be too hard on yourself for not being here when it happened. You know how much Edith loved you. Sorry, I've got to go. I'm being paged. We'll see you tomorrow."

Hanging up the phone, Noelle looked for the nearest restroom. She felt dizzy. Being alone, there was no one to help her, and she needed a wet towel. Seeing a women's restroom at the end of the long concourse, she hurried over. Walking inside, she wet a towel to wipe her face. The cold, damp cloth felt refreshing, but she still felt somewhat unsteady. Grabbing a water bottle from her purse, she walked outside to the nearest gate area and sat down. She wanted to call Alex. She desperately needed to hear his voice. However, she felt too weak to walk back to the phone. Hopefully, Trevor would be able to reach him. More than anything, she just needed to regain her composure and try to relax. Watching a young mother as she tried to catch her runaway toddler, it offered some amusement for the moment. However, thoughts of Edith quickly consumed her. She now felt selfish for putting her wants and needs ahead of Edith's. Why had she left Arlington? How could she have been so insensitive? Alex had totally been right. She had now missed the chance to spend valuable time with Edith. The time that she would never get back.

Noelle walked further down the concourse, thinking that food might give her the strength she needed to stay awake until she boarded the next flight to Hawaii. Finding a noodle shop, she ordered a bowl of Laksa, a thick soup consisting of rice noodles and sweet, sour spices. Purchasing a cup of hot tea, she sat down at the nearest table and tried to consume as much of her meal as she could. Then, feeling somewhat better, she followed the directions along the concourse to her next boarding gate. It was still hours before the flight departed.

Finding a phone, she called Becky. After several rings, she left her itinerary on their answering machine. Deciding to call Alex again, no one answered. Picking up a couple of magazines, she managed to pass the time without falling asleep. She would try to sleep once she boarded the plane. Somewhat over the initial jolt of the devastating news, Noelle now dreaded arriving in Arlington. Edith would never know she'd flown home as quickly as possible. How was it even conceivable that less than twenty-four hours after returning from paradise, fate would bring such overwhelming grief. Wiping her moist eyes, she sat back and waited to continue her journey to Arlington. The only home she'd ever known.

Arriving in Arlington the next afternoon, it was a cold, windy day. After spending the past eight weeks in warm tropical climates, such as Oslob and Bintuhan, Noel had quickly forgotten how cold Missouri could be in February.

"Hey, Noelle, over here," Becky yelled.

"Becky, it's so good to see you. Thanks for picking me up."

"Are you kidding? It's the least we can do. Trevor said he spoke with you yesterday. We're both so sorry for your loss. We want you to stay with us. I don't want you to stay by yourself. I'll take you over to the hospital."

"Thanks. Becky, I can't believe she's gone. I feel like I deserted her. I think it will always haunt me that I abandoned her at an age when she probably needed me the most."

"Noelle, don't be so hard on yourself. Edith would never have wanted you to stay in Arlington. She loved you, and she knew the trauma you went through after your accident. She also knew how hard it was when Alex left on deployment."

"Speaking of Alex, did Trevor ever get in contact with him?" Noelle inquired.

"No. Trevor tried several times, but there was no answer. However, you might be able to reach him once we arrive at the hospital. I think there's a payphone downstairs in the lobby, or you can call him later from our apartment. Let me take your bags. I parked across the street in short-term parking."

"Okay, thanks. Is Trevor on duty at the hospital?"

"Yes. He said to page him once we arrived. But Noelle, Trevor said he doesn't think Alex will be able to come home. So I want you to know that we're going to help you with all the arrangements. We know it has to be hard dealing with such an unexpected tragedy. So don't worry about the fact that Alex might not be here with you. We're not leaving you alone for one moment," Becky smiled sympathetically.

"Becky, that's so thoughtful, but I don't expect you and Trevor to take time away from your busy schedules."

"Noelle, it's not even open for discussion."

Arriving at Methodist Hospital, Becky parked in the physician's parking lot. It was only a short walk over to the hospital lobby. Becky put her arm around Noel as they walked inside. Wait here while I page Trevor. I'll be right back.

Moments later, Becky returned with Trevor. Wearing a pair of green scrubs with a stethoscope hung loosely around his neck, he reminded her of Alex.

"Noelle, how are you? Great timing. I just got out of surgery. How was your flight?" Trevor inquired with frivolous small talk. Trying to lighten the reason for their meeting, it obviously wasn't working. Noelle looked tired and overcome with grief. "Would you like a few minutes before you go up to ICU?" Trevor asked, giving her a huge hug.

"No. I'd like to go up and see Edith," Noelle replied somberly.

"Okay. Do you mind if Becky and I come up with you?"

"No. Not at all."

Taking the elevator up to ICU, not a word was spoken. Reaching the ICU desk, Jodie immediately came over to hug Noelle.

"Sweetheart, we're all so very sorry. If there's anything we can do, please don't hesitate to call us. Unfortunately, Gloria isn't on duty today, but she said to offer her deepest sympathies."

"Thank you," Noelle replied, wiping her moist eyes. "If you don't mind, I'd like to go in and see Edith alone."

"Sweetheart, you do whatever you'd like. Becky and I will be here at the ICU desk if you should need us."

"Thanks."

Walking into Edith's room, nothing could have ever prepared Noelle for what she was about to see. Edith looked pale and lifeless. There was no doubt that only the machines were now keeping her alive. Tubes encumbered her. The constant low hum of the ventilator breathed life into her tranquil motionless body. As tears blurred her vision, Noelle slowly walked over. Trembling, she gently picked up Edith's hand.

"Oh, grandma, how can I ever let you go. You've been the only mom I've ever known. You never once hesitated to put me first in your life. How could I ever thank you? You selfishly gave up your retirement years to raise me. I've always adored you, and you're such a huge part of the person I've become," Noelle lovingly whispered as tears filled her eyes. *"I'm so sorry. Can you ever forgive me? I feel like I abandoned you when I left for the Philippines. It was never my intention. I just felt so lost when Alex left,"* Noelle bitterly sobbed. *"Grandma, I love you. I'll always love you forever. Please let mom and dad know that I'm going to be okay. Alex and I are going to be married as soon as his deployment ends. I only wished that you could have been at the wedding. I know you'll be watching from above."* Gently kissing Edith's hand, Noelle lovingly placed her hand back down by her side. Leaning over, she kissed Edith for the last time as rivers of tears flowed down her face. *"I love you. I'll always love you."*

Walking out to the ICU desk, it was apparent Noelle was visibly shaken with grief. Becky immediately sensed her condition and walked over, putting her arms around her.

"Oh, Noelle, I'm so sorry. Everything is going to be okay, I promise. Why don't we go home? You need to get some rest."

"Trevor, if you have paperwork for me to sign, I'd like to take care of that. I don't want to come back to the hospital. I've said my goodbyes. There's nothing left to say. I don't want to be in the room when she's taken off life support. Do you understand?" Noelle cried, totally consumed with sadness.

"Sweetheart, I'm so sorry. I understand. I'll have Jodie get the legal documents for your signatures right now. Honey, Edith will be moved downstairs to the morgue. It won't be necessary for you to come back to the hospital. She'll simply be transferred to a local funeral home of your choosing. Please go home with Becky and get some rest. I'll see you girls in the morning," Trevor suggested giving them each a hug and kiss.

"Thanks, Trevor. I need to call Alex."

"Definitely. I tried to call Alex several times, but there was no answer. You can give him a call from the apartment. Get some rest."

"Noelle, Trevor is right. I'll take you to our apartment. You can call Alex from our place. You need to get some sleep. That was a long flight, and I'm sure you were under an enormous amount of stress."

"Thanks. Becky, I don't know what I would have done without you both."

"Noelle, we love you, as well as Alex. Trevor and I consider you both family. I got up early this morning and made a ton of lumpia. I also cooked a huge pot of adobo. It's stew. Remember, I made it for you a while back, and you loved it. I made it with fish and fresh vegetables. I hope you like it," Becky mentioned as they walked out of the hospital.

"Thanks. Becky, that was so sweet of you. You're the best."

It was only a short drive to the apartment near the hospital. Walking in, Becky took Noelle's luggage to the guest room and suggested she call Alex.

"Noelle, I'm going to give you some privacy while I warm up our food. Please tell Alex not to worry. Like I told you, Trevor and I are going to help with all the arrangements."

Picking up the phone, Noelle's hands trembled. She needed Alex more than ever. Knowing he was on the other side of the world, her eyes moistened. Dialing his number, she prayed that he would be available. She desperately needed to hear his reassuring voice.

"Good evening, 60th Combat Hospital Support. Lieutenant Garrison speaking, how may I direct your call?"

"I'd like to speak with Major Alex Bennington."

"May I ask whose calling?"

"Yes. Noelle Carrington."

"Please hold for a moment. I think Doctor Bennington just came out of surgery. Let me check."

Remaining on the line, she prayed once again that Alex would be available to take her call. She didn't have to wait long before her prayers were answered.

"Hey, sweetheart, I'm so glad you called. I just came out of surgery. You were lucky to catch me at the hospital."

"Oh, Alex, stop, I have dreadful news. I'm totally devastated."

"Sweetheart, what's wrong?"

Hearing the panic and antagonism in her voice, he instantly cringed. Why was she so upset and bitter towards him?

"Babe, it's Edith. I lost Edith today. She had a massive heart attack."

"What?" Alex answered, completely stunned by the news. "I thought she was doing fine. I just talked to her before I left for Hawaii."

"Alex, I need you. Can you come home? I'm In Arlington. I'm staying with Becky and Trevor," Noelle broke down, letting her emotions entirely consume her. "Babe, I really need you."

"My God, Noelle, sweetheart, I'm so sorry. I'm at a loss for words. When did it happen?"

"It happened about two days ago. I got here as soon as I could. This morning, Becky picked me up from the airport and drove me over to the hospital. Trevor did everything possible, but he said the damage to her heart was extensive and irreversible. There was nothing more that he could do. He kept Edith on life support until I arrived today."

"Noelle, are you okay?"

Before he even asked the question, he knew she was a basket case. Once again, he felt horrible for having to leave. He could hear the resentment in her voice. However, his life was totally dictated by the military. He knew there wasn't even the remotest possibility that he could get leave again.

"No. I need you to come home. Right now," Noelle sobbed.

"Babe, I'm completely devastated as well. Noelle, there's no way that I can come home. Do you understand? I was lucky to get away from here to see you. There's no chance they will give me leave again. Sweetheart, you have to believe me. Trust me. If it were only up to me,

I'd be on the first plane home. But, you know, as I do, that's not how the military operates. Babe, you're strong, and you can handle this. Trust me. I love you. It literally kills me inside to hear how upset you are. Do you even know what that does to me? Sweetheart, you have no idea how much I want to hold you in my arms and comfort you. Babe, I love you. You're my girl. You are stronger than you think."

"Alex, I've never had to deal with anything like this before. I had to sign paperwork to allow Trevor to remove Edith from life support. Do you even know how hard that was for me?"

"Noelle, I do understand, and I'm sorry that I wasn't there for you. Trust me. I know firsthand how difficult that had to be for you. Babe, as a trauma surgeon, I deal with life and death every day. I'm not trying to trivialize the courage it took, but I just want you to know that I understand. Sweetheart, I need to talk to Trevor. I'm sure that he will help you make all the final arrangements."

"Alex, he's already agreed to help. I didn't even have to ask. I just miss you so much. You have no idea how much I miss you. Babe, you were right when you said I should go home and spend time with Edith. Why didn't I listen? Maybe, this would never have happened. I feel like I abandoned her," Noelle sniveled, trying to regain her composure."

"Sweetheart, don't do this to yourself. Edith would never have wanted you to stay in Arlington. She knew how much you needed a break. You did what you had to do. However, I've not read the note you left at the apartment. Perhaps, if anything, that might have been a mistake," Alex mentioned trying to lighten their conversation. "Of course, I think we got past that in Phuket. Babe, I love you. Look down at your left hand. If memory serves, I believe we even replaced your gorgeous ring."

"Alex, I love you too. But, if you're positive, you can't come home. I'll try to understand."

"Now, that's my girl. I'm hoping this deployment might end sooner than expected. I'll send your itinerary to Paris as soon as I know for sure when we're out of Club Med. Babe, will you please have Trevor call me? I want to pay for Edith's burial expenses. Please make all the arrangements the way you would like, no matter the cost. Sweetheart,

I've got this for you. No worries. I love you. I'll try to call you tomorrow. I want you to stay with Trevor and Becky until you feel comfortable enough to move back into our place. Maybe, you could do me a small favor and check on the Porsche," Alex teased. "Sweetheart, I've got to go. I love you. Talk to you tomorrow."

"Alex, I love you too and your silly Porsche."

Hanging up the phone, she felt a bit of comfort and relief despite the fact Alex was on the other side of the world and wouldn't be able to come home. For a moment, she smiled, forgetting her unbearable circumstances. How was it even possible to begin a phone conversation under such duress and end with the hint of a smile? She knew. It was the incredible man she'd fallen in love with, and she couldn't wait to marry him. But unfortunately, the impact of him not coming home was yet to hit her.

"Noelle, everything is ready to eat. Were you able to get in touch with Alex?" Becky asked, walking out from the kitchen.

"Yes. I was able to catch Alex at the hospital. He just got out of surgery. Wow, dinner smells scrumptious."

"I hope you like it. Trevor will get stuck with leftovers tonight," Becky giggled. "How was Alex? Will he be able to come for the services?"

"No. Sadly, he can't come."

Unexpectedly, the significance of her conversation with Alex finally hit her. Alex wasn't coming home. Without warning, Noelle broke down, completely overwhelmed with grief. Crying uncontrollably, she bolted for the privacy of the bathroom. She needed a private place to regain her composure.

"I'm sorry."

Following Noelle to the bathroom, Becky needed to ensure that she would be alright. Standing outside the door, Becky spoke words of encouragement.

"Noelle, no apologies needed. I know losing Edith has to be hard. Her passing suddenly was a total shock. The courage it took this morning for you to let her go had to be extremely difficult. I know she was not only a grandmother but more like your mother. But, please, don't be sad. You're going to make me cry. There are clean washcloths in the bathroom cabinet. Turn on the warm water and wipe your face. Don't worry about dinner. You can eat later."

About ten minutes later, Noelle walked out of the bathroom. Her eyes were red and puffy from crying. She looked distraught.

"Noelle, if you don't feel like eating, your room is ready. Why don't you get some rest? Everything will be warm in the oven if you feel like eating later unless you would rather talk. If that's the case, I'll make us a pot of coffee."

"Becky, if you don't mind, I would like to lie down for a while. The flight was grueling, and knowing that Alex can't come home has taken a huge toll on me."

"Of course, your bed is ready. Get some rest. We'll talk later. Noelle, just one thing before you leave, please don't worry about anything. I want to assure you that Trevor and I will take care of all the arrangements. You just take care of yourself."

"Thanks. Becky, what would I do without you?" Noelle hinted at a smile, giving Becky a huge hug.

"If you need anything, just let me know. But, please, get some rest."

Apparently, the long flight and earlier decision to disconnect Edith's life support had mentally and physically drained Noelle. As a result, she never woke up until the following morning.

Later that evening, when Trevor came in, he was surprised to learn that Noelle had retired to her bedroom.

"Where's Noelle?"

"She's sleeping. At least, I certainly hope she's asleep. But, Trevor, it was heartbreaking. Noelle literally broke down just before dinner. I guess the fact that Alex will not be able to come home evidently hit her pretty hard. It was so sad. I almost started crying."

"Wow, I thought I'd made it clear to her that he probably wouldn't be allowed to come home. For heaven's sake, he's on deployment. I'm truly shocked that he could get away from the base to visit her this past week. But then again, giving a General's daughter the ability to use her legs was pretty significant."

"Are you hungry? I made lumpia this morning and Adobo."

"Is that even a question? I'm starved."

"Well, Doctor Reed, follow me into the kitchen, and I'll fix you a huge plate of delicious Philippino favorites," Becky smiled, pulling Trevor towards the kitchen.

"Oh, I forgot to tell you, I was able to get three days away from the hospital starting tomorrow. The hospital director, Mrs. Maxwell, insisted. I really like Angel. She knows that Alex and I are good friends, and she knew that Noelle would need help since Alex is away on deployment. So, I have the next few days to take care of all the arrangements."

"Trevor, that's wonderful. I told Noelle earlier not to worry that we'd be there for her. But, unfortunately, I think everything is beginning to take a toll on her. I feel so bad for Noelle."

"She's going to get through this. I don't want you to worry. I'll make sure Edith has a beautiful service. I would never let Noelle or Alex down. Even though we have words occasionally, I love Alex like a brother."

"Oh, Trevor, I know. That's what I love you about you," Becky smiled, giving him a quick smooch. "Would you like a glass of wine before we retire for the evening?"

"Yes. That sounds great. Sit with me in the living room. I'm too tired to eat in the dining room. I need the comfort of the sofa and you next to me. Doctor's orders," Trevor winked.

Early the following day, Becky got up to make coffee and breakfast. The day would be busy and stressful. Ensuring that everyone started the day with a hearty breakfast was the least she could do. It wasn't long before the aroma of coffee and bacon brought Noelle into the kitchen.

"Good morning, breakfast smells delicious," Noelle smiled.

"You must be starved. You never woke up to eat," Becky mentioned pouring Noelle a cup of coffee.

"I'm sorry. You went to all the trouble to make dinner for me, and I let you down. I apologize for having a meltdown," Noelle remarked, taking a sip of coffee.

"Noelle, no apologies. It was completely understandable. You've been under a lot of stress. I hope you like blueberry pancakes and bacon."

"Who doesn't? But you didn't have to cook breakfast. We could have easily gotten something later."

"Well, it just happens that Trevor has the next three days away from the hospital. So, I figured I would let him sleep in a while, and I got up and cooked breakfast."

"Becky, I don't want to be an inconvenience. However, I hope Trevor didn't burn up vacation days to help me with Edith's services."

"Noelle, the Hospital Director, insisted that Trevor take a few days away from work to help. She's always favored Trevor and Alex. I have to say they're the best doctors she has on her staff. So, don't worry. I'm sure she wouldn't have let Trevor take the days off if she didn't have the physicians cover him. It will give us the needed time to finalize Edith's services. Would you like blueberry syrup on your pancakes?" Becky inquired, sitting the carafe of coffee on the table.

"Yes. Thank you."

"I think we'll go ahead and eat breakfast while everything is hot. Then, Trevor can eat when he wakes up."

Placing a large stack of warm blueberry pancakes on the table and a platter of crisp fried bacon, along with blueberry syrup and butter, Becky sat down at the table across from Noelle.

"Wow, this looks yummy," Noelle smiled, pouring syrup over her pancakes.

Suddenly, the girls looked up from the table. They were amazed to see Trevor up so early.

"Geez, looks like you girls started without me," Trevor smiled, reaching for a coffee cup.

"Babe, sit down. I thought you were going to sleep in this morning," Becky smiled, giving him a quick kiss.

"Well, it was a little difficult to stay in bed. The smell of fried bacon and coffee was calling my name," Trevor laughed.

"Good morning, Noelle. How do you feel?"

"Oh, I'm much better today. I guess Becky told you about my little meltdown yesterday. I guess I let the fact that Alex couldn't come home get to me. I really feel bad about that. I'm sorry."

"Noelle, you've been through a lot the past twenty-four hours. I think you're entitled to a little meltdown, as you call it," Trevor smiled, taking a huge sip of coffee. "Please, don't give it a second thought. However, I'll have to admit I certainly enjoyed the lumpia and Adobo. Becky only cooks when we have guests," he laughed.

"Trevor, that's not true. Besides, Noelle isn't a guest. She's family," Becky scolded.

"Oh, I know. I just like it when I come home to a warm, home-cooked meal."

"Trevor, you're working such odd hours. It's hard to keep up with your schedule. Your home-cooked meals could become a thing of the past if you don't watch your mouth. You make it sound as if I never cook for you," Becky frowned.

"Babe, it was just a joke. But, geez, calm down," Trevor teased, getting up to give Becky a quick kiss as he walked over to the pantry for maple syrup.

"Noelle, did Becky inform you the hospital gave me a few days off?" Trevor questioned, returning to the table.

"Yes, as a matter of fact, she did."

"Well, I want to get your thoughts on how you would like to proceed with Edith's burial. Did she have a preference for cremation or a more traditional burial? Also, we need to have her body moved to a local mortuary this morning. I hate to ask so early, but we really do have a lot of things to take care of today."

"Trevor, I don't ever remember discussing any of this with Edith. However, I don't think she would want to be cremated," Noelle suggested with a quizzical expression.

"Trevor, don't you think it's a bit too early to be discussing these matters at the breakfast table," Becky insinuated.

"No. We really have a lot to take care of, and I need a game plan. Noelle, I'm not trying to upset you or act controlling. It's just the fact we need to schedule Edith's service for the day after tomorrow. We should run her obituary in tomorrow's newspaper. To do that, we need to know which cemetery she might have preferred, set a time for the service, and which chapel or church you would prefer to use."

"Trevor, I can definitely say that First Baptist is the only place Edith would want her services. She's been a lifelong member of First Baptist for as long as I can recall. Also, I want her buried next to grandpa and close to mom and Dad at Arlington Hills Cemetery. There's an empty plot next to mom. As far as the service details, I would be happy to leave that up to Pastor McClendon. I'll contact the ladies in her Sunday School Class. Her best friends at First Baptist were Mary Godwin and Ethel Peters. I'm sure Clint Harper, one of the Deacons, will be able to provide pallbearers."

"Well, that's a huge start. Why don't you girls make the arrangements for the services at the church and the graveside service? Afterward, make a stop at the Arlington Gazette and provide them with the details for the obituary. If there's time, stop at the florist and order flowers. Don't forget the spray for the casket. I'll take care of the other details. Finally, I'll arrange to have Edith's body taken to Crestwood Mortuary and pick out an appropriate casket. If that's okay with you?" Trevor suggested, shoveling blueberry pancakes into his mouth.

"Thanks. It would keep me from having to make those decisions, and I trust your opinion on the casket."

"Great. I think, with our endeavors today, we'll make sure Edith would approve of everything. Noelle, it's strictly up to you if you want to include a few hours of visitation at the funeral home the evening before the service. It isn't necessary. I'll leave that up to you." Refilling his coffee, Trevor felt confident everything would be taken care of and that nothing would be overlooked. "Oh, you might want to think of reserving a restaurant for after the services," he added.

"You know, after thinking about it, I actually prefer not to have any visitation hours the evening before the service. Emotionally speaking, this is all going to be very hard on me. I don't think I could handle having to be social the day before the services," Noelle suggested.

"Sweetheart, I think you're right. It's totally unnecessary. Well, girls, I think we have a game plan," Trevor smiled. Then, looking down at his watch, he noted the time. "Ladies, can you be ready to leave by 9:00 a.m. this morning? I think that will be ample time to make all the arrangements."

"Yes, Babe, that will work for me. But, Noelle, does that give you enough time to get ready? The apartment has two showers. There's one in the hall bathroom," Becky mentioned as she began to clear the table. "Oh, there's plenty of clean washcloths and towels in the hall closet. Just make yourself at home."

"Thanks. I can be ready to leave at 9:00. It won't be a problem. I just want you both to know how much I appreciate everything. Honestly, I don't know what I would have done without you."

"Noelle, you're family. If Alex can't be here, then we're certainly going to stand in the gap on his behalf. We love you. Now, no more talk about our role in helping you. Let's get ready. We have a long day ahead. Afterward, if you think you'll feel up to it, I'll make dinner reservations for us at Leonardo's tonight. Do you like Italian?" Trevor inquired with a smirk.

"Oh, Trevor, that's sweet of you. I love Leonardo's," Noelle smiled, feeling her eyes moisten.

"Babe, that's so thoughtful. I love you. I guess this means you'll get another great meal this evening," Becky smiled, giving her hubby a quick kiss as she headed for the shower.

Just like clockwork, they were all ready to leave on time. Noelle looked stunning, wearing a black pencil skirt. Matched with a white silk blouse and her long blonde hair swept upward in the back, she gave no outward appearance of worry or dread regarding her somber duties for the next few hours. Dressed relaxed and casual, Becky wore a pair of black denim jeans mixed stylishly with a light gray cashmere sweater with her hair pulled back into a ponytail. The girls were fashionably dressed, even though their taste in attire greatly varied. On the other hand, Trevor wore a pair of denim jeans and a gray sweatshirt. He was just happy to be out of his everyday green scrubs.

"Becky, take the Volvo. I'll take the Beamer. We'll meet back at the apartment. If you run into any problems, page me. Drive safe."

Later that evening, they drove over to Leonardo's Restaurant. Surprisingly, their day had gone according to plan. Trevor was astonished by how quickly everything had come together. Walking in, they were escorted to a candlelit table near the back of the restaurant. Leonardo's reflected the ambiance of Tuscany. The walls depicted an Italian garden mural—red décor and muted earth-tone colors coordinated the furnishings.

"Wow, I've always loved eating at Leonardo's. I love the ambiance and, better yet, their menu. Thanks for suggesting we eat here."

"Not a problem, Becky loves Italian food. Isn't that right, Babe?"

"Yes. Is this your way of making up for your snide remark this morning," Becky laughed.

"Geez, Babe, please, give a guy a little credit."

Dining on a feast of house favorites such as Lasagna, Chicken Alfredo, and Ravioli Florentine, along with a bottle of merlot, the evening was enjoyable and relaxing. Leaving the restaurant later that evening, their memories of making final arrangements for Edith were finally overshadowed by happier moments. The evening had been wonderfully cathartic.

Driving home, it seemed the girls were already falling asleep. Glancing at their tranquil faces, Trevor smiled. It was just what the doctor ordered. It appeared the girls would not have difficulty getting a good night's rest. Tomorrow would strictly be set aside for anything which they happened to overlook. Trevor knew that Alex would be extremely pleased with their results. He would always have Alex's back, even if he were on the other side of the world.

The following day, Trevor decided to get up early and let the girls sleep in for a change. Walking into the kitchen, he made coffee. Deciding his best attempt at making breakfast was probably omelets, Trevor looked through the fridge to see what ingredients he had to work with. Finding leftover ham, the remainder of the bacon, bell pepper, onions, cheese, and a carton of eggs, it looked like he had more than he needed. Quickly gathering the necessary items and preparing and cooking several large omelets took no time. Trevor felt very domesticated and proud of himself as each one turned out perfect. Now, he just had to keep them warm and the coffee hot until the girls woke up. However, that would be sooner than he'd expected.

"Hey, Trevor, what are you doing up so early? Did you get any sleep last night?" Becky inquired, slowly sauntering into the kitchen. Her disheveled appearance made him smile. Her dark black hair was tousled, and she was wearing her rumpled pink bathrobe and fuzzy matching slippers. Surely, she wasn't completely awake.

"Yes. I slept really sound. However, I think you should go back to sleep," Trevor kindly suggested walking over to kiss her good morning. "Sit down and let me pour you a cup of coffee. I think you definitely need it or a hot shower. Maybe both," he laughed.

A few minutes later, Noelle walked in.

"Good morning, everyone."

"Geez, I thought you girls might sleep in this morning," Trevor mentioned pouring Noelle a cup of coffee. "Who's hungry? I made omelets."

"Babe, you cooked?" Becky questioned, rubbing her eyes.

"Sounds great," Noelle smiled, entirely oblivious to Becky's outrageous hair and wardrobe. "Guys, like I said yesterday, you don't have to go out of your way for me. I can easily fend for myself."

"Noelle, I don't consider cooking breakfast as going out of our way. I literally used leftovers from the fridge, but I think you'll like it. At least, I hope that you do," Trevor grinned, placing two large omelets on the table for the girls.

"Wow, Babe, this looks fantastic," Becky grinned, pulling her hair away from her eyes.

"Ladies, enjoy your omelets. Today, there's really not much to do but make a few follow-up phone calls. Maybe you girls might like to go downtown later this morning. I have a black suit to wear tomorrow. However, if you girls need darker attire, I'll give Becky my store cards. Then, you can both go shopping," Trevor suggested, taking a sip of coffee.

"Trevor, that's really kind. However, Alex gave me a credit card with my name on it before he left. However, if Becky doesn't mind, perhaps we could run downtown and check out the women's clothing stores. Honestly, I haven't given any thought to what I would wear. Everything has happened so fast."

"Yes, of course. I'll be happy to take you. I'll never turn down a chance to shop. But, unfortunately, I wished it was for reasons other than Edith's services."

"Babe, maybe you could find a new bathrobe. I think the one you have on is a bit ragged," Trevor smirked.

"Geez, Trevor, thanks a lot. You never cease to amaze me with your remarks," Becky fumed.

"Sweetheart, you took that the wrong way. I was just suggesting you might want to think about a new robe while you're downtown."

"Trevor, I think you should be careful with your choice of words. You might end up on the couch tonight. I'm going to take a shower."

"Wow, Noelle, I'm sorry about that. I really didn't mean to upset her."

"Not a problem. All married couples have minor squabbles. I'm sure when Becky gets downtown and into the stores, she'll never remember your remark. Trust me. When it comes to shopping for clothes, I'm sure it will get her in a better mood."

After spending the entire afternoon shopping, Noelle and Becky found dresses for Edith's funeral. Noel chose a black long sleeve wrap dress, and Becky decided on a cap sleeve trapeze dress. Finally, their wardrobes were complete after purchasing black wool capes to keep them warm and heels. Never once was Trevor's comment regarding her tattered robe even mentioned.

While the girls enjoyed a few hours of retail therapy, Trevor ensured the final details were covered. It was scheduled for 2:00 p.m. at First Baptist Church, with graveside services immediately afterward at Arlington Hills. So finally, everything was at last put in motion.

The following morning, Noelle woke early. Walking to the kitchen, she made coffee. How could she ever be prepared for a day such as this? She desperately needed to hear Alex's voice. It would be the one thing she needed most to make it through the next few hours. Pouring herself a cup of coffee, she walked into the living room. Picking up the phone, she sat down. After several attempts at reaching him, it became futile. Unfortunately, there was no answer. Noelle had to face the hard reality that talking to Alex this morning before the service would never happen. Wiping her moist eyes, the stark realization that once again, he wouldn't be there for her was daunting. Taking a sip of coffee, she had to control her emotions. It was too early in the day to become a basket case.

Trevor once again made breakfast for the girls. Leisurely eating together at the kitchen table, Noelle merely went through the motions. Her stomach was tied in knots. She felt blessed to have such good friends. Without Alex by her side at Edith's services, she would need their strength more than ever.

"I'm going to shower and get dressed for the services. I'm going to leave ahead of you girls today. I want to ensure that nothing is left to chance at the church or Arlington Hills," Trevor mentioned pushing his chair back from the table.

"Trevor, aren't you leaving too early. It's not even 10:00 a.m.?" Becky inquired, a bit confused.

"Not really, I have several stops to make this morning, and I want to ensure the church will be open early for the florists to deliver flowers. Also, don't forget the limo will arrive at 1:30 p.m. I'll meet up with you later before the service."

The morning seemed an endless blur to Noelle. Dressing for the services, she felt faint, nauseous, and out of reality. She was saying 'goodbye' to the only mother she'd ever known. The only family she'd ever had before meeting Alex, and now he was on the other side of the world. Trying one last desperate attempt to reach him by phone, again there was no answer. Wiping her moist eyes, she looked in the mirror to check her make-up.

"Noelle, are you ready? It's almost 1:30 p.m.? The limo should be arriving momentarily."

"Yes, as ready as anyone can be under these circumstances. I just wish Alex was here."

"I know today is going to be difficult. However, I just want you to know that Trevor and I will be right by your side. You're not alone," Becky smiled sympathetically. "We're going to get through this together.

We might not share the same genetics, but that doesn't mean we're not family."

"Thanks. Becky, I truly don't know what I would have done without your and Trevor's help."

"No need to thank us, just remember what I said about the three of us being a family. Oops, I meant the four of us. Poor Alex, I'll bet he's extremely worried about you," Becky mentioned walking down to the car.

Arriving at the church, it was a bitterly cold afternoon. The sun came out sporadically, making the sky overcast and dreary. However, despite the weather, it was evident by the overflow of cars in the parking lot that Edith had many friends. Noelle's legs almost buckled from beneath her petite frame as she stepped out of the vehicle. Catching sight of her dilemma, Trevor immediately ran down the church steps to assist her.

Tenderly putting his arm around Noelle, Trevor carefully escorted her inside. The afternoon sun beautifully reflected the tall, stained glass windows as it immersed the church in a colorful radiance. The fragrance of fresh flowers permeated the air. Every pew was filled as Noelle slowly walked down the aisle toward the front of the church. Viewing Edith's body for the last time, memories flooded Noelle's mind. It seemed her entire life flashed before her eyes. It appeared her earliest memories of Edith suddenly and unexpectedly began invading her thoughts. It felt like a projector was visually replaying her entire life. Then, without a plausible explanation, it appeared Edith had miraculously given Noelle the most incredible gift possible as the remainder of her memories began flooding her mind. Wiping her eyes, Noelle lovingly leaned over the casket, softly kissing Edith goodbye. "Thanks, Grandma. I love you." The odds were infinitesimal that on a day such as this, Noelle's memories would surprisingly return.

Taking Noelle's arm, Trevor assisted her over to the front pew. Noelle was oblivious to the service as she sat next to Becky and Trevor. Wiping tears from her eyes, she now had her precious recollections of Edith to sustain her. Even though the service was short, it was a loving remembrance of Edith's kind, compassionate nature.

After the service, Trevor escorted Noelle and Becky outside to the waiting limo. The drive out to Arlington Hills was quiet and subdued as the limo followed behind the hearse. There were no words spoken. Laying her head back against the seat, Noelle longed to have the comfort of Alex's arms wrapped around her.

Reaching Arlington Hills Cemetery, the limo slowed to a stop. Trevor carefully assisted Noelle out of the car. A cold wind rushed past them as they walked up the steps leading to Edith's gravesite. Just as Noelle had wanted, Trevor ensured Edith had the best possible resting place in the entire cemetery. Taking seats in front of the open grave, they waited for a short time for the pallbearers to place the bronze casket in front of them. Numerous sprays of colorful flowers surrounded Edith's grave. There were beautiful floral arrangements from Trevor and Becky, the nurses in ICU, Edith's Sunday School Class, Clint Harper, and the Deacons at First Baptist. Also, Doctor Edward Thomas, Trisha, James, and Professor Ames at the University of Missouri, sent colorful floral sprays. Noelle viewed the gorgeous flowers and the panoramic vista as friends continued to fill the remaining chairs. Suddenly, her attention was drawn to a taxi parking with the other vehicles at the bottom of the hill. Who in their right mind takes a cab to a funeral? Finally, curiosity consuming her, she stood up, removing her sunglasses to get a better look. Catching a glimpse of a man wearing his dress blue military uniform exiting the cab and sitting his duffle bag on the sidewalk, she gasped. It was Alex. Noelle ran towards him at the speed of light. Momentarily forgetting the somber occasion, her only thoughts were on Alex. She couldn't wait to touch him, to hug him.

"My God, Babe, you came," Noelle cried.

Nothing mattered to her at the moment, only the fact he was here. With tears streaming down her face, she was sure those attending the service figured her to be stark raving mad. But, for once, she didn't care. Her only focus was on the guy in his military blues. Hugging him with every ounce of her being, she couldn't let go of him. Caressing his face, she had to convince herself he was indeed real.

"Sweetheart, God, I've missed you. I love you," Alex smiled. "Noelle,

I think considering the circumstances, maybe you should exhibit a little self-control," Alex whispered, noticing all the stares they were receiving.

"I don't give a damn. Babe, you have no idea how much I needed you to be here today."

"Noelle, I'm only here for two days, but I had to come. I know you too well, and I knew how hard this was going to be for you."

Watching as the scene unfolded, Trevor and Becky walked down the hill to meet them.

"Geez, Doctor Bennington, talk about a 'grand entrance.' I don't even want to know what you had to do this time to get away from the base," Trevor laughed.

"Wow, Alex, what a surprise," Becky smiled, giving him a huge hug.

"Thanks. I'll explain everything later. I think we have people waiting for us. We better walk up and say our goodbyes to Edith," Alex suggested taking Noelle's hand as they walked up the hill.

"I love you," Noelle whispered, squeezing his hand.

Returning to her seat with Alex, it was hard for her to concentrate on the graveside services. She had already said her goodbyes to Edith at the church. Her whole train of thought now centered around Alex and their next two days. It appeared Edith's services were both cathartic and euphoric. How was that even possible? She wondered. However, she already knew. The reason was sitting next to her. It was Alex. Maybe somehow, Edith had played a significant role in today's events. She had restored Noelle's memories of their life together and brought Alex to her. Even in death, it now seemed apparent that Edith was watching over her.

"Thank you, Grandma. Thank you for taking such good care of me. I love you," Noelle cried unexpectedly, releasing a torrent of tears as Edith's services ended.

"Sweetheart, it's okay. I've got you," Alex whispered, holding her in his arms.

"Babe, memories of my life with Edith returned earlier today at the church. Can you even believe it?" Noelle explained, wiping her eyes as she tried to gain her composure.

"Noelle, that's unbelievable. I always told you not to give up hope. Sweetheart, please don't cry. I'm here now," Alex smiled sympathetically.

Somewhat still emotional, Noelle thanked Clint, Mary, and Ethel for attending the services. Everyone was now invited to Leonardo's for dinner. Noel was sure Edith would have approved of her final arrangements.

Finally, after the post-funeral reception for Edith ended, Noelle couldn't wait to get Alex alone. They had only been apart for less than a week. However, so much had transpired. It felt like an eternity since they'd last seen each other.

"You're welcome to stay with us tonight," Becky smiled, leaving the restaurant.

"Wow, Becky, I can't believe you'd even remotely suggest they stay with us tonight," Trevor laughed. "However, there is something I'd like to know. How the heck did you manage to get leave again?" Trevor questioned, stepping inside the limo.

"Trevor, let's just say I attained the status of superhero at Club Med and leave it at that," Alex grinned.

"Alright, but later, Doctor Bennington, I want to know everything," Trevor insisted.

"Geez, Doctor Reed, you and your enquiring mind. Later," Alex laughed.

"Becky, thanks for your offer, but if it's alright with Alex, there's only one place I want to stay tonight," Noelle interjected.

"Where's that?" Becky questioned.

"Our apartment," Noelle smiled. "Alex hasn't seen it since I redecorated. I can't wait to show him how talented I am."

"Of course," Trevor laughed. "I'm sure Doctor Bennington can't wait to see how talented you are."

"Trevor, be nice. They're not an old married couple like us," Becky interrupted.

"We're not old," Trevor laughed. "However, Babe, I'll have to admit you did look sort of frumpy the other day at breakfast."

"Trevor, one more remark like that, and you'll definitely be on the couch tonight."

"Wow. Sweetheart, do they always argue like that?" Alex laughed.

"No," Noelle laughed. "I don't know what I would have done without Becky or Trevor. I've probably stated this a hundred times by now. But, honestly, we have to thank you for letting me stay at your apartment and taking care of all the arrangements," Noelle explained.

"Yes. Noelle is right. I could never thank you enough for being there for my girl," Alex agreed. Pulling Noelle closer to his chest, he quickly kissed her cheek. "Trevor, before I leave, I will cover all the expenses. However, tonight I've got other things on my mind," Alex winked, staring at Noelle. "Trevor, one last thing, I know we've had words over the phone since I've been gone, but it's all water under the bridge. I love you, Buddy. Thanks for taking care of Noelle."

"No worries, Doctor Bennington, just enjoy your evening. I'll have the driver take you to your apartment. I left my car at the church earlier this morning. Let's have dinner before you leave to go back to Club Med. Isn't that what you called it?" Trevor questioned teasingly

"Yes. Sounds good. We'll call you," Alex grinned as Trevor and Becky exited the limo at the church to retrieve their car.

"Wow, Sweetheart, we're finally alone," Alex winked, pulling her even closer. "Noelle, I just want you to know how deeply worried I was about you and the fact Edith passed so unexpectedly. But, I want you to know I also loved her, and I know how much she meant to you. Babe, I'm so sorry for your loss," Alex sympathized with a quick kiss.

Putting her arms around Alex, Noelle felt mesmerized by his kiss. She returned his affection with such passion it sent quivers of excitement throughout her slender body.

"Wow, babe, I've missed you—no more talk about Edith. Today has been filled with enough sadness. Tonight belongs to us," Noelle lovingly whispered into his ear.

Arriving at the apartment, Alex, for a quick second, had thoughts of his Porche parked in the garage. However, he knew it could wait. There was no way he would chance upsetting her. So, not giving it another thought, he followed Noel upstairs. Unlocking the door, he was pleasantly surprised.

"Wow. Sweetheart, the apartment is gorgeous."

"Alex, do you truly like it?" Noelle questioned.

"Like doesn't even cover it," he laughed. Quickly scooping her into his arms, he carried her into the bedroom. "Let me show you how much I like it," he teased wickedly.

Walking past the kitchen, Noelle's note left next to her ring would not be seen until morning. But, just like the Porsche, it could easily wait.

Pulling back the duvet, Alex stopped. Noelle began unbuttoning his blue military dress coat.

"Babe, how did you earn all these colorful bars and medals?" she questioned, lightly running her fingers across them.

"Geez, Sweetheart, seriously, that can wait," he winked, removing his coat and tossing it over a nearby chair.

As Noelle continued to unbutton his dress shirt, Alex lovingly kissed the nape of her neck. Feeling the excitement of his touch against her skin, she melted into his arms.

"Wow, Alex, I must say, I love a man in his military blues," she smiled.

"Sweetheart, no more talking," Alex whispered, kissing her ear.

Taking her hand, he pulled her down to the bed. Feeling the warmth of his body against her was sheer ecstasy. Their entire night was spent in a romantic state of bliss. Never before had she remembered their nights having been filled with such intense passion? Perhaps, it was the stark reality of death they had faced earlier in the day. She wasn't sure. The only thing she knew was the love that they shared could easily transcend this life into the next. Her eyes moistened as she snuggled blissfully into the comfort of his arms. Once again, Noelle knew he couldn't stay. It was getting harder and harder to let him go. She silently wept, not knowing if she could endure lonely future nights without him.

Noelle had not slept as the early morning sun slowly crept in through the curtains. How could she sleep, knowing the handsome man lying next to her would be gone in less than twenty-four hours. Looking over at the clock on the nightstand, it was ominously poignant. Noelle desperately wished she could stop the hands of the clock. Staring at the love of her life, she gently began kissing him awake. She craved every moment that remained. Turning over, he slowly opened his eyes.

"Wow, Sweetheart, what a night," he smiled.

"Alex, every night with you is totally incredible."

Biting her bottom lip, she was determined to keep her emotions in check. There was no time for tears.

"What would you like to do today?"

"Who says we have to do anything?" Noelle smiled. Kissing him intently, she was where she wanted to be.

"Geez, Sweetheart, another kiss like that, and I'll not let you escape," Alex winked playfully, pulling her into his arms. "However, food does come to mind. I don't suppose we have much to choose from in regards to breakfast."

"Sorry. You're right. But, remember, this is the first time I've been back to our apartment. I think we have coffee. If we're lucky, there might be some oatmeal," Noelle mentioned, gently running her fingers through his dark hair. "I'll make coffee."

Reluctantly getting out of bed, Noelle grabbed her robe and walked into the kitchen. The possibilities of oatmeal were enough to entice Alex out of bed. Putting on a pair of pajama pants, he followed close behind her.

Walking into the kitchen, they both stopped abruptly. Staring at the note and ring which had been left on the kitchen table, it demanded their attention.

"Sweetheart, I think we need to talk," Alex insisted, picking up the ring.

Noelle wasn't prepared to deal with the repercussions of her actions so early in the morning, especially after their unforgettable night of passion.

"Alex, sit down. I'll make coffee," Noelle suggested trying to avoid the inevitable.

"Sweetheart, I'm not concerned over coffee right now. I think we have more important things to discuss," Alex demanded.

"Alex, I thought we already discussed this in Phuket. Remember?" Noelle replied impishly.

Picking up the note, he read it carefully. Then, looking up at Noel, he appeared somber.

"Sweetheart, come over here and sit on my lap. We need to talk."

Slowly walking over, she put her arms around him as she sat on his lap. Tears filled her eyes. She had no idea where this was leading or how upset he might be having found the ring and the note.

"Really, Noelle, let me see. I think this is my favorite part. *God willing, one day, hopefully, our paths will cross again.* What were you thinking? Were you truly over our relationship, our engagement?" Alex questioned in a solemn demeanor.

"Alex, you have no idea how much I regret what I did. Can you ever forgive me? Babe, there's never been anyone in my life, but you, there never will be," Noelle answered with tears streaming down her face. After last night and our three days in Phuket, how could you even doubt what we have together? Babe, I was so devastated when you left. Let's just consider it a brief moment of insanity and leave it at that. Please?" she begged softly, caressing his face.

Gently wiping her moist face, he'd merely been playing with her. He'd easily gotten past her fleeting moment of insanity, as she called it when they were in Phuket. But, instead, he just wanted to watch her squirm with remorse. After the night they'd just had, there was no way he could harbor any ill feelings toward her. He loved her more than life itself. He'd waited his entire life for someone like Noelle.

"Well, Sweetheart, let me think. Then, perhaps, you can make up for your evil doings. I'll get back to you on that later tonight," Alex laughed mischievously.

"Alex, really, I thought you were upset. Geez, you just did that to make me grovel. I think you better choose your words wisely. If memory serves, I believe you have something very dear and close to your heart downstairs in the garage. Let me think, oh yeah, I have a key," Noelle grinned.

"Sweetheart, you wouldn't dare mess with my car," he laughed.

"Alex, let's just say she's safe for the moment. Do you consider your Porsche to be of the female persuasion?" Noelle laughed.

"Sweetheart, it's just a car. However, I'm not so sure anymore.

Females are too dramatic and shed way too many tears," Alex joked. Then, pulling her closer and gently brushing her long blonde curls away from her face, he kissed her passionately. Losing herself in the excitement of his kiss, she felt like putty in his arms.

"Wow, Babe, you take my breath away. I almost forgot why I walked in here. Oh, now I remember, coffee," Noelle smiled, getting up from his lap. "So, is this what our married life will be like?"

"After last night, I certainly hope so. What man wouldn't want a wife like that? Just wait till the boys at Club Med hear all the hot, spicy details," he teased wickedly.

"Alex," Noelle yelled. Then, with revenge in her eyes, she ran over, playfully pinching him until he begged her to stop.

"Okay, enough, I'm starved," he laughed, walking over to search the kitchen cabinets for an old box of oatmeal. "I can't believe it. I actually found a box." To his surprise, it now appeared they wouldn't starve.

"Great. I'll brew a pot of coffee, and we can eat in today."

"Sweetheart, Trevor wanted us to have dinner with them later this evening. What are your thoughts?"

"To be honest, I'd much rather spend what time we have left alone, just the two of us. I don't mean to be selfish. I know Trevor would like to see you before you leave, but I've just stayed with them. I'm sure they would understand if we pass on dinner," Noelle suggested, trying to reach inside the tall, upper cabinets for coffee cups.

"Actually, those were my thoughts exactly. Unfortunately, I leave early tomorrow morning, so that doesn't give us much time. I'll give Trevor a call," Alex agreed.

Noting her dilemma, he walked over, putting his arms around her tiny waist. "Sweetheart, let me get those," he winked softly, kissing the nape of her neck.

"Geez, Alex, I thought you were starving?" she giggled.

Enjoying their bowl of oatmeal and hot coffee, Alex had an idea.

"Sweetheart, why don't we check into the Marriott Hotel tonight. I don't think either of us cherishes the thought of spending time in a grocery store, and it appears we're out of everything. Also, it's near the airport. We can order room service."

"I think that's a wonderful idea."

"Great. I'll call and reserve us a suite for this evening," Alex smiled, sipping his coffee. "We'll just move this 'farewell' party over to the Marriott."

"Alex, please don't refer to our night as a farewell party. Do you want me to cry all night?"

"Geez, Noelle, for heaven's sake, you know that I have to leave in the morning. Sweetheart, sooner or later, you're going to have to come to terms with the fact that I'm in the military. You know, you're not the only military spouse in the world. How do the other spouses handle deployments?"

"Babe, I really don't give a damn how the other spouses deal with it. I've just lost the only mother I've ever known. I think that gives me the right to be a little selfish and want you all to myself."

"Noelle, I'm so sorry. I didn't mean to sound insensitive. I know losing Edith was difficult. Please forgive me."

Getting up from his chair, Alex walked over, putting his arms around her.

"Sweetheart, I was waiting to tell you later tonight. There's speculation that our deployment could be ending a lot sooner than originally scheduled."

"Alex, you're just saying that to make me feel better?" She worried his words held no truth.

"No. I would never lie to you. Noelle, trust me, I know how hard this deployment has been on you. Hell, I think we just covered another bout of your insanity a few minutes ago. Babe, as soon as I'm given a definite date, I'll send your tickets to Paris. Why don't you start planning our wedding? I'm told it takes a lot of time to get everything organized. I'm sure Becky would love to help," Alex suggested kissing her on the forehead.

"That sounds wonderful. However, I'm not exactly in the mood to plan a wedding. It's too soon. Losing Edith has taken a huge toll on me both mentally and physically. I haven't exactly been feeling very well, and now I have to deal with the problem of getting my grandma's house ready to put on the market."

"Sweetheart, what are you saying? Are you sick? Have you forgotten the fact I'm a doctor? What's wrong?"

"Geez, Alex, don't be silly. I'm well aware of the fact that you're a doctor. Now you're the one acting crazy."

"Noelle, if you're finished with your oatmeal, let's go sit in on the couch. We'll be more comfortable in the living room."

He was more than a bit concerned over the fact she'd mentioned not feeling well. But, of course, as a physician, hearing those words was always a cause for alarm.

Taking her hand, he led her into their newly decorated living room.

"Noelle, this room is spectacular. You've done an amazing job," he remarked, pulling her down onto the sofa beside him. "Okay, Sweetheart, please explain to me what you meant when you said you weren't feeling well. I have to know as a doctor, but I need to know more than that, as your fiance. What's wrong?"

"Alex, calm down. Honestly, it's nothing."

"Babe, I'm the one with the medical degree. Please, let me be the judge of that."

"Really, it's nothing. I just felt a little dizzy and nauseous at the airport in Jakarta. I was just upset over the news about Edith. I had a long layover, and I just needed something to eat. That's it."

"Sweetheart, look at me. I've been gone for about three months. Are you possibly pregnant?" Alex questioned, needing a cigarette more than ever.

"Maybe," she whispered impishly.

"Oh, my God, Noelle, are you serious? You seemed perfectly fine in Phuket."

"Well, remember, you bought Dramamine for me on the boat ride."

"Noelle, are you telling me that you knew then, and you let me as a doctor buy Dramamine thinking you were simply suffering from motion sickness?"

"I wasn't sure? I was only about two months late."

"What? Sweetheart, why haven't you told me?" he slowly smiled, taking a few minutes for her words to sink in.

"Alex, this is all just speculation. I haven't taken a pregnancy test.

Are you upset? You seem a bit surprised," Noelle inquired with the hint of a smile.

"Sweetheart, maybe the word surprised isn't the correct choice of words. I'm totally elated at the possibilities. However, as your doctor, I highly recommend that you take a pregnancy test," he smiled, pulling her close. "Have you mentioned this to Becky?"

"No. I would never tell Becky before you knew."

"Thank God. I couldn't imagine hearing this news from Trevor."

"Alex, I would never do that to you. For heaven's sake, you're both doctors. Trevor would tease you forever, not once taking into consideration the fact you've been living on the other side of the world."

"Sweetheart, we can either go down to my office at the hospital, and I'll run a urine and blood test, or we can just pick up a pregnancy test on the way to the hotel. If we go to my office, it will be difficult to keep the news private. What are your thoughts?"

"Well, to be honest, I'm still in shock myself. It's not like it was planned. I would prefer that no one knows. But, heck, we're not even one hundred percent sure ourselves. So let's just pick up a pregnancy test. Afterward, depending on the outcome, we'll think about telling Becky and Trevor."

"Sounds good. Man, I could use a cigarette."

The words had simply flown out of his mouth without thought. He knew that Noelle detested cigarettes.

"Alex, do you smoke when you're away on deployment?"

"Definitely not. You know that's a nasty habit."

It seemed safe enough to say at the moment. However, Alex was dying for a cigarette. Noelle would never know that he smoked like a chimney during his time at Club Med or drank himself into oblivion to relieve stress. If she were pregnant, and as a doctor, he knew the probabilities were pretty much stacked in her favor, she didn't need the added stress of knowing.

"Alex, look at me. You seem nervous. You always said you wanted kids. Have you changed your mind?" Once again, she worried.

"Noelle, I totally want children. There was never any doubt about that. I guess it's just the fact that I have to leave tomorrow. I just need to know that you're going to be fine when I leave," Alex winked. "Why don't I call to reserve us a room at the Marriott while you get your things together."

"Okay."

Walking into the kitchen to put everything away, Noelle couldn't shake the feeling that Alex seemed somewhat subdued and shocked. Didn't he understand that he also shared the responsibility of bringing a new life into the world? Geez, he was a doctor," she laughed at the mere thought of him being a physician.

After cleaning the kitchen, she walked into the bedroom. Tears ran down her face as she sat on the edge of the bed. Growing up without siblings, she'd always dreamed of having a large family. Knowing their life might now include a baby gave her hope for the future. However, she cried, knowing Edith would never get the chance to be a great-grandmother. Laying down on the bed, she felt distraught that Alex might be unhappy with the unexpected news.

Alex was surprised to find Noelle lying on the bed as he walked into the bedroom. It bothered him tremendously, and he felt somewhat responsible for the way he'd reacted.

"Sweetheart, what's wrong?"

Laying down beside her, he held her in his arms. Then, pulling back her long blonde curls that were stuck to her moist face, he gently kissed her.

"Babe, are you crying again. Listen, Noelle, I love you more than you could ever know. You have to believe me. Sweetheart, if the test is positive, you'll make a wonderful mother. Of that, I have no doubt. You're gorgeous. This baby is one lucky child. If God allows babies to pick their mothers, sweetheart, it was an easy decision. Noelle, I love you more than life itself. Do you even understand how hard it's going to be for me to leave you tomorrow? Please don't cry. You've been through enough sadness. Get your things. I've made our reservation at the Marriott. Oh, I'm running down to the garage to see if the Porsche will start. It's been sitting for a long time without being driven. I'll be right back."

There wasn't much for her to take over to the hotel. She'd never unpacked after arriving at Becky and Trevor's apartment. Throwing just a few things in an overnight bag, Noelle was finally ready.

Walking into the living room with her bag, she heard Alex bounding up the stairs.

"The Porsche started right up. Can you believe it? Too bad I don't have an extra day or two. We would take her out for a day trip. Are you ready?"

"Yes."

Locking the door, they were finally on their way to the Marriott Hotel located next to the airport.

"Alex, did you remember to call Trevor and let them know that we've changed our mind regarding dinner this evening?" Noelle questioned, getting inside the Porsche.

"No. Remind me once we reach the hotel. I'll call him."

"What will you do with your Porsche if we're becoming a family of three?" Noelle questioned as Alex raced onto the freeway.

"Well, we'll just add to our car collection," he laughed, taking the exit ramp towards the airport. "I'll buy a mid-size family car. Maybe a Beamer like Trevor's?"

"Geez, boys and their toys," she laughed. "Please don't forget to stop at a pharmacy before we get to the hotel."

"Not a chance. There's no way I'm leaving here without knowing if I'm going to be a daddy," he smiled with a wink.

"Thanks, Babe. I love you."

Stopping at a local pharmacy, Alex ran inside. Buying three different pregnancy tests, he felt a little foolish. Getting back inside the Porsche, he handed the small shopping bag to Noelle. Looking inside, she laughed.

"Really, Alex, three pregnancy tests, and you're a doctor," she giggled.

"Hey, are you questioning my abilities as a physician," he laughed.

Arriving at the hotel, Alex parked under the portico giving his keys to the attendant.

"He better not scratch her," Alex whispered as they walked inside the lobby.

After checking in, they took the elevator up to the 10th floor.

Unlocking the door, Alex carried his garment bag, duffle bag, and Noelle's overnight bag inside their suite.

"Wow. The room is exquisite."

Taking a glance around, it was very modern. A king-size bed draped elegantly in a French blue toile duvet sat against one wall. Along the opposite wall sat a beautifully carved mahogany credenza. It held a television in the center and a large alabaster bowl containing fresh fruit. Toward the back of the suite, there was a formal sitting area. A tan leather sofa with a matching love seat faced the sliding glass doors leading to the balcony.

Checking out the minibar, Alex grabbed a local beer.

"So, Sweetheart, what would you like to order for dinner," Alex inquired, handing her a menu from the exquisite Lawry's Restaurant downstairs.

"Well, we've just had Italian food," Noelle mentioned searching the menu. "I think I would like to try their prime rib with roasted potatoes, along with a glass of iced tea.

"Sounds good. I think I'm going to order steak and potatoes, along with a bottle of champagne."

"First, I think you should call Trevor," Noelle reminded him as she removed her shoes.

"Thanks, Babe. I'll do that right now before I forget."

Curling up on the sofa, Noelle picked up a magazine while Alex called Trevor.

"That went well. He understood our need to be alone and the fact we don't have much time before I leave tomorrow," Alex smiled, hanging up the phone.

"Great. I'll invite Becky and Trevor over for dinner next week."

"That would be nice. I left a check to cover Edith's arrangements on the kitchen table."

"Thanks, Alex. It truly means a lot that you covered Edith's final expenses."

"Sweetheart, no problem. She was your grandmother and, more importantly, the person who raised you."

After calling room service and placing their order for dinner, he grabbed another bottle of beer from the minibar and sat down on the sofa next to Noelle.

"Well, are we going to address the elephant in the room or wait until after dinner?" Alex winked, reaching for the bag containing the pregnancy tests.

"Babe, I'm scared," Noelle remarked, becoming emotional.

"Sweetheart, I thank God that I'm here for you to find out. But, Noelle, either way, nothing changes. We've both agreed that we want a large family. So please, don't worry. Let's just take the test. I don't want to wait any longer."

"Okay. If you're sure, you wouldn't rather wait until after dinner."

"Noelle, honestly, why does waiting for dinner make a difference. I know you're nervous, but there's no reason to be scared. I'm a doctor, in case you need to be reminded once again," he winked.

"Alex, you're a trauma surgeon, not a gynecologist," Noelle smiled, wiping tears from her cheeks.

"Sweetheart, did I hear you correctly?" he laughed. "Wow, seriously, Babe, that's it," he scoffed, ripping open one of the boxes.

Taking Noelle's hand, he led her into the bathroom.

"Sweetheart, just so you know, that would be an obstetrician. Not a gynecologist. I need you to pee on this test strip right now—doctor's orders. No more waiting, do you understand," he smiled, handing her the plastic test strip.

"Okay. Don't rush me."

With trembling hands, she did as Alex ordered. Holding her breath, she wasn't sure she wanted to look at the results.

"Alex, you check it. I'm too scared."

"Give it a minute."

Waiting for what seemed like an eternity, she felt faint. Then, finally, Alex looked up.

"Wow," he smiled, staring at her.

"Okay. Tell me. Is it positive?"

"Maybe, I should make you wait until after dinner," he teased.

"Alex, tell me. Right now," she anxiously demanded.

"Sweetheart, we're pregnant," he grinned.

"Oh, my God, I was right," she smiled, throwing her arms around him.

Suddenly, reeling from the news and without warning, Noelle's legs buckled from beneath her small frame.

"Geez, sweetheart, don't faint," Alex cautioned, catching her before she hit the floor.

Not taking any chances, he scooped her up and carried her back to the sofa.

"Noelle, how do you feel?"

"Oh, I'm alright. It's just nerves. What about the other tests?"

"We don't need them," he smiled.

"Alex, you said we would need more than one test. So maybe we should take one more?"

"Wow, Sweetheart, are you questioning my knowledge because, as you said, I'm just a lowly trauma doctor and not an obstetrician?" he winked. "Trust me. You don't need to take another test. However, if you feel the need, here are the other two boxes," he laughed.

"Thanks. I'll be right back. Alex, you purchased them. I might as well use them," she explained, walking towards the bathroom.

"Noelle, if you feel the least bit dizzy, call me."

Hearing a light knock, it indicated the arrival of dinner. Opening the door, the room service attendant pushed a cart laden with food inside their room. After being given a generous tip, the young man was quickly on his way.

"Sweetheart, dinner has arrived," Alex announced loudly.

Walking out of the bathroom, Noelle smiled.

"So, was I right?" he chided.

"Okay. Maybe you did learn something in medical school," Noelle smiled.

"Well, I graduated at the top of my class. But, of course, I might have had a little help from Trevor."

"Alex, can you believe it? We're going to be parents. Isn't this exciting?" she cried.

"Noelle, come over here and sit down. You can't possibly cry for the next seven months. What's wrong? Are you worried? We have less than eighteen hours before I leave for the airport. I need to know that you're going to be alright," he implored, holding her in his arms.

"Alex, it's just that Edith will never see this baby. I feel it's all my fault that I abandoned her," Noelle broke down, sobbing on his shoulder.

"Babe, you have to stop blaming yourself. Sweetheart, call me crazy, but I think Edith's up above working overtime. First, you got your memory back, then I arrived unexpectedly, and this evening we found out you're pregnant. Don't tell me she's not watching over you," he said, wiping his eyes. "Now, you've got me all emotional. We've got to get our act together. This little person is counting on us."

"I'm sorry. I didn't mean to get you upset," Noelle smiled, wiping his eyes.

"It's not you. I guess I've just held my feelings inside for too long regarding Edith. I really loved her. From the very beginning, I saw how much she cared for you when you had your accident. She took on responsibility for you as a newborn when most people are ready to retire. So, if we have a little girl, we can name her after Edith. What do you think?"

"Really, Alex, you would name our baby girl Edith?"

Giving him a perplexed stare, Noelle burst out laughing.

"Alex, I know you mean well and that you're only trying to help, but there's no way on earth that I would ever name our little girl Edith. Are you serious?" Noelle roared.

"Well, at least, I made you stop crying. I think dinner is getting cold. Let's eat. I'm going to celebrate with a glass of champagne. However, young lady, I'm afraid you do not get champagne. Doctor's orders," Alex laughed.

After enjoying dinner, Noelle felt a little nauseous. Noticing her discomfort and the fact they had to get up early to leave for the airport, Alex suggested they turn in for the evening. Unfortunately for him, their evening wouldn't become one of unleashed passion as the night before. However, he went to bed with a huge smile on his face. The beautiful young woman lying so peacefully in his arms was carrying their first child.

Awakened by the sound of the alarm, Alex struggled to wake

up. Leaving the beautiful girl next to him wasn't going to be easy. Deciding to let Noelle sleep in a few minutes longer, he walked into the bathroom to take a quick shower. Standing under the warm water, it felt invigorating. Stepping out of the shower, he quickly dried off, tying the towel around his waist as he walked out to find his uniform. He dressed quietly, unzipping his garment bag, putting on his military blues and shiny patent leather dress shoes. Finally, styling his hair and a quick spritz of his favorite cologne, he was ready to wake sleeping beauty.

"Sweetheart, I hate to wake you. But, unfortunately, we've only got an hour before we need to leave for the airport," Alex whispered, sitting down on the edge of the bed.

"What time is it?" Noelle asked, rubbing her eyes.

"It's almost 4:30 a.m. I'm afraid you've got to get up. I'll order coffee. Do you feel like eating breakfast?"

"No. I'll get something later."

Sitting up, Noelle gasped.

"Wow, Alex, you look so handsome, and you smell heavenly. Can't you stay and simply quit the reserves?" she begged.

"Sweetheart, you must be dreaming. Seriously, you should know by now how ridiculous those questions are. I'm really sorry you have to get up this early, but I need you to drive me to the airport. Afterward, I want you to go home and get some sleep. I'll call you from Aviano when I arrive."

Slowly getting out of bed, Noelle walked into the bathroom. Turning on the warm water, she wiped her face. Then, pulling her long hair into a ponytail, she walked out to find her clothes.

"Geez, babe, you look incredibly sexy this morning," he winked, walking over to give her a quick, passionate kiss.

"Right. I have no make-up, and I'm still half asleep," Noelle gestured.

"Well, it works for me. But, unfortunately, I'm out of here in a few minutes," Alex winked, picking up the phone to call room service.

"Good morning, this is Major Bennington in Suite 418. I'd like to order a carafe of coffee and a large glass of milk. Also, could you add two bowls of oatmeal to that order? Thanks."

"Yes, sir. I'll have that sent right up."

"Alex, I'm not hungry. I told you I didn't want anything to eat. It's too early," Noelle frowned, getting dressed.

"You have to join me in a final bowl of oatmeal," Alex insisted. "At least do it for the baby," he winked.

"I'll try, but if I get sick, you're the cause of it."

"Noelle, there were so many things we didn't get the chance to discuss. Things like selling Edith's house and getting you to the right doctor. Do you have any questions about being pregnant? I'll not be here if you have questions. With Edith no longer with you, you can always call Becky. Don't forget Trevor's a doctor and a damn good one at that. However, he's not an obstetrician. He's a cardiologist. Babe, I'm honestly worried about leaving you in this condition," Alex mentioned closing his duffel bag.

"Alex, women have been having babies since the beginning of time. I'll be fine. However, I would like your recommendation for a doctor."

"I'm thinking of Doctor Chang, but let me get back to you on that. I'll call you once I've made my decision."

Hearing a soft knock at the door, room service had arrived.

"Good morning, sir," the attendant smiled.

Carrying a tray that contained coffee, milk, and oatmeal, the young man sat it on the credenza. After Alex had given him a generous tip, he was on his way.

"Sweetheart, sit down on the sofa. I'll bring your milk and oatmeal."

"Really, Alex, I hate milk," Noelle giggled.

"Well, Sweetheart, I'm afraid you better get used to it. Doctor's orders," he once again reiterated. "Oh, that reminds me, you're going to need prenatal vitamins. Doctor Chang can prescribe them. Although, I'm not sure he's taking any new maternity patients. I'll have to check on that."

Walking over to the sofa with their oatmeal and beverages, Alex insisted that Noel finish her entire glass of milk and eat at least half of her oatmeal.

"Geez, Babe, maybe it's a good thing you're leaving for a while. I hate milk," Noelle teased.

"Well, you fell in love with a doctor, and you're carrying our baby.

I think you better get used to it, at least, when I'm home. That reminds me when I get back to Club Med, I'll give you an update on my return date. I'd still like you to meet me in Paris if you feel up to it."

"What miss out on Paris? Are you kidding? If your deployment ends in the next thirty days, I won't be that far along. I'll be there."

"That's my girl. My aunt rents an apartment close to the Eiffel Tower. You'll love Paris. I stayed there a lot as a young boy before we came to the states. I can't wait to show you the City of Lights," Alex explained, looking down at his watch. "Sweetheart, I'm afraid we have to leave. My flight leaves at 6:00."

Grabbing their few items from the room, Noelle followed Alex to the elevator and downstairs to the lobby. Requesting the Porsche at the front desk, Alex and Noelle walked outside to the hotel entrance. The sun was barely coming up as the attendant drove the Porsche around to the front of the hotel. He opened Noel's car door and waited for her to fasten her seat belt before gently closing her door. Walking around to the driver's side, Alex got inside, closing his door. It was only a short drive to the airport.

"Sweetheart, it's not necessary for you to come inside the airport. I'll just park temporarily at the terminal entrance, or would you rather I park in short-term parking."

"Alex, you better park in short-term parking. I'm coming in with you. I'm walking with you to your boarding gate."

"Alright. I was just trying to make it easier on you."

Parking the car, Alex grabbed his duffel bag and quickly rolled up his garment bag.

"Noelle, here's the key to the Porsche. She's a great car and shouldn't give you any problems while I'm gone. If God forbid something goes wrong with her, please call Trevor first and have him check it. She should be fine. I'm hoping to be home in less than thirty days if everything goes according to the rumors I've been hearing."

Taking Noelle's hand, he led her inside the terminal. Standing in a long line of passengers waiting to check-in, the airport was always busy at this time of the morning. Approaching the check-in counter, Alex checked in for his flight and received his boarding gate information.

"You're all set, Major Bennington. Enjoy your flight."

"Thanks."

"Well, that didn't take long, considering the length of the line," Noelle mentioned wiping her eyes.

"Sweetheart, please don't do this to yourself. I think you should have dropped me off at the entrance instead of coming inside. It would have been much easier for you," Alex mentioned noticing her tears.

Slowly walking toward the boarding gate, Noelle pulled him close. Clinging to him with every ounce of her being, she didn't want to let go of the handsome man in his military blues. Finally, her heart broke, watching as Alex checked in, reaching the gate. Afterward, they found vacant seats and sat down.

"Sweetheart, how are you feeling? I certainly hope you don't get dizzy. I should never have let you come inside."

"Geez, Alex, I'm not going to lay in bed all day because you think I might just happen to pass out, and nothing would have stopped me from walking with you inside the airport and to your boarding gate."

"I know. I just worry. Maybe you should call Doctor Chang tomorrow and see if you can get an appointment. Tell him you're my fiance. Heck, I'll call him from Aviano."

"Alex, I'm going to miss you," Noelle frowned.

"Noelle, hopefully, it'll just be a few weeks. Please hang in here for me. You can do this. You're stronger than you give yourself credit. Heck, you went to the Philippines and then to Sumatra. Sweetheart, that took a lot of courage to leave Arlington. Trust me. You're going to be fine. I think you'll find the amenities at our apartment more modern than what you had in those countries," Alex smiled. "Speaking of our apartment, as a reminder, I left a signed blank check for Trevor on the kitchen table. Just enter the amount. Also, there's more than enough money in our joint bank account to cover any expenses you have while I'm away. My pay goes in by direct deposit, and you know the drawer where I keep our checks. Do you still have the credit card that I gave you?"

"Yes."

"Then, you'll be fine, at least financially speaking. I'm more worried about the fact you're pregnant. You have to take care of yourself. Do you promise?"

"Alex, stop worrying. I certainly hope we don't have neurotic children."

"Sweetheart, that's not funny. There's certainly never been anyone unstable in my family. However, I'm not so sure about yours," Alex teased.

Suddenly, Noelle cringed, hearing the boarding announcement.

"Good morning. We're ready to begin our boarding process at gate twenty-one. All first-class passengers, as well as those boarding with small children and anyone needing assistance, is welcome to board at this time," the gate agent announced.

"Oh, my God, Alex, this is it," Noelle gasped. "Will you please call me when you get to Aviano?"

"Yes. Noelle, go home and get some rest. You've got to go grocery shopping later," Alex reminded her.

"At this time, we'd like to continue our boarding process with all passengers sitting in rows one through twenty," the gate agent continued. "Welcome aboard."

"Sweetheart, that's me. I love you more than you know. Be a good girl, and take care of my baby. I love you," Alex smiled, pulling her close to his chest.

Quickly, giving her a short, passionate kiss, he gently withdrew from her arms. Then, holding onto her hand, he slowly let her fingertips slip through his hands as he walked towards the jetway.

"I'll call you," Alex spoke inaudibly before losing sight of her.

Noelle wiped her eyes. For a brief moment, she found herself becoming scared and vulnerable. She took a deep breath and watched his plane as it was slowly pushed back from the gate. Then, gently, placing her hand over the lower portion of her abdomen, she no longer felt alone. She now carried a tiny piece of Alex within her, growing safely close to her heart. Walking away, she smiled.

Chapter Fourteen

Aviano Air Base, Italy

Arriving at Aviano Air Base, Alex had a short layover. In a few short hours, he would board a military transport which would take him once again inside the war zone and finally back to Club Med. Looking down at his watch, it was almost midnight in Arlington. Despite the late hour, he'd promised to call when he arrived. Hopefully, Noelle would still be awake. Finally, after the third ring, she answered.

"Alex, you remembered to call. I love you. I thought you might forget," Noelle answered.

"Sweetheart, I love you too. But, please, give a guy a little credit. I promised to call you. We just arrived about a half-hour ago. So how's my little mommy this evening? How are you feeling? Have you had any dizzy spells since I left?"

"Alex, I'm fine. Calm down. I came home from the airport and took a nap."

"Did you go grocery shopping? We were out of everything."

"Not yet. Don't worry. I stopped at the Quick Mart and bought a few items until tomorrow. Babe, I'm not going to starve. Don't be silly. How was your flight?"

"Tired and boring. We had a short layover in Germany before

arriving in Aviano. Sweetheart, I have to go. Some of the other guys are waiting to use the phone. Please take good care of yourself and try to contact Doctor Chang. I'll try to call you later this week. I love you more than you know."

"Oh, Alex, I love you too. But, please, don't worry. Keep safe. I love you."

Hearing the sound of her voice, he smiled. Thoughts of becoming a dad amused him, even if it wasn't planned. He'd never loved her more. Hopefully, news of an early return awaited him at Club Med.

Boarding a C-141 transport, he was on the last leg of his trip. Arriving in the desert at Club Med, he was exhausted. Colonel Williams sent a driver to meet his aircraft.

Club Med

"Welcome home, sir," the young airman smiled, throwing Alex's bags in the back of the jeep.

"Thanks. So how are things at Club Med?" Alex smiled.

"We've just experienced one of the worst sand storms. You're lucky. The flight line just reopened for business this afternoon."

"Wow, great timing. I'm pretty tired. You can just drop me at my tent if it's still there."

"Oh, we were given notice regarding the impending weather. The hatches were battened down, so I'm sure you'll find things as you left them."

"Great."

Exiting the jeep, things appeared pretty normal. Then, walking inside, he threw his bags over to one side of the tent. Even though it was early afternoon, his only thoughts were to get some rest. Tomorrow would come soon enough, and he would have a full day of surgeries.

As Alex walked to the operating room the following day, he ran into Craig.

"Geez, Doctor Bennington, your home," Craig grinned, catching a glimpse of Alex. "How the heck did you manage to get away for the second time? Oh, let me guess, your superhero status. I feel snubbed. You didn't even stop by to say you were leaving."

"Noelle lost her grandmother, and Colonel Williams let me take leave to attend her services. Everything happened suddenly."

"I'm sorry to hear that. How did Noelle take the news?"

"Much better after I arrived. However, I really owe Trevor and his wife, Becky, for standing in the gap for me. Trevor made all the arrangements. They met Noelle's incoming flight from Indonesia and insisted she stay with them. I've got to run. I have a young man on the operating table waiting for me to put his fractured leg back together. When you get off from work, come over to my casa. I've got some surprising news. Oh, pick up our usual friend, Jack."

"Okay. Pizza and Jack Daniels it is. See you later."

After being in surgery for over two hours, Alex tossed his surgical mask in the hazardous waste bin. He was craving a much-needed cup of coffee. Only two minor surgeries remained on his schedule for the afternoon. Walking toward the cafeteria, thoughts of Noelle and the baby consumed him. For a brief moment, he wished he'd never signed up for the reserves. However, his regrets were short-lived as he remembered the young soldier on his operating table. The casualties who were brought in each day deserved his best. They were willingly and unselfishly defending the greatest nation on earth. The least he could do was offer his knowledge and skills to ensure they went home. Hopefully, alive and in good shape.

Quickly consuming two cups of strong coffee and a grilled cheese sandwich, it was time for his next surgical patient. She was an extremely lucky young lieutenant. She'd only received lacerations to her face as a result of a roadside bomb exploding near her Humvee. Alex knew his expertise was not the specific skills of a plastic surgeon. However, he knew he could suture well enough to get her stateside with minimal scars.

Finishing his last surgery of the day, Alex quickly shed his scrubs. Feeling exhausted from his recent flight, he excitedly left the hospital.

Hopefully, Craig would soon arrive with pizza and Jack Daniels. The two staples had managed to sustain them throughout their long hours of deployment.

"Hey, Doc, are you home?" Craig teased, pulling back the flap to Alex's tent.

"Yes, come in. I hope you didn't forget the pizza and Jack Daniels. I'm starved."

"Not a chance. Get some glasses. I'll pour us a round. I hope pepperoni pizza will work. It was all that remained this evening," Craig smiled, walking inside the tan camouflaged tent. Opening the bottle, he filled two tall glasses.

"Wow, just what I needed," Alex mentioned throwing back the entire drink in one huge continuous gulp.

"Geez, Doc, rough day in surgery," Craig laughed, passing him the bottle.

"No, basically routine. So what's the latest news on the length of our deployment?"

"Well, you might want to pour yourself another round. I'm afraid the news isn't good."

"What? You've got to be kidding. I thought we were getting out of here early?"

"Sorry. It appears things have changed. I hate to disappoint you on your first day back, but you know the drill around here," Craig frowned, stuffing a large slice of pizza in his mouth. "You seem shocked."

"Yeah, well, that would be an understatement. I thought we were practically on our way home," Alex fumed, lighting a cigarette. "I told Noelle that I would be home soon."

"Really, Alex, you should have known better. You're in the military, and things always change. So, let's have it. What's the surprising news you were going to tell me," Craig questioned, leaning back in his chair with anticipation.

Snapping back from his disgruntled thoughts, Alex smiled. "Noelle's pregnant. We're going to have a baby."

"Wow. You work fast. Congratulations," Craig smiled. "No wonder you're so disappointed by the news of our extension."

"Thanks. It seems Noelle has known for a while. She never mentioned it while we were in Thailand. However, we're both really excited."

"Well, that demands a toast," Craig smiled, pouring them a refill.

"Here's to a healthy, beautiful baby girl or handsome little boy," Craig toasted.

"Thanks, Craig. I'm pretty stoked at the idea of becoming a father. Noelle seems really happy," Alex smiled, lighting another cigarette. "Can you even imagine?"

"That's great news. I'm excited for you."

"It was so hard leaving her. It was probably one of the hardest things I've ever done. She's been experiencing morning sickness, and now with Edith gone, she's pretty much on her own except for Becky and Trevor."

"I'm sure she'll be fine, but I can understand your worries. Isn't your friend Trevor a doctor? That should give you some comfort knowing he's there."

"Yes. Trevor's a cardiovascular surgeon. However, I know Becky will be a great help to Noelle," Alex replied, taking another slice of pizza from the box. "I just want to be home when the baby's born."

"That's certainly understandable. But, things could change, nothing is for sure around here, and we could be sent home sooner than we think. So, now, I'll have to make a trip down to Missouri," Craig smiled, lounging back in his chair as he lit a cigarette.

"We'd love to have you come down to Missouri. But, as I said, you should consider taking a job at the hospital. I'm friends with the Hospital Administrator."

"Well, you never know, I might just take you up on your offer," Craig mentioned.

Later, Craig looked down at his watch as he took the last slice of pizza. It appeared they'd easily spent the past two hours drinking and complaining about Club Med.

"I suppose we should call it a night. I have to be at the hospital early in the morning. Unbelievable, we've managed to kill both bottles and finish two pizzas. We certainly have an interesting life at Club Med. It appears that pizza and Jack Daniel's have become our closest friends."

"Yeah, well, I'm ready for a change," Alex smirked, standing to stretch his legs.

"Wow, Dad, I'll bet you are," Craig laughed. "See you at the hospital."

Arlington, Missouri

The morning sun cast a warm glow inside the bedroom, waking Noelle. She felt terrific. No signs of morning sickness consumed her. Sitting up in bed, she began to make a mental note of things that needed to be done. First, she would restock the kitchen cabinets. Grocery shopping was a priority. Next, she would contact Doctor Chang and schedule a prenatal appointment. Afterward, if time allowed, she would consult a realtor and begin listing Edith's house. The house had no mortgage attached to it. Unfortunately, it was an older home with dated interior and appliances. The kitchen and bathrooms would require significant updates. However, with the help of a local contractor, it could quickly be brought up to date. Hopefully, the sale proceeds would be enough to purchase a more extensive, modern home—a home with enough bedrooms that would adequately accommodate a growing family.

For a brief moment, Noelle contemplated waiting for Alex's return. Unaware of the news Alex had received upon his arrival at Club Med, she had no way to know his deployment might be extended. Ridding Edith's house of its contents would be a daunting, monumental task. It was a living museum of her life with Edith. She could easily use Alex's help and expertise in the house's sale and bringing it up to today's standards. Edith's life was too similar to that of a hoarder. She always saved everything. Alex could help her decide which things needed to be kept and which items needed to go to Goodwill. Pulling the covers over her head, she felt completely overwhelmed.

Hearing the phone on the nightstand, Noelle eagerly reached over to grab the receiver. Hopefully, it was Alex.

"Hello," Noelle answered excitedly.

"Good morning. I hope I didn't wake you," Becky queried.

"Oh, no, I was awake," Noelle reluctantly replied with a hint of disappointment.

"Geez, Noelle, I'm sorry. Were you expecting a call from Alex?"

"No. Alex called last night," she mentioned trying to cover her frustration. "What's up?"

"I was calling to invite you out to lunch. I know Alex left yesterday, and I thought you could use some company. I know you must really miss him, and I didn't want you to spend your first day alone. How does Leonardo's Restaurant sound?"

"Great. Should I come over and pick you up?"

"No. I'll stop by your apartment around 11:30. Will that work for you?"

"Yes. I look forward to seeing you. I have some exciting news to share with you."

"Really. What's going on?"

"I'll tell you over lunch."

"Okay. I'll see you at 11:30."

"Thanks. See you later this morning."

Finally, getting out of bed, Noelle grabbed her robe and walked into the kitchen to make coffee. Perhaps, it was a good thing Becky called. It would give her a chance to tell her about the pregnancy, and with Alex away, she could certainly use a close female friend.

She began making a list of things a baby would need as she sat at the kitchen table sipping coffee. Perhaps, after lunch, they could go shopping. A crib seemed like the perfect place to start. It appeared her list of things to do was growing. Finishing her coffee, she took a shower and got dressed. It seemed the morning was off to a good start. Later hearing a knock at the door, Becky had arrived earlier than expected.

"Hey, Becky, come in. You're early," Noelle greeted.

"I know. I hope it's okay."

"Of course, it's not like I have a lot to do here in the apartment. Would you like a cup of coffee?"

"Thanks. I'll take it black, no cream or sugar."

"That's good. It seems I'm out of everything. I need to go grocery shopping."

"Please have a seat on the sofa. I'll get the coffee," Noelle mentioned walking into the kitchen.

"Wow. I'll bet Alex loved the way you redecorated the apartment. You did an amazing job."

"Thanks. I think Alex loved it. You know men. Sometimes I think they hardly notice those things," Noelle smiled, sitting a tray with coffee on the sofa table.

Taking a sip of the hot beverage, Becky paused, staring at Noelle.

"Okay. Let's have it. We have plenty of time, and I'm dying to know. What were you going to tell me?"

"Well," Noelle paused. "I'm pregnant."

"Wow," Becky gasped. "Congratulations."

Becky tried to hide the fact she wished it had been her news instead of Noelle's. It appeared she and Trevor had secretly been trying to conceive a child for over a year with no luck. However, Noelle was her best friend, and she needed to support her.

"That's wonderful. When is the baby due?"

"Oh, I'm just a little over two months. I'm guessing September. Of course, I haven't seen an obstetrician yet."

"I bet Alex is really excited about becoming a daddy."

"Yes. Alex certainly seems thrilled. He's a little overprotective, but I think that's because he's a doctor," Noelle smiled. "It was so hard for him to leave yesterday. I was feeling a little dizzy and nauseous. He was worried."

"Well, that's easily understood. However, I want you to know Trevor, and I will be here for you. If you need anything day or night, just give us a call. Wow, I can't wait to tell Trevor. He's going to be excited. Alex and Trevor seem more like brothers than close friends."

"Thanks, Becky. Alex is supposed to be home soon. I can't wait, but I have so much to do. I have to put Edith's house on the market, and it needs updates. I've thought about waiting until Alex is home. It's going to be quite an undertaking."

"Well, I don't know a lot about selling houses or doing renovations, but if there's anything we can do to help, just let us know."

"Thanks. I'm sure we'll simply hire a contractor to do all the upgrades. I think the worst part will be disposing of Edith's things. She never liked to get rid of anything. In her mind, she could always envision another purpose for things or reasons to hang onto stuff. I always teased her that she was a hoarder."

"Wow, as I mentioned, if we can help, please don't hesitate to give us a call. Are you ready to eat? Leonardo's opened at 11:00."

"Yes. Let's go. There's certainly nothing to eat here," Noelle laughed.

After lunch, she suggested they make a quick stop at Kids Boutique to check out cribs and mattresses. It held an endless supply of nursery furniture and décor. What should have been a short visit quickly turned into hours of careful, detailed inspection of showcased cribs, changing tables, matching armoires, and accessories? Afterward, Becky took Noelle to their local grocery store, ensuring she had an ample supply of staples. Everything possible that a new mommy to be might crave was added to their cart. Finally, after hours of shopping and the fact Becky's Volvo couldn't hold anything further, they drove back to Noelle's apartment. Getting everything upstairs and put in its proper place was the most challenging part of their day.

"Why don't you stay, and I'll cook dinner?" Noelle inquired after everything was put away.

"Thanks, but Trevor will be home soon," Becky answered, noticing the time on the kitchen clock. "I need to get home and cook supper. He thinks I never cook anymore," Becky added.

"Well, thanks for lunch, spending time with me at Kids Boutique, and taking me to the grocery store. Becky, you're such a good friend. I honestly don't know what I would do without you," Noelle smiled, giving her a quick hug.

"What are friends for if we can't help. Get some rest and take care of yourself. I'll call you tomorrow. Remember, if you need me anytime, just give me a call."

"Thanks, Becky. I'll talk to you tomorrow."

Closing the door, Noelle lounged back on the sofa. She felt exhausted. However, she now had a game plan for the type of nursery furniture she wanted. It was a significant first step in setting up a baby's room. Suddenly, the thoughts of Alex made her miss him terribly. With moist eyes, she gently caressed her tummy. She took comfort in the fact she carried their unborn baby—a new little being solely dependent upon her. Then, remembering Alex's demand that she drink more milk, she got up from the sofa, walked into the kitchen, and poured herself a huge glass of milk. Then, downing it with a couple of crackers, she was ready for bed.

Turning off the kitchen light, she walked down the hall toward the bedroom. Changing into pajamas, she was ready to slip under the warm duvet and watch television until she fell asleep. At least that was her plan until the phone rang.

"Hello."

"Hey, Sweetheart, how was your day?" Alex asked.

"Hey, Babe, it was good. Becky came over and took me to lunch. Then, we went to the Kids Boutique to check out nursery furniture. Afterward, Becky took me to the grocery store. You'll be happy to know the kitchen pantry is fully stocked once again. Doctor Bennington, so that you know, I drank a tall glass of milk before coming to bed tonight."

"Wow, that's my girl. It sounds like you've been busy."

He was pleasantly surprised to hear that she'd had a wonderful day with Becky. However, he knew what he was about to tell her would more than deflate her pleasant mood. However, there was no way around giving her the shocking, unexpected news regarding his deployment extension. It was killing him emotionally. Nonetheless, she had to know, and the sooner, the better before she started to make plans for his return.

"Sweetheart, I'm afraid I have some rather unexpected news. There's not an easy way to say this," he paused, knowing the impact his following statement would have. "Our deployment has been extended. It looks as if we're here for several months. I'm so sorry. Noelle, you have to know how much I was looking forward to coming home soon. The news of my extensions has been a huge disappointment."

There was nothing but silence on the phone.

"Noelle. Sweetheart, are you there?"

Suddenly, Alex distinctly heard muffled sounds of crying. It was killing him. He couldn't be there to hold her in his arms and convince her that everything would be alright.

"Noelle, it's only time, nothing more. Do you understand? God, I wish it was within my power to change this. I love you. You're a strong, brave, courageous young woman, and you're carrying our child. I have to know that you can handle this."

"Oh, Alex, you don't understand. I need to put Edith's house on the market, and it's going to require a lot of work. Once the house is sold, we can buy a much nicer, larger house. Do you understand?" Noelle cried. "I wanted to be settled into our new home before the baby was born. I've dreamed of decorating a baby's room and furnishing it with everything a newborn would need, and now you tell me that you're not coming home. What if you're not back before the baby is born?" she cried hysterically.

"Sweetheart, please calm down. Being this upset isn't good for either you or the baby."

"I don't care. Alex, I need you. I was counting on you coming home. Do you understand?"

Hearing the tone in Noelle's voice was horrifying. She was distraught, and there wasn't a damn thing he could do about it. For a brief second, he almost contemplated going AWOL, absent without leave. However, to entertain those thoughts were complete stupidity.

"Noelle, you've got to calm down. There's always a slight chance I could leave sooner. We don't have to move into a new house before the baby is born. Trust me. A newborn will never know the difference between sleeping in our room or a nursery. We have plenty of time to find the perfect home. Sweetheart, I love you. You have to understand if it were possible for me to change things, I would. Babe, I love you."

"Oh, Alex, I'm sorry. I didn't mean to get so upset, and I know it's not your fault. I know that being in the military means being separated a lot of the time. I'll be alright. Please, don't worry about the baby or me. We'll be fine. I promise. I love you too," Noelle wept, trying to control her emotions.

"Babe, I can't stay on the phone. I got an impending surgery patient waiting to arrive. I love you. I'll try to give you a call tomorrow or the day after. Please, take care of yourself. You're carrying our baby. Did you call Doctor Chang?"

"No. Today was a busy day. I'll call his office tomorrow. Don't worry, I'm not going to let anything happen to either the baby or me. Babe, I love you. Trust me. We'll be fine. Guess we'll just see you whenever your deployment ends. Take good care of yourself. I love you."

"Sweetheart, I love you more than you know. Get some rest."

Hanging up the phone, Noelle buried her head into her pillow. She cried herself to sleep, resting her head on the moist pillowcase. Alex was right. Everything was out of their control. A lot of things would merely have to wait. Selling Edith's house, purchasing a new home, setting up a beautiful nursery, even their trip to Paris would all have to wait. Hopefully, he would be back in time to witness the birth of their first child. Nothing else mattered.

Chapter Fifteen

Arlington, Missouri

Unbelievably, six months passed quicker than she could've ever imagined. Alex was finally coming home. Her ever-expanding belly now prohibited her from simple mundane tasks like tying her shoelaces or bending down. She felt like a blimp. Her only solace was the fact Alex would soon be home to rub her back, bring her chocolate ice cream, and set up a small crib in their bedroom.

Deciding to decorate the living room with balloons and festive streamers for his arrival, Noelle drove downtown to a large discount store. Grabbing a shopping cart, she filled it with every imaginable item one would need to decorate for a homecoming. Staring at the things in her cart, it was obvious she had gone overboard. However, she didn't care. She would find a place for everything.

Parking the Porsche in the garage, she barely managed to get everything upstairs in two trips. Finally, unlocking the door to the apartment, she put all the bags on the floor and sat down on the couch. She was exhausted. Finally, after resting for a few minutes, she stood up to empty the bags. Suddenly, she froze, feeling unexpected sharp cramps in her lower abdomen. Perhaps, she had run up the stairs too quickly. Deciding it would probably be a good idea to sit down, she laid back on the sofa. Surely, it was just Braxton Hicks contractions. She knew all about the pre-birth pains associated with pregnancy. Dismissing the sharp pains from her mind, she would simply rest for a while. The decorations could wait. Alex wasn't even sure of his exact arrival date.

Club Med

"Well, Doctor Bennington, have a great flight home. It's certainly been enjoyable having you as a drinking buddy. I'll try to get down to Arlington to see you, Noelle, and the new baby when it arrives. So take care, Buddy, and keep me posted."

"I will, and give some serious thoughts to taking a job at Methodist. See you in Arlington," Alex smiled, walking across the tarmac to board the C-141 cargo plane.

Colonel Williams made special arrangements for Alex to be on the first plane out of the desert. Civil Engineering was dismantling the hospital, so there was no longer a need for an operating room. Knowing Noelle was eight months pregnant, Colonel Williams felt Alex should be allowed to leave as soon as possible. As Alex boarded the plane, there was only one stop in Germany before he arrived in the states. He was eager to surprise Noelle by arriving a few days early.

The military flight, as usual, wasn't as restful as flying commercial. Still, Alex was grateful to be on his way home. He couldn't wait to hold Noelle in his arms and feel the soft kicks of the baby. Filled with anticipation, he couldn't wait to discover the sex of the baby, as Noelle had decided to wait until he was home to share in the excitement of the sonogram. Sitting back in the narrow rows of canvas seats aboard the C-141 Starlifter, Alex anxiously waited for the long, arduous flight to be over.

Ramstein Air Base, Germany

Arriving at Ramstein Air Base, Germany, the cargo plane taxied over to the terminal. It was expected to be a short layover. However, unbeknown to Alex, unforeseen plans awaited his arrival. It appeared General McFarland had been in contact with Colonel Williams and made aware that Alex was on board the arriving C-141. As a result, he requested that Alex immediately be taken to the Landstuhl Regional Hospital upon his arrival. It appeared that a close personal friend of General McFarland, Colonel Whiteman, had been involved in a serious auto accident on the A6 autobahn. Colonel Whiteman was in grave condition, and General McFarland knew there was no better trauma surgeon than Alex. Therefore, the C-141 cargo plane would continue to the states minus one passenger, Doctor Alex Bennington.

Sending a driver out to the tarmac to meet Alex's plane, a young lieutenant exited the car and briskly walked towards the soldiers leaving the aircraft. The troops aboard the aircraft were given a few hours layover while the plane was made ready to continue the flight. Also, other troops were waiting to board the continuing flight to the states.

"Doctor Bennington, Doctor Bennington, over here," the young officer loudly repeated. "I've been sent to pick you up. I know this is unexpected, but General McFarland has requested that you be immediately brought to the Landstuhl Hospital. It appears Colonel Whiteman, a close personal friend of General McFarland, has been in an auto accident on the A6 autobahn and is in critical condition. General McFarland contacted Colonel Williams and was made aware you were incoming to Ramstein. You're needed in surgery immediately. One of the doctors will brief you on the details once I get you to the hospital. Afterward, General McFarland wanted me to inform you that he will personally see to it that you are flown to the states on a military Lear jet."

"Wow, I must say this is an unexpected surprise. However, I would never say no to General McFarland. The general has been more than accommodating to me in the past. I owe him," Alex remarked, following the Lieutenant to the parked car.

Arriving at the Landstuhl Hospital, Alex was quickly briefed by Colonel Whiteman's doctors. After carefully reviewing his x-rays, it appeared that Colonel Whiteman had a broken pelvic bone, a dislodged hip, and broken bones in both legs. It wouldn't be an easy surgery, but

Alex felt confident he could ensure the Colonel would get back the full use of both legs. Quickly, dressing in a pair of green surgical scrubs, a team accompanied him to the operating room.

Finally, after four hours of intense surgery, Alex was exhausted. Pleased with the outcome, the surgery had been a huge success. Now, he just needed to unwind from all the drama. Finding his way to a temporary residence for physicians, Alex found an open cot and fell asleep. However, while he was sleeping, it appeared the drama surrounding his stopover at Ramstein only grew worse. Without him knowing, the fate of his decision to perform the surgery on Colonel Whiteman had inadvertently saved his life. The news was just coming into the base the following day. The C-141 cargo aircraft never arrived in the states. Unfortunately for those on board, it had tragically gone down before a refueling stop in Bangor, Maine, killing all on board.

Club Med

The crash was just beginning to hit all the major news channels. Craig instantly felt sick hearing the devastating news that the C-141, which had departed Club Med, had gone down, killing all on board. He knew from the logistics of the flight that Alex was on board. His legs almost buckled from beneath him when he thought of Noelle and the baby. He was utterly devastated, and the news concerning the tragedy was horrifying. Opening his wallet, he pulled out a business card that Alex had given him. It had his home phone number on the front of the card. Now, he felt obligated to notify Noelle. How could you ever inform someone they had lost a loved one, especially someone in Noelle's condition. He questioned if he should be the one to notify Noelle or wait for the military to send someone to her door. As if by fate, he just happened to turn over the business card that Alex had given him. On the back was Trevor's contact information at Methodist Hospital. Maybe it was a sign that he should call Trevor. Debating his next step, Craig felt it might be better to notify Trevor first. He was closer to Noelle, and maybe it was meant for him to somehow break the news to her as gently as he could under the circumstances. The irony of his plan would be that he had no way to know that Alex had remained in Germany and wasn't a passenger on the doomed flight.

Finding the nearest phone, he called Trevor. Amazingly, Trevor answered on the third ring.

"Doctor Reed."

"Doctor Reed, this is Captain Daniels. I worked with Major Alex Bennington. Our units have been deployed together over the past several months. Regrettably, I'm afraid that I have tragic news regarding Alex. I hate to inform you that Alex was killed in a plane crash earlier today. I'm not sure if you've heard the news regarding the C-141 that went down near Bangor, Maine, which killed everyone on board, but Alex was on that aircraft. I actually spoke with him yesterday just minutes before he boarded the flight. I'm truly sorry," Craig explained.

"I'm sure you've probably been given some erroneous information," Trevor suggested in disbelief.

"I know it's hard to believe. The news of the crash has just made the headlines. I'm sorry. The reason for my call is to ask that you inform Noelle. I believe it would be kinder coming from you. I've never met Noelle. However, I feel as if I know her. Trust me, Alex loved her more than life itself, and I know she's eight months pregnant."

"Alex was like a brother to me. This can't be possible. Are you sure?" Trevor paused, feeling sick in the pit of his stomach.

"Yes. I'm sure. I witnessed Alex boarding the doomed aircraft. Do you want to call Noelle or wait for the military officers to contact her? I think Alex would want you to inform her."

"I think you're right. I believe Alex would want me to tell her, but how do you tell a pregnant woman her husband has died," Trevor asked in a state of shock.

"I have no idea. I'm truly sorry. I really have no answer, but I trust you will somehow come up with the right words. I'm afraid I can't talk long on this phone, please let me leave my contact information. Would you kindly let me know about the services or memorial for Alex? I would like to attend."

"Yes. I'll give you a call," Trevor added after taking Craig's contact information. "We'll be in touch."

Hanging up the phone, Trevor's hands were shaking. He was visibly shocked. He desperately needed a strong drink. However, he was on duty at the hospital. There wasn't even the slightest possibility of soothing his nerves with alcohol. It was so hard to believe that Alex was gone. They were closer than brothers. The tragic loss would haunt him for years. Picking up the phone, he called Becky. There was no way he was going to see Noelle without Becky. She answered almost immediately.

"Becky, I don't know how to tell you, but we lost Alex this morning."

"Trevor, what do you mean?" Becky gasped.

"Sweetheart, someone by the name of Captain Daniels just called to inform me that the C-141 carrying Alex and returning soldiers from the Middle East went down this morning near Bangor, Maine. No one survived the crash," Trevor started nervously in total disbelief.

"Oh, Trevor, my God, what about Noelle," Becky cried.

"We have to tell her. I need you to go with me. To be honest, this is the hardest thing I've ever been asked to do. Sweetheart, I'm coming home. I'm going to need your strength to get through this. I'm completely devastated. I loved Alex like a brother."

"Trevor, I know. I know," Becky softly reiterated. "I'll be ready."

Driving over to Noelle's apartment, not a word was said. Instead, they were simply consumed with sadness. Trevor held tightly to Becky's hand as they ascended the stairs. Then, knocking on the door, Trevor's breath hitched. He felt like he couldn't breathe.

"Hey, guys, what brings you over? Come in. I could use your help with decorating the apartment. I can't believe Alex will be home soon. Can you even believe it?" Noelle smiled. "Have a seat. Can I get either of you something to drink? Maybe coffee?" Noelle rambled excessively, unable to contain her joy. The excitement of Alex's homecoming could be heard in her voice. She exuded happiness.

Listening to Noelle's idle chatter only made things worse as Becky's eyes moistened with tears. She could hardly contain her emotions.

"Noelle, why don't you sit down. I'll get everyone some coffee,"

Becky suggested. She needed privacy in the kitchen to regain her composure and wipe the tears from her eyes.

"Becky, sit down. We'll get coffee in a few minutes," Trevor interjected.

"Trevor, what's wrong? You seem awfully nervous. Why aren't you at work?" Noelle inquired, sensing something wasn't right.

"Noelle, sweetheart, I'm afraid we have some tragic news," Trevor paused.

"What are you talking about? You guys are beginning to scare me. Don't you know it's not good to scare a pregnant woman, and on top of that, I've had some strong contractions earlier today?"

"Noelle, I received a phone call regarding Alex," Trevor stated reluctantly. His voice was shaky, barely audible, and his hands trembled.

"What's up? Is he stuck somewhere with a long layover? Are you here to tell me that he's not going to make it home this week?" Noelle interjected.

With tears flooding down Becky's face, she stared at Trevor. Noelle's words were almost prophetic.

"Becky, what's wrong? Why are you crying?"

Becky knew that Trevor was having a difficult time trying to find the right words. She knew it would probably be better if she told Noelle. Putting her arm around her, she pulled her close.

"Noelle, the reason we came over was to tell you that Alex will not be coming home," Becky cried softly.

"What do you mean?" Noelle trembled.

"Sweetheart, there's no gentle or kind way to say this. Alex was tragically killed in a plane crash earlier this morning. The C-141 cargo plane went down near Bangor, Maine killing all onboard," Becky cried, embracing Noelle.

Pulling away from Becky, Noelle screamed.

"Trevor, is she telling the truth?" Noelle insisted hysterically.

"Yes. I'm sorry. Becky is telling you the truth," Trevor slowly answered, unable to face Noelle.

"Oh, my God, this can't be true. It can't be true," Noelle screamed.

Then, getting up from the sofa, she frantically began pacing back and forth. "I don't believe you. I don't believe either of you," Noelle yelled.

Suddenly, Noelle's legs buckled from beneath her small frame. Trevor caught her just before she hit the floor. She was out cold.

"Becky wet a washcloth," Trevor instructed as he laid Noelle on the sofa. Hurry, you need to warm it under the hot water."

"Okay. I'll be right back."

Running back with the warm washcloth, the warmth of the cloth had no effect on Noelle.

"Becky, I'm running downstairs to the car to get my medical bag. First, I need to check her blood pressure and vital signs. I'll be right back. Keep wiping her face."

"Alright, but hurry. What if she goes into labor?"

"Well, let's just hope that doesn't happen."

Rushing back inside the apartment, Trevor was pleased to see that Noelle had regained consciousness.

"Thank God. I was worried that I might have to admit you to the hospital," Trevor smiled. "I'm going to take your blood pressure."

Everything looked fine as Trevor checked her vital signs.

"Your vital signs all look great. Can you stand for a moment?" Trevor instructed.

"Oh, my God," Noelle screamed. "My water just broke."

"Well, I'm not an obstetrician, but I would say that you're right. Do you have an overnight bag ready for the hospital?"

"No. I'm only eight months. I thought I had a few weeks to pack a bag."

"I think your time just ran out. Becky, can you grab a few items from the bedroom. Maybe a robe and slippers. Everything else can wait. Noel, once your water breaks, and it's pretty apparent that just happened, you have to go to the hospital. Becky and I will drive you over to Methodist, and I'll get you checked in."

"Trevor, I'm not full term. I can't lose this baby and Alex too." Noelle panicked, crying uncontrollably.

"Noelle, as I said, I'm not an obstetrician, but the baby will be fine. A lot of women deliver early and have perfectly healthy infants."

Walking back into the living room, Becky carried a small overnight bag.

"I think I have everything. I packed your robe, slippers, and a few toiletry items. You can make a list of things you might need later. I'll come back and grab those for you," Becky smiled.

"Okay, let's get you to the hospital. Oh, Becky, grab a towel."

It was only a short drive over to Methodist. Trevor checked Noelle into labor and delivery and paged Doctor Chang. Once she was connected to all the fetal monitors, Becky came in to stay with her.

"Noelle, Doctor Chang will be here soon. You're lucky. He's in the hospital. But, I don't want you to worry. Becky can stay with you. I've got rounds to make. You're in great hands, and I'll check back with you later," Trevor assured her.

"Oh, Becky, I'm so scared. What if the baby doesn't make it?" Noelle cried.

"That's utter nonsense. You're both going to be fine."

Becky's heart was breaking. She prayed for Noelle and the baby. Suddenly, life seemed extremely cruel. How was it even possible for someone to lose their fiance and be faced with an early delivery within minutes of hearing the tragic news? She couldn't imagine the worries Noelle must be experiencing.

"Ms. Carrington, I'm Julie, and I work in labor and delivery. I'm going to start an IV. We want to keep you hydrated. It also gives us a line to administer any medications that might be necessary. Is this your first baby?" Julie questioned with a smile.

"Yes," Noelle answered, softly wiping her eyes.

Noticing her emotional state, Julie felt sympathetic. She routinely witnessed the fears and worries that new mothers often experienced.

"Oh, honey, please don't cry. Do you have any concerns? You're in great hands at Methodist, and Doctor Chang is a wonderful doctor? Is there anything that I can get for you?" Julie smiled.

"No. I lost my fiance earlier today," Noelle exclaimed.

"Oh, my God, I'm so sorry. Sweetheart, you have my deepest sympathy. Was he the baby's father?" Julie inquired, biting her bottom lip. She was trying desperately to keep her emotions under control. Julie had worked in labor and delivery for many years, and she couldn't remember a more horrific set of circumstances.

"Yes," Noelle cried as tears flooded her face.

Witnessing the conversation between Noelle and Julie, Becky sat frozen in her chair. She was still reeling with shock. It seemed unbelievable that Alex was gone. Noelle had just buried her grandmother. It wasn't fair that she would now lay to rest her fiance. Silently, Becky asked God to give Noelle the strength to deliver a healthy baby. She feared Noelle would have a difficult time over the next few days processing the horrendous fact that Alex wasn't coming home. Remembering her decorations in the living room sent chills down Becky's spine.

As Julie walked out of the room, Becky went to Noelle's bedside and gently took her hand. Noelle looked up with tears streaming down her face.

"Becky, I can't do this. I can't," Noelle cried. "I don't want to have this baby. I just want to die and take the baby with me. Then, at least, we would all be together."

"Noelle, that's crazy. Stop right now. Do you hear me? You're stronger than you think, and this baby is going to need you. Noelle, I'm sorry, but you're acting selfishly. I don't mean to sound callous and cold-hearted. I love you. I can't wait to meet this little one, and hold him or her, and kiss their sweet little cheeks."

"Becky, I need a miracle. What if I lose the baby?" Without Alex, Noelle's emotions were consuming her.

"You're not. Please, don't even think it. You're both going to be fine."

Just at that moment, Doctor Chang entered the room. Walking over to Noelle's bed, he was at a loss for words.

"Noelle, you have my deepest sympathy. Trevor gave me the tragic news. I'm so sorry, and I don't mean to sound disrespectful, but I need you to focus on bringing this baby into the world. Our goal is to deliver a healthy baby," Doctor Chang stated empathetically. Do you have any questions?"

"How long will I be in labor? These pains are starting to become extremely uncomfortable," Noelle wept, reaching for a tissue.

"Well, giving birth isn't an exact science. Each birth can vary on length of time in labor and whether you might require a cesarean. However, I expect this to be a normal delivery. It's your first baby, and they usually take longer. I'll be checking on you periodically. If the contractions become unbearable, I can give you something to help ease the pain and make you more comfortable. Hang in there. We're all here for you. You're doing great," Doctor Chang smiled, leaving the room.

"Thanks, Dr. Chang."

"Wow. He seems like a nice doctor. Trevor really likes him," Becky stated with the hint of a smile. There had been enough tears, she thought.

Two hours later, Noelle began experiencing excruciating pains. Buzzing for the nurse, Julie walked in.

"Hey, Sweetie, what can I do for you?" Julie smiled.

"The contractions are extreme. Doctor Chang said he could give me something for the pain," Noelle grimaced.

"Okay. I'll let the doctor know."

Within a few minutes, Doctor Chang walked into the room.

"Julie said your contractions have become significantly painful. Let me check your progress, and we'll give you something to make you comfortable."

After performing the usual cervical test for dilation, Doctor Chang removed his gloves and smiled.

"Well, it appears you're a candidate for an epidural. I'll have our anesthetist administer it. The epidural will relieve the pain, and perhaps you can get a little sleep. He'll be right in. Hang in there. You're doing great."

"Noelle, that's good news. I think you should try and rest. I'll be right here," Becky mentioned. "It might be a long night."

Looking up at the clock, it was almost 5:30 a.m. Finally, Noelle was, at last, ready to give birth. But, as the medic wheeled her to the delivery room, once again, she panicked.

"Becky, you're coming with me. I'm not doing this alone. I need you," Noelle begged frantically.

"Okay. If I'm allowed, but no more crying. I'll page Trevor."

Hurriedly putting on green paper scrubs and booties, Becky followed Noelle's gurney into the delivery room.

"Oh, Becky, Alex isn't here. He'll never be here. I don't want to have this baby without him," Noelle cried bitterly.

"Well, Noelle, I hate to tell you, but this baby is coming with or without Alex. I'm excited, and I think you should be too. For heaven's sake, you're about to become a mom. You're about to meet this new little person you've been carrying for the past eight months," Becky smiled.

"Noelle, I need you to give me several strong pushes," Doctor Chang instructed.

After several powerful pushes, the cries of a newborn filled the delivery room. It was music to Noelle and Becky's ears, as well as the attending personnel who worked in labor and delivery.

"Congratulations. You have a beautiful baby boy," Doctor Chang smiled, holding the infant up.

Laying his warm, tiny body on Noelle's chest, she cried. However, these tears were much unlike all the tears shed earlier in the day. Instead, these were tears of joy. Noelle was thrilled to be holding her newborn son. Quickly counting ten tiny fingers and ten toes, he was perfect.

"Congratulations. Noelle, he's beautiful. I'm so happy for you," Becky smiled.

"Thanks. Becky, look at his cute face. He resembles Alex. He has curly black hair. Can you believe it?" Noelle smiled.

"He looks a lot like his father. What a handsome little guy," Becky immediately agreed.

"Wow, I heard someone just had a baby boy," Trevor teased, walking into the delivery room. "Congratulations, let Uncle Trevor take a look at his little nephew. Wow. He resembles Alex. Poor little guy," Trevor grinned.

Walking over to Becky, Trevor put his arm around her.

"Sweetheart, don't worry," Trevor whispered. "I know how much you want a baby. Trust me. It will happen," he reassured her. Then, taking the back of his hand, he wiped the tears from Becky's eyes.

Handing the newborn over to the nurses to be weighed and measured, Noelle again broke down, letting her emotions consume her.

"Oh, Becky, I don't even have a crib. What am I going to do?" Noelle cried.

"Noelle, don't worry about a crib. I'll buy the best baby bed Arlington has to offer, and I'll have it all set up before you go home. Uncle Trevor and Aunt Becky will ensure our little guy has the very best," Trevor announced with pride.

"Thank you. As always, I don't know what I would do without you," Noelle answered.

"Your little guy weighs 6 lbs 9 ounces, and he's 20 inches long," the nurse smiled, handing the newborn to Noelle. He's a handsome little boy, and I see a lot of newborns," she recalled, passing the tiny infant back to his mom.

"Thanks," Noelle smiled softly, kissing her sweet little boy. "Mommy loves you, and Daddy loves you too," she whispered.

Ramstein Air Base, Germany

Boarding the Lear jet, Alex was more than anxious to be on his way home. Having just received the news of the crash, he made several attempts to reach Noelle at the apartment. Finally, he gave up and simply left a message. She was probably out shopping for the baby and was totally oblivious to the fact the plane had gone down. However, she had no way to know that he wasn't a passenger on that aircraft, and she never watched the news, so the chance of her even hearing about it was slim to none, or so he thought. He was sure that he would be home before she was even made aware of the tragic event.

After an eight-hour trip across the Atlantic, Alex was looking forward to arriving in Arlington. Now, only three and a half hours stood between him and the love of his life. General McFarland had been more than generous flying him to the states onboard a private military jet. Craig was right. Once you reached superhero status, life got a lot easier.

Sitting back in his seat, he knew that General McFarland had no doubt saved his life by requesting that he remain behind in Germany. His heart went out to the families who had lost loved ones onboard the tragic flight.

"Would you like a beverage? Coffee perhaps?" the flight attendant inquired.

"Yes, thanks. Coffee would be wonderful."

His only thoughts were of Noelle and the baby as he took a sip of the hot coffee.

Finally, the aircraft began its descent into Arlington Air Force Base. Once they were on the ground, Alex walked into the small terminal and called for a cab. There was no need to call Noelle to pick him up. He loved the element of surprise. However, what he could have never known was the surprise that awaited him.

Running up the stairs to the apartment, he eagerly unlocked the door. Looking around, he was shocked to discover Noelle wasn't home. Checking out the decorations which remained behind in the living room, he laughed. Why had she gone to all the trouble to purchase balloons and streamers and not finished decorating? Walking into the kitchen, the pantry was fully stocked. Noticing several large boxes of oatmeal, he laughed.

Thinking Noelle might be with Becky, Alex picked up the phone to call Becky and Trevor's apartment. Again, there was no answer. Rubbing his forehead, he couldn't fathom why no one was at home. Surely, Trevor could enlighten him on the girl's whereabouts. Deciding to call Trevor's office, again, there was no answer. So much for a welcome home committee, he smiled. Getting desperate, he decided to call the hospital and have Trevor paged. Within minutes, Trevor answered.

"What the hell!" Trevor exclaimed. "You're supposed to be dead. Craig called and said, your plane went down near Bangor, Maine, killing everyone on board."

"It did. But, I wasn't on it," Alex explained. "Where are the girls? I'm at the apartment, and there's no sign of Noelle. There are just a lot of decorations scattered all over the living room floor. Guess she decided not to finish decorating."

"Alex, Noelle is at the hospital."

"What?" Alex interjected without waiting for Trevor to explain the reason for his statement.

"Alex, Noelle had the baby early this morning. She's fine. Becky is with her."

"What?" Alex interrupted once again.

"Congratulations. You have a son, and he resembles you. Can you believe it?"

"Trevor, did you say that I have a son?" Alex asked in disbelief.

"Yes. I think you should get over to the hospital."

"I'm on my way. But, please, don't let Noelle know that I wasn't on that plane. I only have one chance to come back from the dead, and I can't wait to see the expression on Noelle's face."

"Alright, if that's what you want, but I have to tell you she's been through hell. The news of your death devastated her, to put it mildly."

"Trevor, I'm hanging up. I'll be right there. Don't say a word."

Running downstairs, Alex opened the garage and started the Porsche. Racing to the hospital, it was a good thing it was only a short drive. Otherwise, he surely would have been arrested for reckless driving.

Arriving at Methodist, Alex parked in the physician's parking lot and ran inside the hospital.

"Congratulations. Welcome home, Doctor Bennington," Angie smiled, passing him in the hallway. "Wait, aren't you supposed to be dead?" she curiously questioned.

"Well, does it look like I'm dead," Alex scoffed.

Hurriedly taking the elevator to the second floor, Labor and Delivery, Alex raced down the hallway to the nurse's station.

"Which room is Noelle Carrington's?" Alex inquired.

"Wait, you're supposed to be dead," Julie screamed in a state of shock.

"Yeah, well, I keep hearing that but does it seriously look like I'm dead," Alex countered.

"She's in room 212 at the end of the hallway."

Racing down the hall and into the room, Alex smiled.

"Noelle, I'm so sorry I wasn't here," he apologized, rushing to her side with tears in his eyes.

"Oh, my God, my God, Alex, you didn't die in the plane crash," Noelle gasped as tears of joy streamed down her face. "You're home."

"Noelle, I can explain everything."

"You're here. We have a son. There's nothing to explain," Noelle smiled, placing the tiny infant into Alex's arms. "My world is perfect."

Epilogue

Bringing their new son, Benjamin Alexander, home, it was apparent the one-bedroom apartment was no longer adequate for a family of three. So after selling Edith's house, Noelle finally purchased the home of her dreams and planned a lavish Christmas wedding. Honeymooning in Paris, Noelle fell in love with the City of Lights.

Alex continued to serve in the reserves. However, Noelle now had a growing family to give her purpose when Alex was deployed.

A baby girl, surprisingly named Edie, joined her brother two short years after his arrival. Finally, after the adoption of Ian, and Isabella, their family, was complete.

It quickly appeared Arlington, Missouri's population was growing by leaps and bounds as Becky and Trevor excitedly announced they were expecting twins.

Watching from above, Edith smiled.